Immersed in Murder

Alison Lingwood

About the Author

Alison Lingwood lived in Hale, Cheshire, attending Altrincham Grammar School for Girls. Married to a Contracts Manager, she has two adult children and two grandchildren.

After training as a teacher she worked for many years as a lecturer in Further Education before setting up her own business.

She retired in 2009 and now lives with her husband in north Staffordshire, where she turned to writing, publishing her first novel at the age of sixty.

Immersed in Murder is Alison's sixth novel. The first five, Portal to Murder, The Bridport Dagger, A Wild Kind of Justice, Stains of Suspicion and The Calibre of Death are also available through amazon.co.uk in paperback format or on Kindle.

Reviews for Alison's earlier books

'A great read.' SS

'I have just finished reading Portal to Murder and thought it was excellent.'
                                    SafariGirl

'...an excellent read, lots of twists and turns and the plot kept me guessing right till the end.' KR

'...a scary description of how social media can be manipulated.' C

'Brilliant! Excellent story, characters and setting.' KP

'A really good read. I found the characters interesting and the way they all came together intriguing.' Mr & Mrs D

'...what a fantastic read... it kept me totally engrossed.' KR

'Have just finished reading your first book. Enjoyed it, very good.' ML

'Intricately woven and the leaves the reader guessing.' JG

'Enjoyed this murder mystery, didn't want to finish it. Hope there's more.'
                                    Hollystar

"One sin I know, another doth provoke. Murder's as near to lust as flame to smoke."
                                         Shakespeare

By the same author

Portal to Murder
The Bridport Dagger
A Wild Kind of Justice
Stains of Suspicion
The Calibre of Death

for my brother-in-law Ken Roberts

Before

For Susan Jennings a particular autumn day in 1987 was not memorable. Although pivotal to her future there was little that the eight-year old could later recall about that date with any certainty of accuracy.

She had been shooed out into the garden by her mother soon after breakfast, but before long she had abandoned the outdoor play to come and spend the morning with her dolls in the bedroom.

At mid-morning the little girl had been sent outside a second time by her mother to ask her brother whether he and his friends wanted a drink. Resenting the interruption to her solitary play, she stomped down the garden as only a petulant eight-year old can. She scuffed with bad grace across the frost-encrusted lawn towards her brother's hiding place. Her game had been interrupted to take the message and she was not happy.

It is a well-known fact that sound travels clearly across water but the grass silenced her approach and she was not sure how to respond to what she was seeing. For a long moment she stood silently sucking on the pebble necklace she wore, loving the texture of the various grey stones. Then …

'Neil! Mummy says …' Her voice faded away and her steps slowed as she approached the boat. Wide-eyed she stared, the necklace dropped and her thumb crept unbidden into her mouth in a habit overcome at least four years previously.

Solemn-eyed she eventually made her way back to the kitchen door where she removed her shoes. They were damp from the frosty grass and she would feel her mother's anger if the kitchen floor was dirtied, no matter what the circumstances.

'Well?' her mother's hand was poised over the kettle, 'do they? I hope you told them they'll have to come up and get it – I've no time to be traipsing up and down the garden after them.'

'They don't,' she said, 'they don't want any. They're busy ... playing.'

Her mother sighed, 'I hope you didn't go pestering them. You took long enough out there. Neil's grown up now – he doesn't want a little kid hanging around all the time. And take your thumb out of your mouth, what are you? A baby?'

Her mother scooped up clean mugs she had set out on the counter in preparation. There were five of them.

Susan wondered how many friends her mother thought Neil had out there with him. Was she the only person who knew that there was one friend, just one?

* * *

At lunchtime she was again sent outside, this time to tell her brother that his meal was ready and his friends must go home for their lunch.

Susan called to the shadow she could see through the cabin window. There seemed to be shouting, 'You're to come straight in. Now.' Having thus delivered her mother's words verbatim, the prim little girl was more intent on not slipping on the melting frost, on her way up the sloping lawn as she returned to the house. She was happily anticipating the roly-poly pudding she had been promised once her main course was eaten.

The pudding never materialised. Indeed she had barely started her main course before mayhem ensued. She was told to remain in the kitchen to finish her lunch and was left alone with the doors closed, even when her plate was empty. Her father arrived home from work; a move unprecedented at this time of day. He had barely been gone a couple of hours, but he passed her by without a greeting, just as police officers arrived. She recognised them as such from pictures in books and on television, though she had never talked to one before.

It was busy, so busy – ambulance people pushing past the police officers, running in the kitchen and down the garden. Then the scene moved to slow motion. The ambulance men, in their green suits stood around to one side of the garden. One was smoking and she watched in wonder as her father, normally so censorious, failed to comment, seemed hardly to notice. After what seemed like forever, on a word of command from one of the police officers the ambulance men pushed a gurney across the damp grass and Susan was whisked away into the sitting room, there to gaze in wonder at the pretty female officer who wore make-up and ill-fitting uniform trousers.

She sat awkwardly, pinioned on the sofa between her parents whilst the police asked her about going down the garden, what she saw, what she heard and this she related to the policeman as well as she could understand it, while the policewoman wrote things down in her notebook, filling several pages with indecipherable squiggles. Susan began to cry, then she began to scream.

* * *

There were a lot of tears, and much muttering and mumbling of lowered voices as she was calmed and sent to her room to play; and still the promised pudding had not materialised. To her surprise the policewoman accompanied her and started packing clothes into one of the small suitcases. Downstairs her mother cried and her father paced. There was much banging of doors and several times the telephone rang, then at just after seven o'clock her grandparents arrived and took her home with them for the night – an unexpected treat.

The next few days were odd, a holiday at Gangan and Pops', yet without the joy and laughter of holidays. No school, yet schoolwork appeared as if by magic, which she did supervised at Gangan's kitchen table.

After eight or nine sleeps Pops took Susan home in his car, back to normality. Well, relative normality. Mummy seemed to spend every day in her nightclothes, seldom washing and not going further than the back door. The old boat had gone and was never mentioned. At the next school holidays she was sent to stay with Aunty Viv and Uncle Bob, and never permanently returned home. When she did go home Neil was not there. She was never to see him again.

2017

Chapter 1

Early that November morning a number of events were fatally converging.

In Newcastle-under-Lyme Carly Broadbent swore mildly as she knocked her alarm clock off the bedside table in an attempt to stop its cacophony. Turning over sleepily she smiled as she remembered what day it was and why she had to get up so early. Today her new business venture was opening to the public for the first time. She would need hard work and dedication to pull it off, and more than a little good luck. Sending a silent prayer to who-knew-where, she swung her feet out of bed.

When the future of the fruit farm Strawberry Fayre had been threatened the previous year because of the proposed route of the HS2 rail link, Carly Broadbent, manager of the farm's café, decided to take the bull by the horns and set up business on her own account. With the help of a small legacy from a relative, she had taken the lease on an empty shop in

Audley village, capitalising on the closure of the library in the spring and opening a café incorporating a second-hand book shop.

This was an idea culled from smart city-centre bookshops and she felt that her only concern would be the combination of her baking in conjunction with paperback books. She decided the risk was worth taking. Books were, in her opinion, so devalued these days by e-readers and Kindles, that a few jam or cream splatters here and there would be of little matter.

She had worked out her budgets carefully and decided that she could manage to employ the elderly Josie as cook. They had worked well together at the farm and been made redundant when Strawberry Fayre closed.

Josie had grumbled a little about her part-time hours – all that Carly could afford, and grumbled more at the limited menu not doing justice to her talents, which was true. When Carly showed her the tiny kitchen and the budgets, she agreed that Carly's suggestions were realistic.

The two of them had spent happy hours planning, visiting other tearooms, seeing what worked and what failed. They went to Dagfields, Slaters, Marks and Spencer for afternoon tea, then out to Oak Tree Farm and Amersham near Stone for lunch.

'We need to stop the research now and just get on with it,' Josie suggested at last. 'I couldn't zip my trousers up this morning. What are those?'

Carly had carried through from the car a large box of crockery. Much of this she had inherited from the aunt who had left her the legacy; some was her mother's, and some she thought may have been her grandmother's.

She looked through it sadly. 'I hoped to use this in the café, but there isn't a complete set amongst it. The cups suffer first, losing handles and getting chips around the lips. I'll have to buy new.' She was disappointed, but Josie had an idea.

'Use it mismatched,' she said, 'it's all pretty, and if the whole place has odd cups, saucers and tea-plates it will look intentionally different. Plus it doesn't matter if we have any breakages. If you buy matched, you're going to have to get something you can be sure to match in the future.'

'I hadn't thought of that.' Carly tried a few combinations. 'It works,' she said at last. 'I knew there was a reason why I'd taken you on. It will save a fortune too.'

'When we next go on a recce round the charity shops for more books we can look for crockery at the same time,' Josie suggested.

As yet the shelves were not completely filled. They had browsed charity shops as well as buying redundant stock and some of the surplus shelving from the library before it closed in the spring.

They went to an auction in Hanley and bought an enormous Welsh dresser. It was very cheap – no doubt because it would be far too big for most domestic settings, and the delivery costs were more than the auction price. The only way it could be accommodated in the café was because one of the plate glass windows was cracked and the dresser was carried through the gap and in situ half an hour before the new window was fitted.

'If the business fails it will have to stay there,' Carly laughed.

'If the business fails, you and I will be using it for firewood over the winter,' Josie told her.

'Better not fail then. Come on, let's get it cleaned down and some crockery on display.'

They worked on happily, sometimes arguing over placing tables, menus and hours of opening, but mostly working well together as they had done at Strawberry Fayre.

The opening was taking place on the first Saturday in November. The Stoke Sentinel newspaper had run an article and carried Carly's adverts. Signal Radio had been plugging them for weeks, and the interview with Radio Stoke had gone well. Leaflets had been delivered locally. In a nod to Roald Dahl, each had attached to it a *Bookends Café Golden Ticket*. These asked for suggestions as to what facilities locals would like to see provided once the café opened. There was to be a prize for the best idea. A gratifying pile of responses had been received and Carly's plan was to wait a couple of weeks, get over the first excitement, then draw the winning ticket and announce the prize for the best idea.

Putting the tickets to one side for now Carly charged up her phone for photographs and Josie had her hair done. The press and local radio stations would be there, as well as several local councillors, and the MP, always happy for a positive photo opportunity, was performing the opening ceremony.

A strategically placed sign at the till, suggested that books purchased were either returned or donated to charity shops once finished with. They were priced very reasonably according to their condition, with no expectation of profits, they would be regarded as a loss leader to lure customers into the café. Each table carried a card asking for ideas of what people would like to see in the café in the future.

Standing back, Carly admired the signage: *Bookends Café*. She was ready.

She was not to know then that the café opening would vie for front-page coverage on the Sentinel newspaper's front page with news of one of the strangest crimes in Staffordshire.

* * *

At Manchester Airport the same morning a Boeing 747 just landed from Orlando was disgorging its bleary-eyed cargo, including the Fraser family, into the arrivals lounge on a day that was to prove memorable for all of them.

The holiday had been a tremendous success. It had been considered unacceptable by the powers-that-be to take the children out of school during term-time, but the Fraser parents were not prepared to pay what they saw as extortionate prices to visit America in August, and so a political illness had been called into play.

Travelling at the beginning of the October half term holiday, and taking an illicit week afterwards, had given them time to visit Disney World for a week, then go on for a further week to stay with Edward's brother in Vermont. The children would need to be primed about the illness they had supposedly suffered on their return home, but she would plan that when she was less jet-lagged.

The outward journey is always more exciting than the return. So thought Caroline Fraser as she closed the curtains against the dawning light and tucked the children under the covers.

They would all sleep now, and waken when their body clocks dictated. Tomorrow would be a day of laundry and sorting out, followed by a return to their usual routine on Tuesday.

Succumbing to the inevitable exhaustion as she and Edward tumbled into bed, Caroline was not to know just how long it would be before life returned to anything like normality.

It seemed like moments later she was dragged from a deep sleep by her daughter's shrill voice. She peered bleary-eyed at the clock – 14.53. It took her brain a moment to engage, hmm – Sunday afternoon. Six year old Mary stood beside the bed, tousle-haired, and spoke through the thumb clamped in her mouth.

'Mummy, who is that funny lady asleep in the bath? She doesn't smell very nice.'

Chapter 2

At first Caroline had believed that Mary was playing games with her, and had only stirred out of bed when eight year old Robin had confirmed that what his sister said was the truth.

Entering the bathroom in the gloom of a November afternoon, she saw at once the figure of a mature woman lying face down in a bathtub full of water. The smell was foul. Fighting the urge to vomit, she dashed back to the main bedroom and woke Edward, who immediately dialled triple nine.

Now she began feeding the washing machine with dirty laundry from the suitcases as they awaited the arrival of the police.

* * *

In the Timothy household excitement had been running high for several weeks. Laura, four-year old daughter of DCI Christopher Timothy and his wife Pippa, was now just a few days short of her first outing as a bridesmaid. She got out of bed and put on, inevitably, her white socks and the shoes selected for the wedding day.

She had tiptoed noisily into the main bedroom and whispered sotto voce in Pippa's ear, 'Is it the wedding day today?'

Half-awake her mother told her that it was two weeks away and far too early to be out of bed. She must go back to bed quietly and not disturb her little sister. Laura did as she was told, but the excitement at the prospect of being a bridesmaid was too much for her to contain and before long both sisters could be heard from the adjacent room. There seemed little point in waiting for the alarm clock's clarion call. Pippa got out of bed and into her dressing gown in one swift movement and made her way to the kitchen.

* * *

The personal relationship between DS Frances Hegarty and DI Pete Talbot had become general knowledge in the office about twelve months previously.

The prospective groom, who had been Chris's sergeant for a number of years, he had lost the previous year on secondment to the vice team at County HQ. Pete had acted up into the Detective Inspector role during Chris's recuperation from an attempt on his life, and had sufficiently proved his competence to now be made up permanently into the DI role at Stoke on Trent. As a much larger police authority Stoke on Trent had a three-man Detective Inspector team in the Major Crimes Unit and Pete had been offered one of these.

Once his transfer was made permanent from Newcastle to the neighbouring division, he had felt able to declare his feelings for Frances and the romance had blossomed. It would have been frowned upon whilst they were working together but now it was what she had hoped for. The romance developed quickly. Pete's team in Stoke tended, necessarily, to work different hours to hers, yet they had still contrived six dates in four weeks. Dates sounded such an outmoded term – yet that was what they had been.

And now their wedding was nearly upon them. After the ceremony they would be taking two weeks' leave, for a honeymoon on the Greek island of Santolini, after which the couple would return to live locally in Pete's cottage in Miles Green.

The Timothy household viewed this wedding in different ways. Chris's wife Pippa and their elder daughter Laura, who was to be a bridesmaid, were delighted. In the case of the latter there was a high degree of excitement and Laura had been intent on breaking-in the wedding shoes around the house at every opportunity. Pippa had feared that the shoes would be worn out before they were broken in, and may need to be replaced.

Husband Chris's thoughts were more concerned with the further depletion of his team for the period of two weeks after the wedding. The honeymoon effectively made Chris's team, albeit temporarily in the case of Hegarty, down by two experienced officers and in these times of austerity such losses were seldom replaced. Thus short-staffed he hoped, without much confidence, that the Newcastle-under-Lyme criminal fraternity would remain quiescent in the run-up to Christmas.

Pippa's mobile rang, and she asked Chris to sort out the little girls' tea while she spoke to Florence, her half-sister. Florence's mother Sonja was a recovering alcoholic but her latest spell of abstention had not seemingly lasted very long and she was once again a patient in The Priory.

As Laura clattered into the kitchen wearing the inevitable wedding shoes, Chris allowed his mind to switch off and he prepared her meal before picking up the local newspaper. An article at the foot of the front page was about a new bookshop/café opening that day in Audley village, and a familiar name caught his eye – Carly Broadbent. A moment's thought brought it back to him. She had been the manager at the café in the fruit farm, scene of a fatal shooting the previous year. So she was moving on. The food, he remembered, had been excellent. If she had been able to poach the chef into joining her in the café venture, he felt that her success would be assured. He chuckled at his own wit as he carried his younger daughter downstairs after her nap. The telephone call was finishing.

'How is Florence?'

'Much more sanguine. I think she's coming to terms with Sonja's illness now. She'd like to come here for Christmas if that's okay.'

'Of course it is. I hope you told her straight away – you didn't hesitate?'

No. I said it would be fine and we'd love to see her. I also said she could come over this weekend if she wants. The visits are so brief now she's getting older, I miss her.'

'I'll go up and collect her.'

'Don't you dare! You can offer, but she loves the train journey nearly as much as my Gran does. You can meet her at Stoke station.'

'Will she be here for the wedding?'

'I don't know if she's invited. Pete and Frances aren't exactly close to her.'

'Pete wouldn't mind. I'll ask him. Florence would enjoy a wedding.'

'Stop it. You can't go inviting random relatives to someone else's wedding, it isn't done.'

He laid down the paper and went into the kitchen intent on persuading his elder daughter out of the wedding shoes she had been wearing since she first got out of bed, when his mobile phone rang.

His wish for a quiet period was evidently not to be granted just yet.

Chapter 3

The initial telephone call had been logged at the Guildhall at 15.08pm on Sunday November the sixth. The police surgeon grunted, confirmed that life was extinct and sent for the Newcastle under Lyme pathologist, Ben Hanchurch.

The Fraser family sat huddled together on the enormous leather sofa, the children watching CBeebies and playing on a Smartphone respectively, their faces grey under the suntans. The parents looked shell-shocked. Caroline was tall, slim and beautifully groomed with hair that looks like a model's, but her eyes were huge, like those of a terrified animal. Edward constantly raked fingers through his hair. DCI Christopher Timothy sat opposite to them, with DC Harris beside him taking notes.

'The flight was on time,' Caroline explained. 'We landed in Manchester just before half past six this morning and customs was very easy. We got home at about half past eight and went straight to bed.'

'Did nobody use the bathroom before you settled down?' This seemed unlikely.

They looked at each other and she shook her head.

'Both the children went to the downstairs loo as soon as we got in, then I put them straight to bed while Edward brought the luggage in. We didn't bother about their teeth or anything. I washed quickly in the en-suite shower room, and Edward brought a cup of tea up to bed.'

Edward took up the story, 'I used the shower room as well. Next thing I knew Caroline was shaking me awake saying there was ...' he glanced at the children and lowered his voice, 'a woman in the bath and she seemed to be dead.'

Chris decided to separate them.

'Mrs Fraser I wonder, could I take you up on your earlier offer of a cup of tea? DC Harris will give you a hand.'

'Absolutely.' In one graceful movement she rose to her feet. Chris thought she could have been a model, although she was a bit on the heavy side compared with the size-zero preferences these days. Nevertheless she was a very attractive woman.

Once they had left the room Chris leaned forward and said quietly, 'Sir, are you quite sure you have no idea who this woman might be?' He thought he had seen a flicker of fear.

Edward Fraser bridled with indignation. 'Certainly not. I am quite sure I have never seen her before. I resent the implication.'

Chris made a note, thinking that perhaps he protested too much. Nobody could have been sure from that brief viewing that the body was not known to them unless they had moved the body before the police arrived, which they both denied doing.

'Do you have a burglar alarm, sir?'

'Yes, but it wasn't set. It's rather temperamental. Last time we were away it went off a couple of times at night and upset the neighbours. Sharon asked us to leave it off.'

'Sharon?'

'Next door. She has a key. She was popping in to keep an eye on the place while we've been away.'

Caroline returned, followed by the constable carrying a laden tray. Before she had chance to sit down the doorbell rang. Both children jumped up, but Edward quelled them with a word as DC Harris went to the door. A moment later he put his head round the door. 'It's the neighbour sir, Sharon Welland.'

Chris excused himself and left the room, closing the door behind him.

In the hall stood a thin woman, whose waif-like body was untroubled by curves. She was visibly shaking.

'This is terrible. I can't believe it, a woman found in the house, and I've been coming in, even bringing the baby and there could have been a killer...'

For a moment DC Harris thought she would faint and rushed to place a hall chair where she could flop into it. Chris handed her the untouched cup of tea he was still holding. 'Drink this. You've had a nasty shock. How did you know about it?'

'Caroline phoned me directly she had called you.'

A voice came from upstairs, 'We're ready to move her, chief inspector.' Chris went up to speak to Ben.

The photographer took pictures at each stage of the process of moving and examining the body. Chris had seen few drowning victims – a drunk pulled from the Caldon canal the previous year and, more distressing, the accidental drowning of a toddler when he was mere rookie. He dredged his memory for something pertinent to ask.

The body was of a small, very slim woman. Her hair was short and dark, but would appear lighter no doubt when it was dried out.

'I'd like to move her as soon as possible Chris. The process of putrefaction would have been slowed by immersion, but will be significantly accelerated now that she is out of the water.'

'Any idea on the time of death?'

Ben shook his head, 'Not much. What parameters do we have?'

'The family went on holiday on 22nd October and found her this afternoon.'

The head shaking continued and Ben looked at his watch, 'The sixth today. That's a span of two weeks. I'd say probably earlier in that period rather than today or yesterday, but I can't be sure. I may know more when I open her up.' He looked up at Chris. 'There are so many variables...'

Chris tapped him on the shoulder, 'I know Ben, just anything you can give me. When's the PM?'

'I'll get onto it this evening. Do we know who she is? Any clothes or belongings?'

'None, and she's not going to be easily recognisable. It may be down to teeth I'm afraid, or linking her effects, if we ever find them, to a missing person.'

* * *

Once the body had been removed, the detective went downstairs to Sharon.

'Mrs Welland, at the moment we have no idea who this woman is and we need to identify her as soon as possible, do you understand?'

A shuddering gasp and a nod.

She took a gulp of tea and asked, 'I won't have to look at her, will I?'

Chris doubted whether many people could look on the recently dead with equanimity, certainly not the recently murdered. But although there was no spirit left in the woman in the bath, her body had been dead for some time and was therefore unpleasant to look at.

'Of course not. I want you to go home now and have a good think about any callers, any friends of Caroline or Edward you can think of and put a list together. Can you manage that?'

Again she nodded.

'You spoke of a baby, Mrs Welland. Where is the baby now?'

'At home, next door. My husband Billy is with him.'

As the stretcher reached the waiting ambulance Billy Welland came out in search of his wife. He moved down the path, exceeding quickly for someone with such a strange gait, having bandy legs such as are seldom seen these days. DC Harris nipped down the drive and intercepted him. He too shook his head.

The baby began a feeble wail as fireworks banged and cracked through the darkness.

'Sharon, I don't want you gettin' involved. I don't want that nosey cow next door prying into everything.' His wife glanced at Chris and nodded uncertainly.

'Do you and your husband live alone with the baby Mrs Welland?'

'Yes, well no – not at the moment. My half-brother is staying with us.'

'Is he at home?'

'No. He's gone to work. He works nights helping out driving for a friend.'

Having arranged to speak to the Wellands and Sharon's half-brother next day, they released the couple, and turned back to Edward and Caroline Fraser.

'I don't know what state she will be in tomorrow morning. We often heard them going at it hammer and tongs again just before we went away, nothing unusual there. You'd be better leaving it till he's slept off tonight's hangover.'

Chris was not so easily intimidated.

Edward Fraser looked up from his newspaper, 'Now if it had been her found in the bath that would have been understandable.'

His wife nodded sagely. 'Absolutely.'

'I won't keep you much longer for now, but I'm afraid there will be a police presence searching the house for some time.'

'Searching! Why searching? We've told you we don't know this woman. What are you searching for?'

Chris took a moment. These people may well be totally innocent, touched by a horrible crime taking the joy out of what had evidently been a happy holiday. On the other hand, until eliminated, they had to remain key suspects.

'It is difficult to see how this woman arrived at your house naked. Somewhere must be her clothes, a bag perhaps, purse and keys, jewellery, probably a phone, something to identify her. She entered your house apparently without breaking in. That suggests that she or someone knew that the house was empty, and also that they have access to a key.'

'I must get the locks changed,' Edward Fraser began.

'I'm sorry, sir. That can't be done just now. After the search we will speak again. Please do not continue with your laundry Mrs Fraser. Our officers will empty your machine and the contents of the sump will be taken for analysis. The forensic team will go over the whole house and you will have to remain here in the meantime. I'm sorry.'

They looked bleakly at each other.

'Do you leave your central heating on while you are away?'

'Absolutely. Well yes, it comes on twice a day – morning and evening, then is off during the day unless anyone advances it, and of course it's not on overnight.' Chris sighed. This was not going to help establish the likely temperature of the house or the water, nor how long had passed since the woman was killed.

'And my final question for the moment: does anyone else have a key to the house? Cleaner? Gardener? Anyone.'

Caroline thought, 'Absolutely not. I am here when the cleaner comes on Mondays, she has no need to let herself in.'

'And while you're on holiday, does Sharon let her in?'

'Certainly not. She doesn't come. I let her have a holiday. Paid of course. The gardener comes on a Wednesday. He absolutely never enters the house. He brings all his equipment with him. Other than that, there's only my mother. She has a key for emergencies. She lives in Madeley, but it's a bit too far for her to pop over all the time, so we leave the key with Sharon.

'There used to be someone who came in to walk the dog, but that's years ago. We lost touch. My son has an allergy and the dog had to go when he was just a baby.'

'I'll need their details the cleaner's, your mother's, the dog walker's if you can find it, and the gardener's.'

'Absolutely.' She moved to a drawer and extracted a calf-covered address book, noting down the details of her two employees. 'May I call Mother and speak to her? She doesn't know we're back yet, and it would be a terrible shock if you just turned up on the doorstep, she's quite frail.'

'Of course. Do it now please, Mrs Fraser, and in here.' He was not letting her make any calls in private until he had a better idea of what was going on.

* * *

On the evening of Hallowe'en in the Pitman's Lamp public house, Anthony Whitfield had stared gloomily at the bottom of his glass and debated ordering another pint. Perhaps he had drunk enough. If she came now ... he glanced at the clock behind the bar, eight fifteen. Who was he kidding? Over an hour late, there was no way she was coming now.

He gestured to the barman with his glass, 'And a whisky chaser please, mate.' He was angry now and getting more so. For two pins he'd go round there and ... he forced his clenched fists to relax. Losing his temper had got him into trouble before. He would finish his drink and go home, then think what to do tomorrow.

He was reluctant to leave it. They had seemed to be getting on so well. Why had she accepted lunch from him? And a present? Had she been taking him for a fool all along? Perhaps she had got cold feet or someone, her ex-husband perhaps, had stopped her coming.

Anthony tried to telephone her next morning, and throughout the day but the phone went straight to voicemail. He left a message saying that he had been disappointed that she was unable to meet the previous evening. He hoped she wasn't ill and that she would suggest an alternative meeting.

Nothing happened for a couple of days, then he received a text:

Sorry about not meeting you; something came up – bit of a family crisis. I will contact you to rearrange soon.

He would give her space, take no further action until he heard from her. When no call came after a further week he made up his mind to reluctant acceptance.

'Forget it. Forget her, the bitch,' he muttered into yet another pint, and so her absence, if not unnoticed, went unreported.

Chapter 4

In the no-man's-land between Scot Hay and Alsagers Bank, beyond the speed delimit signs for either, stands a row of cottages. The fourteen modest dwellings are set back from the lane and overlook Woodpecker Woods, the north tip of Shropshire and, on clement days, the Welsh hills beyond.

There was space enough in front of the cottages for a single car to be parked clear of the road, a wise move since the sharp elbow in Scot Hay Road made visibility a challenge. Towards the middle of the row Bob lived with his son Ray in a permanent fug of cigarette smoke and inadequately-washed clothes. The two had lived together fairly amicably since the younger man's mother had left home years previously.

Ray worked at the big garden centre on the Shropshire border, a routine job, not particularly well paid, but sufficient for his needs. His father had never considered it a man's job, called it *messing about with flowers,* but with his father's pension it kept them ticking along nicely, and until quite recently the younger man had been able to put some money by in the Building Society, though for what he never considered.

That evening as he returned from the pub his father sat tight-lipped, the very silence harsh and condemnatory. Each tiptoed around the other, with wary glances on the old man's side and a clenched jaw on his son's. Someone had to break the impasse and pick up the thread of their earlier discussion.

'It's not right, Dad. She's younger than I am. You'll be a laughing stock.'

'What's age matter, lad? Loads of couples have years difference in age.'

It was true. He tried again. 'Why now, Dad? We've been okay since Mum went haven't we? We've enough money for what we need. You can have the heating on all day in the winter; you can walk to the Gresley for a pint or I drive you if it's wet.'

It was all true. They went to France twice each year to visit Bob's daughter. They'd toured the Highlands of Scotland last year – Dad had enjoyed all those whisky distilleries – and this summer they'd been to London. Dad had seen Westminster Palace and the Changing of the Guard. He had baulked at going on the London Eye, but relished a nostalgic river trip to Greenwich.

'Why, Dad?' Ray repeated, 'Why now?'

'That's only a couple of weeks a year. It would be company. I'm on my own all day, it would be nice to have someone bustling round in the kitchen. Sometimes I don't talk to anyone all day when you're at work. She's on her own too, a quiet person, seems to like me.' He paused and dropped his voice. 'Lonely at night too.'

'Oh! That's it! An old man's itch …' Well he could understand that, he too was lonely at night, but the idea of his dad and that Gayle revolted him.

It was true that she was younger than he was himself but only by a few months. He remembered her from school. She had never ventured away from Audley and there could be no secrets in a village.

She had worked in the fruit and vegetable shop

– she possibly still did. Greenery not being a feature of their family's diet he had not crossed the threshold for years. She would no doubt try to make his dad eat sprouts past their sell-by date, he remembered her as a woman cautious with her money. He smiled to himself.

'What's so funny?' his father snapped, 'and less of the *old*. I'm in my prime,' he leered unpleasantly. 'I could give you a little brother or another sister yet.'

The younger man, himself no longer young, tried not to show the disgust on his face. What age was his Dad? He was uncertain, somewhere in his early sixties he supposed. And Gayle, she must be the same as him – early forties. With horror he realised that this could happen – just.

'And where would she sleep, Dad?' He decided to get the worst over. Now his father was looking embarrassed although his son had misunderstood the reason, 'With me of course. The King James Bible says a man shall *cleave to his wife and they shall become one flesh.*'

'His wife! You're going to marry the gold-digger!'

Bob wagged his finger, 'Less of that talk. I told you there ain't nowt wrong in it.'

'With me on the other side of the wall?'

His father was bright red now and fumbling to light a cigarette, 'Well son, that wouldn't be...it would be better if ...'

He was incredulous, 'You're throwing me out?'

* * *

When at last they turned the sign to *Closed* Josie and Carly were tired but euphoric. The opening day could hardly have gone better.

One young mum had asked about story time, someone wanted a book club and a local author had offered to do a talk and perhaps read from his latest book.

Some things of course had gone not so well. One woman had brought in a – fortunately small – dog, which had lifted its leg against a table, and a local businessman had got the new lock stuck on the lavatory door. These proved to be minor matters, easily resolved with a mop and bucket and a screwdriver.

Carly looked around and sighed contentedly. Not a computer in sight – well only her old laptop in the back room, which would be used for ordering and keeping her accounts.

She had toyed with the idea of banning technology from the café altogether, in keeping with the retro image, but dismissed it as impractical.

Tiredly she collected the vivid blue cards off each of the tables, and piled them on the dresser with the other Golden Tickets. Later would do for going through the suggestions, they had decided to leave them out for a week before deciding on the winner.

At least the press had turned up, promising a good spread in Monday's Sentinel. Carly looked forward to reading it.

* * *

The morning after the body was found, the Frasers' neighbour Sharon Welland looked even more fragile in the wintry light. In spite of the season she wore a faded loose dress in denim blue over a grubby white tee shirt. As she opened the front door the fair hairs on her forearms stood erect and an angry purplish bruise showed on her wrist. Seeing him glance at it she quickly turned away. The baby, a boy judging from his blue outfit, was young – younger Chris thought than his own second daughter Rachel. It crossed his mind irrelevantly that his wife Pippa would have been envious of how quickly this young girl had regained her figure.

He followed her into the living room, where her husband was standing, and soon saw the reason for the summery attire. The room was stifling, with heat beating out from a radiator, and a gas fired turned low, before which a rack full of nappies and small baby-grows was drying. The aroma of young baby was unmistakable.

'Mrs Welland, did you manage to put together a list of names – visitors to next door during the last three weeks?'

She flushed and held the baby in front of her like a shield, 'Not really. You see, I couldn't think of anyone. All their friends probably knew they were away so why would they call round? Of course someone may have knocked on the door, but nobody I saw.'

Chris nodded. 'Any strangers?'

She gave him a shy smile and he saw how pretty she was.

'Of course, in a manner of speaking.' She handed the baby to her husband who took him as if bestowing benison rather than taking his share of responsibility. He plonked the child down in an old-fashioned pram that took up much of the available space, before leaving the room. Sharon moved through an archway to the kitchen and filled the kettle with her back to them.

'It's been Hallowe'en and Bonfire Night since the Frasers went away. We've had no end of Trick or Treaters and Penny for the Guy; of course there have been strangers.'

'Did you recognise any of them?'

'Only little versions of Miss Piggy and Margaret Thatcher.' Again she gave him the beautiful smile, 'Oh, and a couple of clowns.'

Chris sighed. He had forgotten the celebrations. Hallowe'en, another import from America that seemed to have become a cult with bored youngsters over recent years. His head was whirring. Would they need to track down every Trick or Treater and Penny for Guy seeker? They would need additional resources.

'Is your brother here?'

'Not yet. He's at work up in Manchester. He said he'd be back for lunch.'

'DS York will stay and speak with him.'

* * *

It was only ten minutes after Chris left that DS York heard a door bang, muted conversation then a young man wandered into the room, barefoot, chewing a slice of pizza and concentrating on his phone.

'This is my half-brother, Ryan Lee. Ry, put your phone down. The sergeant wants to talk to you.'

He belched unattractively and nodded.

'Is this your permanent address, Mr Lee?'

'What? Yeah – for now.' He spoke through the pizza, glancing at his sister.

'It's not, Ry.' Sharon's glance flew anxiously to the door through which her husband had disappeared, 'You know it's only temporary. I've told you we an't got room enough, not with the baby'

She turned to DS York. 'He lived in a flat with his mate but they fell out so he was homeless. We said he could stay here for a bit, just till he found somewhere else.' The baby started to grizzle quietly in its pram.

The sergeant asked her politely to please let Ryan answer for himself. Huffily she swooped up the baby, startling him into a wail of distress.

'Now look what you've done.' She glared at him and slammed the door behind her.

'You left your flat when you and your friend fell out?'

'His flat, innit?' Finishing the pizza he wiped sticky fingers down his jeans. 'I didn't have any choice. I came to Shaz's for a bit but then I lost my job and couldn't pay rent or a deposit anywhere else.' He tossed the phone onto the chair arm.

'But you were at work yesterday when I spoke to your sister.'

'Got a job now, haven't I? Driving for a mate.'

DS York wondered whether this was cash-in-hand but decided it was not likely to be relevant to the current enquiry. If Major Crimes Officers were expected to pick up on every minor offence they came across in the course of their investigations, the job would never get done. He moved on, 'But you still live here?'

'Yeah, well. No law against that is there?'

'None at all, Mr Lee.' DS York could well imagine the nice little billet he had secured for himself, and guessed that he would not hurry to move on.

'Did you know the people next door?'

'Dunno. Might have seen them comin' and goin' but I don't know them, don't know anyone in the road.'

'How long have you lived here, Mr Lee?'

'Must be...' he thought, picking a bit of pizza from his teeth, 'six months, mebbe a bit more.'

'Have you heard your sister or brother-in-law talking about the people next door at all?'

'Nah. Don't listen, do I? They're always rabbiting about this and that. The kid's always squawking. I don't listen.'

'One last question Mr Lee. Think carefully. Have you seen any visitors next door in the last few weeks?' Ryan was shaking his head before the question was finished. He had picked up his phone again before the officer left the room.

Afterwards DS York was to wonder what it was that he should have asked.

Chapter 5

In the case of a suspicious death an immediate report is submitted to the Coroner, who issues a warrant in the name of the pathologist – in this case Ben Hanchurch – for the post mortem to be carried out. Generally a member of Chris's team would be assigned to attend that post mortem, often a constable. This officer would take the roll of Coroner's Officer and maintain liaison between the coroner and Chris's team to ensure continuity of evidence. There would thus be no danger of the Criminal Prosecution Service refusing subsequently to prosecute on the grounds of a technicality. Given the unusual nature of the current situation, with no certainty as yet that this was a serious crime or a suicide, Chris opted to attend the post mortem himself. Seven o'clock that evening found him facing Ben across the mortuary table.

Head injuries still upset Chris after a period in a coma after a head injury some time before. He looked at the victim in front of him and could not avoid seeing what might have been. With difficulty he dragged his mind back to the pathologist's discourse.

'There are a number of issues with this one, Chris. It's a while since I had a drowning and I've been doing a lot of looking up.' Ben gestured to the open page on his computer.

'I have four questions only, although I doubt you can answer all of them,' Chris told him.

'Fire away.'

'How did she die; was it an accident, suicide

or murder; how long has she been dead, and who was she?'

Ben gave him a long look before pulling back the sheet that covered the body.

'I'm sorry to disappoint you Chris, but I can't answer any of them, not for definite.'

Chris puffed out his cheeks. 'Okay, tell me what you've got.'

'Firstly, how did she die? Answer: in one of two ways. There is evidence of water in the lungs, and widely through other tissues of the body, but you would expect that if she had been dead already then left immersed in water for any length of time. There is no evidence of frothing from the lungs but that would disperse fairly quickly after drowning. There is no evidence that the water involved was anything other than fresh water. This would be rapidly absorbed into the blood stream, causing transient electrolyte dilution. The effects of, say, sea water, would be quite different. However, chlorine and other chemicals would disperse quite quickly so that doesn't really help either.'

'Can't you do a diatom test?'

Ben thought for a while, 'That's only really helpful immediately after death, and to be honest, it's very controversial.' He indicated the computer. 'There have been cases of diatoms found in the lungs where drowning has not been the cause of death. Because there are diatoms everywhere in the air, it is almost impossible to avoid contamination, so whilst it may support other findings, on its own it's not enough.'

Chris wandered thoughtfully to the far side of the laboratory and looked at the rows of specimen bottles containing various body parts. He turned one of the jars slowly.

'Pretty on the inside aren't we?'

'Colourful anyway,' Ben agreed.

'Why do you keep all this stuff? It's a bit ghoulish isn't it?'

'Not at all.' Ben was indignant. 'Think of it as a reference library.' He indicated adjacent jars, 'That's a healthy liver and this is the liver of an alcoholic who died of cirrhosis. I can use these for comparison purposes, they're not there for fun.' He sounded tetchy. 'Shall I go on?'

'Sorry, Ben. Yes please, I'm just trying to assimilate all this.'

His friend smiled, 'Sure.'

'Question two …' Chris started but Ben interrupted him, 'Hang on, I haven't finished with question one yet.'

With the assistance of the mortuary technician Valerie, he turned the body onto her side, and pointed to an area at the base of the skull.

Chris bent to look, 'She was hit?'

'Perhaps. Or she banged her head on something, possibly as she fell, but I'm inclined to say that she was hit, with something tube-shaped but with a right-angled projection.'

'Like a bath-tap? That would suggest a fall.' Ben was shaking his head. 'No, a tap would be the wrong shape, too narrow for what actually hit her, and too broad for the projection. That is narrow – about 1.5cm diameter.

'And then there is this depression to the side, like the edge of something smooth. Any matter would have been washed away but it was smooth like the corner of a cupboard, rather than something like a brick. The indentation is a clear line.'

'Wouldn't explain the tap-like protrusion though, would it?'

'It wouldn't.' Ben moved on, 'Now whether that was before or after death I can't say. All the blood has leached away obviously and you can see the state of the skin. That's going to be one I don't think I can go into the dock with. I'm going to have a closer look though. If I can get any more information from the wound I'll let you know.'

Chris understood. Ben's pride had taken a hit a few years earlier, when he had made a critical mistake in diagnosis. From time to time Counsel, and more cruelly the press made reference to it, and these days he was much more cautious. Chris considered it good for Ben to be fallible; it was unhelpful for a jury to believe an expert witness because of who he is rather than what he says.

'Fair enough. Now question two?' Chris raised his eyebrows.

'Deliberate or not? I'm sorry Chris, there's no way of knowing. She could have been struck from behind, fallen into the bath, or fainted and struck her head as she fell, but given that this is too narrow an injury to have been caused by a bang against a tap, that's unlikely. I don't see how it could be an accidental death in a stranger's house, and why had she no clothes or effects with her? Sorry that's your job.'

'Guess for me. I won't hold you to it.' Chris smiled.

'Someone else had to be involved hadn't they? If only after the event to take away the clothes, or to take her to the house naked. My guess, since you ask, would be that this was no suicide, too chancy. Normal people phone the ambulance after an accident, whether it's drowning or a due to an accidental blow. They don't clear off with the victim's clothes.'

'That was my thought too. Have you any idea of the time of death?'

'Time? No.' But I may be able to pin down a little detail.' He nodded at Valerie to put the body back into the refrigerator. 'Come into the office.'

Once there he brought up pictures of the cadaver on the screen.

'Maceration of the hands and feet when exposed to immersion, is likely to be well established during the first week.'

'You speak like a text book, what do you mean?'

'Softening and breaking down of the skin. It happens first on the soles and palms. That's beginning to establish here, so don't go getting any ideas that we may be able to lift fingerprints. What happens is that nerve fibres in the digits are triggered. These constrict the blood vessels. With me so far?'

Chris nodded.

'Because the resistance blood vessels in the digits are not uniform – they are tighter nearer the joints, and looser at the tips so that we can grip things – the pressure on them is uneven causing wrinkling and eventually for the skin to pull away in parts. By the end of a week in water the skin shows signs of separation of the digits.

If the body has been immersed for much longer – say two weeks – I would expect much greater detachment of the skin, and not just on the fingers and toes. That has only just started to happen, so I reckon she has been in the water for about seven to nine days.'

Chris was looking at the images on the screen and comparing them with a text book showing the result of a more advanced immersion. The difference was very evident.

'So that would make it before Bonfire Night and probably around Hallowe'en?'

'Perhaps. Is that significant?' Ben was wary.

'No idea. Did she wear any rings, a wedding ring?'

Ben had a closer look at the screen. 'No jewellery, but if you look here,' he pointed at the left-hand ring finger, 'once we'd dried her out, you can see from the colour of her skin that she has been used to wearing a ring. She was quite tanned. Whether that was taken off at the time of death or maybe she took it off herself earlier I have no way of knowing.'

'It could even be a relationship, marriage gone wrong so she stopped wearing it.'

Ben nodded. 'Of course we have no idea of the conditions under which the body was kept before it was put in the water. Nor the temperature of the water. For instance if someone was visiting the property twice a day and topping the bath up with really hot water, the effects would be very different from a body put in cold water and left alone for a week. Also we don't know the ambient temperature inside the house. Was it consistent? Was the central heating on twenty-four hours a day in case of frost? It's unlikely, so there were possible fluctuations.' He looked at Chris's face as Chris puffed out his cheeks.

'I'm sorry, it's complicated isn't it?'

When Chris failed to respond, he continued:

'Question four, identification – I'm afraid that one isn't my province Chris, but you wouldn't really expect me to be able to help with that one.'

'Not unless she had a very distinctive unique artificial limb, a Titanium plate or something and she hadn't. What about teeth? What about DNA?'

Ben leaned back in his chair, making it creak. 'Do you know I get sick of watching crime programmes so-called on the TV when they get a perfect match to a victim's teeth, or DNA. I could give you details of a sample of DNA and we'll certainly keep it, but at the moment what are you going to try and match it with? A hair sample for comparison – no problem, except we have nothing to compare that with either.'

It was unanswerable. Until they had some possible missing persons, a DNA sample was useless.

'Teeth?' Chris was getting despondent now.

'The same proviso applies. I will take impressions of course and photographs, but this lady had not visited a dentist for some years. There is only one tooth that has been capped – a lower front, which I reckon must be at least twelve years old. That would be needle in a haystack time, Chris. Sorry.'

Ben paused, but Chris knew him well.

'But?' he prompted, and Ben smiled his conspiratorial grin.

He indicated a photograph of the woman on his computer screen.

'You can see that although her nose and mouth are completely under the water the top part of her back and shoulders is exposed to the air, now look at this.' He pressed a button that homed in on a small section of the woman's back, just below the left shoulder-blade.

Chris leaned forward to see. A small cicatrix mark was clearly visible on the skin, slightly puckered round the edges.

'What am I looking at?'

'Interesting isn't it? It's thickened tissue, I'd say a scar of some sort. It goes deep, through the hypodermis, that's the lowest layer of the skin, into the tissue beneath. I think she's perhaps had a mole or a cyst removed and it's been a deep incision. Deep enough to require anaesthesia.'

Chris looked again. If Ben was right and this was a deep scar requiring a local or general anaesthetic, then there would be records, either at a hospital or a Health Centre.

Chris sighed heavily. He had come across the nightmare of bureaucratic confidentiality within the NHS before.

But Ben had not finished with him yet. 'I'll put out a few feelers at the local hospitals, Stafford, The Royal and Leighton. See what I can find out.'

Chris was about to thank him and got up to leave, but Ben continued: 'We've got another bit of interest here. Possibly this may be the most useful bit yet.' He changed the images on the screen, this time showing what looked like a filament of cotton thread.

'This is magnified considerably. It is barely visible to the naked eye, and we found it tucked in one of the interstices of the body, a crease just below the left ear.'

'What is it?'

'I'm not sure yet, but it seems to be part of a plant of some sort. I've bagged it ready to send to the lab for analysis, as soon as you have signed the docket, it seemed best not to waste any time.'

And there's another trace of some sort of plant life in the alveoli, that's the small air-sacs at the ends of the bronchioles. Looks to be the same thing. She must have inhaled it while she was submerged. I've sent it away for analysis.'

Ben had shared what he knew for now. He took his leave, 'I hope to have more for you when I've examined the organs and had a closer look at that wound. One thing I can tell you though, I don't think she died there.'

* * *

'Said that, did she? Cheeky mare.' Jayne Hardcastle looked like a domestic servant straight out of a television production. She wore a pair of black leggings, topped by a cross-over apron of the type not seen by DC Dearing since her grandmother was alive.

'Half pay! Half pay and hardly any notice. Pretended she'd told me about the holiday ages ago she did, but she hadn't and she knew it. I swear Lady Caroline blushed while she was telling me.'

When exactly did she tell you, Mrs Hardcastle?'

'Must have been four or five days before. She said they would be flying on the Saturday and she wouldn't need me again until ...' she rummaged in a capacious handbag for a small pocket diary, 'the thirteenth of November. Look.'

Dearing took the proffered book, and confirmed that it showed three consecutives entries of *no work* against the three relevant Mondays.

'So, she told you this the week before? The

seventeenth?'

'No,' the cleaner seemed reluctant to admit it, 'she told me on the tenth.'

In a fair approximation of Caroline Fraser's accent she said, '*I shall need you next week Mrs H, but after that not for three weeks.* She said as they were flying back on the Sunday she wouldn't want me the Monday 'cos they'd be absolutely jet-lagged. Makes sense I suppose.' This last was offered grudgingly as she put her hand out for the return of the diary.

'Was it usual for her to ask you to stay away when they went on holiday?'

'Had to, didn't I? She wasn't for handing a key out to the likes of me.'

Having ascertained that it had always been Mondays that she cleaned for the Fraser household, and that over the three years of her employment there it was quite normal to be given just two weeks' notice of holidays, Dearing took her leave.

Chris was becoming despondent. They seemed to have so little to go on, no ID, no clothes, bag or phone, just a watery death. There was enough water round the area to keep them searching for months.

He began to think he was in need of a miracle, and ready to leave it for the day, when the telephone rang. A woman had gone missing from Silverdale.

Chapter 6

Nicola Storey was reported missing by her friend. They were supposed to go to a Hallowe'en party in Hanley on 31st, but the friend, Maddie, couldn't get hold of her on the mobile or on Messenger for a couple of days before. She can't recall exactly when she realised she wasn't getting through but she had last spoken to Nicola on the previous Saturday. DS Hegarty reported back on her conversation with Maddie.

'Nicola was mid-thirties, had no boyfriend that her friend knew of, and Maddie felt it unlikely she would have met someone and not let her know. Nor was she aware that Nicola ever wore a ring on her wedding finger.'

'Does Nicola live alone?'

'Yes. She had a flat-mate who moved out a while ago, but seems her dad pays the rent and she hasn't bothered looking for anyone else to share. She did ask Maddie to share with her, but Maddie was still thinking about it. It seems Nicola wasn't the brightest star in the sky, and Maddie was worried that she may be roped into looking after her, rather than just being a friend. She didn't want any responsibility, she said.'

'Hmm,' Chris wondered whether there had been previous occasions when Nicola had acted in a way that left Maddie feeling that she needed to be responsible for her. What about now, now that Nicola had effectively disappeared?

'She did stress, rather a lot actually, that

Nicola isn't stupid, she's just not terribly bright. I asked whether she felt Nicola might make decisions that weren't very sensible, and she got a bit uppity, said that was exactly what she meant. It wasn't for her to comment on her friend's decisions.

'I felt I'd lost a lot of ground so I just asked her about the scar. She said she wasn't aware of anything but it would be just like Nicola not to want to share anything like that.

'I asked at the other flats in the block, but no-one is saying that they know anything. Several had no idea who I was talking about. The people next door said that she didn't seem to go to work, but they didn't think they had ever spoken to her. The woman on the other side said she kept herself to herself. The people downstairs said that the neighbour who said that was a right nosy cow and no-one in their right mind would share anything with her unless they wanted it spread round the neighbourhood. Oh, and Nicola has long blonde hair. It's not much.'

* * *

Ben Hanchurch arrived at the Guildhall as the team was assembling for the afternoon meeting. Chris found him looking out of the window across the outdoor market, where a few hardy stallholders were still trying to peddle their wares, in between battening down awnings against a capricious wind.

'Ben rang earlier this afternoon and I asked him to go through the details with all of us. This is important and we have little enough to go on.' Chris nodded to Ben to address the team.

'The lab has identified the scrap of plant life

found on the body, and in the lungs, it's the same plant, called Cladophora. It's a small filamentous algae. Pond weed, if you like. The lab has also done toxicology tests and the plant life contains traces of copper sulfate and monolinuron.'

He sounded excited. Whilst not ghoulish, the occasional mystery cadaver must make a change from the more routine road traffic accident and *anno domini* victims, Chris supposed. Like a vet faced with an exotic reptile in amongst all the domestic dogs and cats.

The pathologist looked at a sea of blank faces.

'What's that?' DS Hegarty asked what they were all thinking.

'It's an algaecide used to help prevent standing water going green with algae. So you may be looking for someone with a garden pond, or maybe a swimming pool.'

'The Frasers have a garden pond,' Chris said, 'but it's covered over with a mesh in a solid frame that looks as if it has been in situ for years, because of the children I expect. It would take some shifting if you wanted to drown someone. Anything else Ben?'

'The fact that these two chemicals were still evident in the sample on the body gives us some more information. It means that the tap water from which the plant had probably been transferred to the body, had been treated, from the amount of saturation, probably some weeks before the plant dried out.

He pointed to the photographs. 'If you recall the head was turned slightly and the back of the left ear was out of the water, but the water that drowned her did not come straight from any bath tap.'

Chris checked what he was saying. Ben was

right. The crease behind the left ear was not underwater, and if the body had been left in situ for a week or so then the water was treated very recently before that.

'So she could have drowned in a pond and been moved? It's certainly treated water rather than just tap water?'

Ben nodded. 'Or a domestic swimming pool, not a river or stream or canal anyway. And not fresh tap water.'

DS York was despondent, 'Wow! That really limits the number of options.'

'Don't shoot the messenger, Yorkie. I'm doing what I can.'

'I know, Ben. I'm sorry.'

'Another question, Ben.' Chris was still examining the pictures. 'If she was drowned in a pond and then put in the bath, how long could she have been dead between the two?'

'Remember, as we said before, she may not have drowned at all, but the Cladophora being in the lungs would suggest she breathed it in and so was alive when she went into water somewhere, although she may have been unconscious. You don't ask the easy ones do you?'

'Sorry Ben, best guess?'

'This does give us a greater indication that immersion was contemporaneous with her death, but it would still depend on the conditions in which her body was kept. I'm sorry I can't help you more.'

Young DC Harris flushed to the roots of his wispy hair. 'Sir, my parents have a swimming pool.' He waited for the ribald laughter to die down, and the calls of *Oooh – get you.*

'And?'

'They would never use copper sulfate to keep it from greening, because it discolours the water. It's more likely to be a garden pond, perhaps someone who keeps Koi carp.'

'Bit of an expert are we, Harris?' called some wag from the back of the room.

'Actually,' Harris said, grinning broadly, 'My parents keep Koi carp as well.'

More hoots of laughter, which Chris quelled with a look.

'I don't know about everyone, but they are very careful to keep the two means of algae control separate.'

'Thanks, constable. That's useful.' Chris meant to be encouraging to the young detective, but privately wondered how many fish ponds there were in the area. He was concerned that they might have to find out. He wondered too what percentage of homes in Staffordshire included a swimming pool indoor or outdoor.

Not many he guessed, the climate hardly being conducive. Although the use of copper sulfate pointed more towards a pond, no-one would deliberately discolour the water in their swimming pool.

Chapter 7

Next morning over breakfast Chris looked moodily at the headline in the local newspaper, *Did she fall or was she pushed? – DCI Timothy remains tight-lipped about the cause of death of a mystery woman found in the bath of a house near Audley at the weekend.*

To himself privately he added: *or drowned or hit with something or... what?* The article went on to relate, it seemed to Chris, all the mistakes and errors of judgement he had made throughout his career. He threw the paper aside. Usually the press, particularly the local newshounds, were very helpful in an enquiry, but when they felt he was being obstructive they could be very negative.

The Assistant Chief Constable, normally one to delight in press conferences, was on holiday and Chris had conducted the meeting himself. Floundering in the investigation, he had the start of a headache and was taciturn. His younger daughter Rachel was teething and he had a disturbed night.

Chris was abrupt with the media: *No, we don't yet know who she is; no, we don't know how she died; or when; or where.* Even to his own ears it sounded like a catalogue of failure.

Afterwards he stared gloomily at the coffee DC Georgia Dearing placed in front of him, uncertain where to begin.

She put down a pile of reports for Chris to go through. As the enquiry continued, the piles of paper would grow and grow until hopefully they had sufficient evidence to present a case to the CPS.

'House to house, sir. Not much. One of the Frasers' neighbours, Jack Morgan, got up during the night, but he can't remember exactly which night it was. He thinks Sunday thirtieth or Monday thirty-first of October, but can't be sure. He thought he heard something. There was a street light out just here.' She indicated on the large map on Chris's wall.

Chris surveyed the map closely. The other street lamps had been marked and were some distance from the Frasers' house.

'He lives almost opposite the Wellands' house.'

'Did you get to speak to Sharon Welland's brother?'

DS York checked his notebook, 'Yes, sir. He's a bit vacant. Was out on a driving job in Manchester, but got back soon after you left. Says he knows nothing about anything, and doesn't know the neighbours. Spends a lot of his time in the pub or watching TV. As he pointed out, it is a while ago.'

Chris agreed, 'I doubt I could tell you what I was watching last week. What about the Welland husband?'

''Both he and the wife say he never went next door. She had checked the house each day, closed the front curtains before it went dark at tea-time, then nothing till she opened them after breakfast next day.' He looked over at Chris, 'I didn't know you had them in the frame, Sir.'

'I don't particularly. I just want to dot all the I's. What else have we got? Hegarty?'

'Usual crank calls. A few random sightings of

the mystery woman, fitting the description of the woman we put out, some clearly rubbish, all being checked out. One even claimed to be after we'd found the body.'

'Nothing short of miraculous that one. Is that it?'

'Anything remotely tenable is being followed up, but I doubt it's going to bring us anything helpful.'

She turned over the page in her notebook, 'There is one thing, the window cleaner, sir, Krystal Kleer. The owner is Jason Castle. They visit a few houses in that road, including the Frasers'. They did their rounds on Monday – that would be the thirty-first of October.

'Anyone talked to them yet?'

'No sir, they'd already gone out to start work when I went round to the owner's house first thing. His wife rang him, he'll come into the Guildhall at his lunch break.'

'I'll see him. I want to check for his latest visit, but also previous visits. If he has others working for him or with him, I'll need you to talk to them this afternoon.'

Hegarty made a note.

Chris felt as if he was clutching very slender straws, but the sergeant had saved the best for last.

'Ben Hanchurch wants to meet you at the lab at ten o'clock. I said that'd be okay if he didn't hear different.'

Chris checked the clock before leaving for Stafford.

'Sounds interesting, then that's where I'll be this morning.'

He addressed DS York, 'Arrange for me to see

Jack Morgan again this afternoon after the window cleaner. Otherwise, the usual routine.'

DS York allocated jobs: interviewing, checking, visiting and revisiting.

He told DC Dearing, 'Go back to the Wellands again and check if the window cleaner visit jogs any memories for any of them. Then run a check on Ryan Lee, Sharon Welland's brother, and Billy, the pugilistic husband.'

'Based on?'

'Instinct. They were close at hand and had access to a key. And then I'll get onto Missing Persons. See if they have any other possible matches locally for our lady in the bath.'

* * *

Ben Hanchurch was a first-rate pathologist, but so much more. He could see that to look at the body in isolation could limit his findings. A murdered body impacted on its environment and vice versa. Ben had the skill of making that connection.

'Chris look at this,' he was clearly excited but Chris dreaded this moment. The chemist and Ben stood to one side and Chris peered down the microscope, no idea what he was looking at.

'What is it?'

'I'm not sure but I think it's paint. A fragment of paint stuck inside the area of the wound.'

'Paint?' Chris's mind went into overdrive. He could picture an image of the woman's body, dead or unconscious, lifted into a car, banging her head, but the balloon was quickly deflated by the chemist.

'Definitely not car paint, wrong constituents, it

looks to me like a paint you would use on plastic. I'll have to do more analysis. I'll get onto the PRA.'

'Remind me.'

'The PRA, Paint Research Association. They'll be able to match it, almost certainly. My worry is that it is so small, if we damage it in testing, then bang goes our evidence.'

'Could it be from the weapon?'

'I would think so.' The chemist nodded enthusiastically.

Ben was in one mind with Locard, whose Exchange Principle says that every criminal brings something, however insignificant, which he leaves at the scene, and also that he similarly takes something away. Chris was less sure.

'So you're saying that somewhere is a piece of plastic missing a bit of paint,' Chris sounded dismissive.

'Hang on a minute. What I'm saying is that this flake of paint is missing, almost certainly off a piece of plastic and quite possibly off the murder weapon. If you come across that piece of plastic you may be able to make the link. It may give you a clue as to where she died and even how.'

'Okay, okay. I get it.' He grinned, 'Plant life and plastic – all the clues I need.'

* * *

Hegarty was approaching the house opposite the Frasers' when she heard Caroline's Fraser's strident voice behind her.

'Oh, hello there! Detective! Constable is it? I must protest.' She hurried across, meeting Hegarty in the centre of the road.

Hegarty introduced herself and gave her rank, receiving a scathing look in return.

'Sergeant, there are police all over my house. All my clothes pawed over, even my underwear. We can't even go upstairs, we're having to use the downstairs lavatory, and that policewoman asked me to check whether any of my clothes were missing, as if that …that …thing …that body may have worn them. I feel absolutely violated.'

'I understand how you feel, Mrs Fraser. Unfortunately this woman has suffered a much worse violation.'

'Yes well …' Caroline sounded as though she was not so sure, 'and what are they doing in the garden?'

'You have a garden pond, madam?'

'Yes, but …'

Hegarty disliked holding this discussion out in the road, but the woman had begun it. She chose her words carefully.

'We believe that a garden pond may have played a part in the woman's death.'

'Oh, really! I have young children. That pond has been covered up for years. I should report you for this. It has nothing to do with us.' Her anger was mounting.

'Mrs Fraser, a woman has been murdered and her body found on your property. Whoever she was, whatever her life held, she was entitled to that life just as you are to yours. You must report me if you see fit, my name is Detective Sergeant Frances Hegarty, but I cannot believe that you really expected us just to take the body away and make no enquiries.'

She let the silence lengthen.

Quietly the other woman said, 'Yes, of course. Sorry. Do whatever you need to. It's just such a strain.'

'Just one more question, do you use Krystal Kleer window cleaners and if so, do you know whether they cleaned your windows while you were away?'

Giving a grudging affirmative Caroline Fraser gave a disgruntled sigh and went back across the road, slamming the front door behind her.

Hegarty continued on her way to speak to the neighbour. She smiled quietly to herself. Poor woman – inconvenienced by a murder to the extent of needing to use her downstairs loo.

Chapter 8

Identification via the scar on the woman's back was proving more difficult than Ben Hanchurch had suggested, with no evidence of the surgery having been carried out in any of the local hospitals. Chris asked Ben to spread the net wider, to Trusts in the surrounding area. Then Ben had a bit of luck. An administrator at a Birmingham hospital phoned Chris to say that she thought the photographs may be of a colleague's work.

'We can trawl through the records for you but it may take some time. It is the sort of thing one of our surgeons specialises in, but there are hundreds he's done spanning the length of his career. It may not be identifiable.'

There was a pause. It sounded as though the woman on the other end of the phone was eating. 'Of course,' she continued, 'all the records are confidential so it will have to be an internal trawl as and when we can spare staff to do it.'

'I'd be grateful for anything you can do. It may be our only hope of identifying this woman.'

'The specialist says that from your photograph he would say the most recent the scar can be is twelve months ago, so we'll start there and go backwards. It's a long shot though. Hopefully it won't be too long ago, before the records are computerised, all that old stuff has been archived.

'I don't want to get your hopes up, chief inspector. Comparatively few operations have photographs taken, only if they are interesting or of use as training aids. Luckily the surgeon is Mr McLeod who is punctilious about keeping notes. Drat.' There was a pause, then: 'Sorry, shouldn't be trying to eat and talk at the same time.

'Where was I? Oh, yes. Mr McLeod is very meticulous, but if he took no photographs and we are just comparing his written notes with your snaps, well Chief Inspector Timothy, you will appreciate the difficulties.'

Chief Inspector Timothy appreciated the difficulties only too well. He briefly considered applying for a Court Order but decided that cooperation and patience was, in this case, more likely than coercion to produce results.

It was just on twelve o'clock when Chris, recently returned from seeing the pathologist at Stafford, was called by the front desk. The window cleaner had been as good as his word, arriving just as Chris decided a sandwich was needed to sustain him through the afternoon. In Chris's absence, Hegarty was preparing to talk to him, and Chris decided to put lunch on hold and join them.

It seemed that Jason Castle had just an hour he could spare and he would like to get something to eat as well please. He was not about to delay his afternoon's work for anyone. Chris and Hegarty took him over to the Roebuck Centre where they found a table in the atrium café. With the Hallowe'en and Bonfire nights over, the shops were ramping up their Christmas crusade, in vain competition against on-line shopping.

Officers often used the café at lunchtime and there were a couple of other detectives at a corner table. The staff recognised their urgency and quickly provided sandwiches and tea, of which Jason took a big gulp before he spoke.

'I started the firm from scratch,' he said proudly, as Chris investigated the insides of the sandwich and evidently found it satisfactory. He waited for the window cleaner to be served his hot meal. Hegarty settled for a coffee, and got out her notebook.

'Essential this is,' the window cleaner explained, 'a hot meal in the middle of the day, especially in this weather. People who sit in offices don't know what it's like to be out in all weathers.'

Chris nodded wisely. He doubted whether the younger man knew how much of a police officer's life was spent in the open air, and how well he could understand.

'I specialise in the estates where houses are close together and you can get a lot done in the day. A government start-up loan got the business off the ground five years ago and now I employ three lads full time.'

Chris was suitably impressed and told him so, then paused while the waitress placed a fresh cup of steaming coffee in front of his interviewee.

'I know what you want of course. I don't think I can be much help. Perhaps you should tell me exactly what you want to know.'

He forked spaghetti expertly while Chris looked on enviously, deciding that a hot meal would have been an excellent choice.

'I want to talk specifically about when you were in the area of the house where the woman was found. Do you have a regular round that you can check up on?'

'I do but we can't always stick to it, obviously the weather plays a part and the time of year makes a big difference 'cos of the daylight. You can't go climbing ladders in a really high wind, nor if it's piss...sorry, bucketing down with rain.' He wiped the back of his hand across his chin, 'People resent paying for what they can't see.'

He reached into his jacket for a small notebook. 'I had a look at this before, thinking it would help with what you needed. I have a number of customers who pay by cheque, usually every few months or so. I generally let it go about three months then hand them a little bill, a bit of a reminder like. That way it doesn't get out of hand.'

Chris decided to let him tell it his own way. The window cleaner stabbed one of the pages with his fork.

'This is Mrs Dawson, she pays every three months by cheque. Now I can use her payment as a guage of where I was and when. Ahead of her September payment in the book is number two, that's a big house so it's fourteen pounds, then here is Mr Price at number seven. He's the only customer I've got that pays that amount, so I know it's him.'

Chris was unsure that he needed so much detail but felt reluctant to interrupt, Jason Castle was trying so hard to help.

'Now here is Mr Price again in October so that was the same day as I cleaned the Frasers' windows. See no payment because they were away. You ask Mrs Fraser, she'll tell you they came home to a ticket like this,' he handed Chris a slip of paper that read:

Windows cleaned
Date:
Amount owing:

'And that according to my book,' he sat back in his chair to deliver the finale, 'was 31st October.'

'Are you able to tell me when in the day that would have been, Mr Castle? Morning or afternoon?'

Jason Castle sucked in his cheeks, and showed the notebook to DS Hegarty. The detective had gone off-piste now. After a great deal of thought and reference to the little notebook, Castle made his pronouncement, 'Late afternoon.'

'Are you sure about that?' Seeing the hurt face Hegarty went on, 'What I mean is, are you certain or is that the closest estimate you can remember?'

'We'd had our dinner in the van that day, but that was up on the High Street. It's not always handy like this to get somewhere to eat. We had soup in a flask. By the time we got there it would have been gone four o'clock. Gets dark about half past and we usually finish this road and the next one along then finish.'

'You say usually, how sure can you be?'

'Pretty definite. It was that cold, we'd had enough but forecast for the next few days was bad so I said to the lads we'd just get that far then finish.'

Chris thanked him, having reluctantly been given contact details for the men who worked for Jason.

'They don't know about this stuff,' he persisted, 'they won't be able to tell you anything I can't tell you.'

But there, as it turned out, he was wrong.

Chapter 9

'The report is back from Missing Persons, sir.'

'Tell me,'

'It's not good news. The lists are nothing like up to date, there isn't the manpower to chase them up and mostly people don't bother to let the police know when people are found.'

'What are the figures?'

'Staffordshire alone there are currently over sixteen hundred women on the register aged between twenty-two and thirty-nine. Some of those will have been missing for years. This year a total of nine hundred and sixty-four adults in that age range have been reported, over half of them women.'

DS York had overheard. 'Then we would have to consider our close proximity to Cheshire and Shropshire. She could have come from there.'

'Cheerful Charlie!' Chris growled at him, 'Dearing, get a couple of PCs over to trawl the phones. Divide this year's list between you first and phone each family to see the outcome. Be sensitive and check the exact age of the missing person, Ben has narrowed it down to mid or late thirties. Anything that looks likely drill down more deeply, see if there has been an operation resulting in a scar in the last couple of years. Check the photographs with the PC's so they know exactly what they are asking about.'

* * *

DS Hegarty sat opposite Darren, one of Jason's acolytes. It had taken some time for him to untangle himself from gloves, scarves and jacket, and he sat now with grateful fingers around a mug of steaming tea.

'So, let me get this straight. You cleaned the Fraser's windows with Jason in the afternoon while the other two were working at number seven? And what did you see?'

'Nothing then. It was later on. Short cut home from the girlfriend's isn't it?'

'And what did you see?'

'There were steam coming from the central heating vent at the back and water running. There was no light on though, I thought it was funny that someone was having a bath in the dark at nearly two in the morning.'

The sergeant made a mental note to check with the Frasers' the timings of their central heating clock.

'Were any other lights on that you noticed?'

'No, and I would have done, 'cos that street light wasn't on.'

'Have you not seen about this in the papers?'

'No, I'm not much of one for reading.'

Hegarty tried not to let her exasperation show, 'Didn't Jason say that we were making enquiries about that house?'

'He did. I reckoned if you wanted to know anything off me, you'd come and ask me.' He gave Hegarty a broad smile, 'and now you have.'

* * *

Before leaving the office for the evening DS York reported to Chris on progress so far.

'We started with the most recent missing persons in Staffordshire. DC Dearing and the two PCs are now looking for the most recent on the Shropshire and Cheshire lists, but we have two hopefuls locally. Paula Fielding is a married woman, left the family home on 28th October after a row. Hubby said he presumed she had gone to her mother in Werrington, then on the Tuesday, which was Paula's birthday, the mother phoned and hadn't seen her. So that kicked us into action.

'The other is Nicola Storey as you know. DS Hegarty spoke to her mother, and she's more worrying in that she has special needs. Not physically but her mum was worried that she wouldn't cope very well on her own. She's been very sheltered and although she's thirty-five, she's hardly ever out by herself, and speaks to the family every couple of days at least.

'Uniform spent a lot of time talking to the sister who they said was a bit cagey. They thought there may have been a falling out with her friend that the sister was keeping quiet about.'

'And the scar?'

DS York shook his head. 'Not that any of them know of.'

'We need to talk to the mother again.'

'Paula lives in Bucknall near the park. She's a married woman with no children. She had a row with her husband; one of many regular rows according to the neighbours, on the evening of Hallowe'en. About seven o'clock this was, so the husband says.

'She'd left him before but only to go to her

mum's. Each time she'd stayed a night or two then come home, either of her own volition, or he'd gone and fetched her. He described her as a little bit unstable.

'This time, he says, she told him she wasn't going to her mum's. Mum is just out of hospital and she didn't want him going bothering her.'

'Did she say where she was going?'

'He says not. She went on foot, they have just the one car and it's still there in the driveway.'

'There would be buses running into Hanley or to get her to the station that early in the evening. Did she take any luggage?'

'Just a black leather handbag he says. He was happy enough to show me the wardrobes and he's quite probably right. He said her heavy coat's gone and her boots – black with quite high heels – but nothing else that he can see.

'He phoned the mother eventually on the 3rd November but she hadn't seen her. It was the mother who actually reported her missing.'

'Do either of them know the Frasers or the Whitfields?'

'They say not. I believe the mother. He's more difficult to read.'

'What does he do?'

'He's a gents' hairdresser, a barber in Hanley.'

'What about the scar. Does she have anything like that on her back?'

DS York looked at the floor. 'Damn. Sorry sir, I forgot to ask.'

Chris ran his hand over his hair, 'Never mind, I could do with a haircut. Before I do, what about the other misper?'

'Nicola Storey. I have an address in Hanley for her, a flat, but there's no-one home. I've left a PC there to call me when any of the neighbours turn up.' He gave a massive sigh. 'Sorry sir.'

Pete Talbot had always joked that DS York could not survive for more than a couple of days and was not happy unless he had a computer in front of his nose. He was not the strongest member of the team out in the field but he was a whizz with the electronics.

* * *

John Fielding cut Chris's hair in comparative silence, then after Chris had paid he produced his warrant card.

'I know who you are and I can guess why you're here. Give me a minute.' After barking instructions at a couple of the stylists and checking the appointment book, he indicated with a nod for Chris to follow him into a tiny cupboard-like room, where a washing machine whirred quietly in the corner.

Without speaking he went to a coffee machine and made himself an evil-looking concoction, then cocked his head at Chris questioningly.

Having refused coffee, Chris sat down at the table, moving a pile of warm, fluffy towels to use the surface for his notebook.

'You recognised me?' he asked, 'I don't think we've met.'

His professional persona slipped, 'Come on, I had a copper round this morning, then you present a very distinctive head with a very distinctive scar. Your face was all over the papers when you were attacked; heads and hair are my livelihood, how could I not recognise you? Paula's Mum been shouting her mouth off has she?'

'She is concerned for her daughter, Mr Fielding. What I need to know from you now is whether your daughter had a scar below her left shoulder blade, just about here?'

'Don't know about a scar. She had rather pitted skin. She'd had bad acne as a teenager, so she had marks and stuff.'

'Has she had any operations on her back in the time that you've been together?'

'No, no operations.' Had the answer come too quickly? Too emphatically? Chris was unsure.

* * *

Having spent an enjoyable evening with Pete Talbot, Chris was surprised to receive a phone call from him first thing next morning, but it cleared up one mystery, 'Paula Fielding's mother has been on the phone. Her daughter doesn't want her son-in-law to know where she is. He's violent and she stayed a couple of nights in a hotel, now she's gone to her mum's for a bit. She's leaving him but she's frightened.

'Paula'll be at her own house at three o'clock this afternoon to get her things.' He paused with a laugh, 'We can talk to her there if you want. She says if we can send the biggest, burliest officer in uniform you can find, that would help her too. Put the wind up John Fielding I'm thinking. Would you like me to send PC Grimes round to talk to her? He's built like a brick outhouse with a bullet head and crew cut. He also has a very mean-looking facial scar.'

'Good of you Pete. He sounds perfect. Let me know what he gets out of her, but she certainly isn't our Jane Doe.'

'No problem, the mother lives in my patch anyway. Of course it's really only to check her ID, but I like to think of it as crime prevention as well.'

'Very laudable. Doesn't help our current problem though does it? We've no further news on Nicola Storey at this stage.'

'Do you think we need to get onto Cheshire?'

'Done. Hopefully they are trawling records even as we speak. It's like looking for a needle in a haystack.'

DS York came and stood beside Chris's desk. 'We've heard from Nicola Storey. She had left a note saying she was going away for a few days with a girlfriend, but somehow the note got thrown away. She's home and fine. DC Dearing spoke to her this morning.'

Chapter 10

DS York spoke up at the team meeting. He had again taken up his preferred position in front of the computer screen and found some information, although as yet, its relevance or otherwise was unknown.

'As a matter of routine a DNA test had been done on the woman's body. It has identified a probably fraternal connection with a known offender. This was a youth who had been convicted as a juvenile for soliciting men in Hanley bus station years and years ago. He was then aged fourteen.

'He had spent a brief time in a Residential Special School in Cheshire, now defunct, but the education department must still have records, we've got them doing a search. There have been no convictions since he was fifteen, he fell off the radar so we have no clue to where he or the sister may have been since. His name is Neil Jennings. We're trawling records for her Christian name now.'

From her position in front of the crime scene photographs, DS Hegarty followed Chris into his office. She was plucking up courage, denouncing herself for being nervous with him.

'Sir. Could I ask you something? It's not to do with work.'

She was well aware that Chris was punctilious about keeping work and social life separate. She and Pete regarded him and Pippa as friends but that was strictly for outside working hours.

He looked at her stricken face and red eyes.

'Of course, Frances.'

'It's the wedding, she said, 'you know my dad had a stroke last year. He's suddenly decided he can't face up to giving me away. His speech and his walking are very difficult and he says he's been really worrying about doing it. I don't want to put him through it when it upsets him so much. I wondered whether I could ask you to stand in for him.'

He smiled at her immediately. 'Of course I will Frances. We'll talk later on about what's involved. My wedding day to Pippa passed in a bit of a blur. I'm afraid I can't remember clearly exactly what her dad did. I must admit I'm very relieved. I thought if it was all off I wouldn't only have you and Pete to deal with, but Laura would be devastated.'

'Thank you, Chris.' Her relief was apparent. She passed him an envelope. 'And here's Florence's invitation. Would you pass it on to her at the weekend please?' She leaned in and gave him a peck on the cheek. A step too far in the office perhaps?

'Right Hegarty,' Chris said briskly, 'Let's get on. What were you so absorbed in about the photographs?'

Together they returned to the incident room and approached the photographs of the dead woman, Hegarty's head tilted to one side. She had taken a couple of hours' leave for shopping with her and Pete's mothers for their wedding outfits and was spending some time catching up on activity during her absence.

'I think I knew her,' she said at last.

'Why on earth didn't you say so?'

'I didn't recognise her, sir. It was when Yorkie said Jennings. When I knew her we were at school.

Suzy Jennings she was known as then,' she looked thoughtful. 'When Yorkie said about the youth in the bus station it sounded familiar and now looking again at the pictures I'm sure it's the same person.

'There was some tragedy in the family. I can't quite remember... I think her brother died or someone in the close family when she was really young. I remember as her friends we were all at a loss to know how to talk to her when she came back to school. We were very young.'

'How young? Teenage?'

'No, no. I met Suzy when we were in Primary School. We must have been eight or nine. I remember now, it was her brother – a good few years older than her, but still at school I think. He died and it turned the mother a bit strange. Suzy virtually moved in with an aunty and uncle and they brought her up. I don't think I've seen her since.'

'Hmmm.' Chris was losing interest. Susan Jenning's death – or whatever she was called now – could hardly link back to her childhood. The truth must surely lie in her much more recent life.

As she began her lunch Hegarty pursed her lips, she was not so sure. She determined to find out the names of relatives with whom Suzy had been sent to stay, and to find out whether there was anything further they could reveal.

'Good work, Hegarty. Get on to the records office, find out is she still single. Otherwise her married name and her last known address.'

Almost at once PC Gregory put his head around the incident room door. He was ebullient.

'We've got something, Sir. Ben Hanchurch has been on the phone, and we've got an ID on the dead woman. Susan Chell, née Jennings, was admitted to the Queen Elizabeth Hospital, Birmingham eighteen months ago.

'A Mr McLeod carried out an operation to remove a cyst from her back. It was supposed to be done under local anaesthetic but ended up needing a general. It was an unusual case so they took photographs of the procedure and the finished result.'

'Photographs?' Hegarty pushed her yoghurt to one side.

'Yes, sergeant. It's a teaching hospital. They do that.'

'I hope you haven't brought us any.'

'I have, but Ben Hanchurch has looked at them already so you don't need to.' He grinned as Hegarty threw the remaining yoghurt into the bin.

'The surgeon looked at Ben's photos and recognised his own work, seemingly. And the two pictures of the scar – Ben's and the surgeon's –are virtually identical. Even I could see they were the same. The dead woman lives, or lived I should say, near the Gresley Arms at the top of Alsagers Bank.'

'What news of her family?'

'There is the husband or ex-husband living locally. Both parents are dead, Dad of cancer about five years ago. Mum had been very strange for years – since her only son died. That was Susan's brother of course. He was just a teenager. The mother died quite recently. She was in Homedean after being in various hospitals for years.'

'Let's have the Alsagers Bank address.'

Having gained details of Russell Chell's home, Chris and DS Hegarty made their way via the A34. Traffic was bad with one lane closed. A pothole had grounded an SUV, causing the traffic to crawl past in a single lane. It took them forty minutes to reach Alsagers Bank.

Although no more than a few miles from his own home, Chris had never before driven down the unmade road beside the Gresley Arms car park. Of course he knew of The Poplars, the Residential Care Home with discreet signage on the High Street, and Hegarty had been called out to the home a couple of months ago, but neither of them were aware that there was also a small row of houses clinging precariously to the steep hillside.

Before approaching the house he stood and looked at the view. It was almost the view from his own house, except a panoramic version, without the interruption of trees and rooftops. Today the air was so crisp and clear that he could see the white tops of snow on the peaks of Snowdonia in the far distance.

He had thought at first that he approached a bungalow, with an integral garage to the right of a large front window, but looking beyond the garage it was clear that there was a second floor, below the one on which he was entering.

The doorbell was answered eventually. They waited so long that at first it seemed the house was empty, but after a few minutes a man of indeterminate years opened the door a fraction. DS Hegarty thought he had a look of Hugh Grant, with hooded *come-to-bed* eyes that she was sure would crinkle attractively when he laughed, and hair deliberately styled to emulate the actor.

'Mr Chell? Russell Chell?'
'Who wants to know?'
'Police, Mr Chell.'

'What do you want?'

He looked awkward, then ruffled his hair in a gesture familiar to rom-com lovers.

'This is the address we've been given for Mrs Susan Chell, sir. Is this information correct?'

'Sort of yes. Susan Chell lives here, yes.'

'For how long, sir?'

'It must be five years since we married.'

'And this is still Mrs Chell's address? You don't sound very sure.'

Again there was the little-boy ruffling of his hair to best effect.

'Where is Susan, sir?'

He still seemed unconcerned, 'She's not here at the moment.'

'Where is she supposed to be Mr Chell?'

He picked up immediately on the phrase, Chris's mechanism for starting to alert him to a problem.

'Supposed to be, what do you mean? She's house-sitting for a friend.'

'I'm afraid we need some details, sir. We really would be better inside.'

With bad grace he let them in as far as the hall.

This entrance doubled as a space for dining. Other than a huge modern table and ten chairs that dominated the room, and in the middle of which stood the bust of a phrenological map, the only other decoration was a crystal decanter and set of tumblers displayed on a side table islanded on the expanse of cold tiled floor. Beneath them stood a telephone and directories.

The only adornment was an amateur but rather pleasing water colour of a canal side scene featuring a small boat, which hung on the wall facing the table. He saw them looking.

'Sue's father painted that years ago. He didn't want to keep it and never painted again apparently after his son died. All his pictures were of boats and the canals, you know the sort of thing. Sue is devoted to it.' He seemed to remember who they were and closed the front door sharply.

'Now what is all this?'

'May I ask what you do for a living, Sir?'

Chell looked bemused. 'I'm self-employed. I work as a management consultant – go where the work takes me you know. You're lucky to find me here. I have to be in Birmingham this afternoon. Now,' he sat down on one of the dining chairs, 'what is all this about?'

I'm afraid we may have some very bad news for you sir. We have recovered a body whose description matches that of Susan Chell.'

'Description, what description? I've not given anybody a description. What do you mean?'

'A scar on her back has been positively identified by the surgeon who removed a cyst eighteen months ago. Did she undergo such an operation, Mr Chell?'

'But it can't be Sue, Sue isn't missing.'

'When did you expect her home?'

'I wasn't sure, I thought I'd probably got it wrong.'

'Did you try phoning or texting her?'

He hesitated, then, 'Yeah, there was no reply,' said uncertainly.

'And the people she was house-sitting for, who are they?'

'What? Oh, Diane and Anthony Whitfield I think.'

'Did you try the Whitfield's landline?'

'No, just her mobile. Sue didn't leave me their number'

An old-fashioned flip-up index stood on the table beside Hegarty, next to the telephone. She flipped it open at *W*.

'The number's right here, Mr Chell.'

'That's Sue's, not mine. Don't you need a search warrant to do that?'

'That seems a strange reaction in the circumstances, sir.' He moved to gaze at the painting on the wall.

'You seemed remarkably casual sir, about when she was due home.'

'To be honest Inspector, she'd gone off before, stayed away for a few weeks then come back with her tail between her legs, usually when she ran out of money or the latest love of her life didn't live up to expectations. She quite frequently spent time away from home. More so latterly.'

He turned to face them, 'Where's her car? Sue's car?'

'There was no car at the Whitfield house, sir. We'll need the details and her mobile number, and of course to check your own garage. Would you have expected her to take her car to Mrs Whitfield's?'

'Of course I would, it's miles away. How else would she have got there?'

'You didn't answer my question about the scar, Mr Chell. Did Susan undergo such an operation on her back?'

He had gone pale. Frowning he said, 'Yes, but

I don't understand. Sue can't be dead. If she's been in an accident why didn't you come straight to me? You said a surgeon identified her, why did a surgeon get involved? Had she been taken to hospital?'

Briefly Chris told him about the body found in the Frasers' bath; that it was naked with no bag or clothes and that was why the scar had been used for identification.

'Would you like to sit down, Mr Chell? The sergeant will put the kettle on.'

Eventually Chell nodded and led the way into a lounge that utilised the whole of the rear of that floor, with floor to ceiling doors opening onto a full-width balcony, and the spectacular view.

Hegarty almost gasped and Russell Chell looked suitably gratified; no doubt this was the response he expected from everyone.

'Stunning isn't it?' he said, while Chris wondered about a man who, in these circumstances was prepared to waste time discussing the view, however spectacular.

Chell moved to a grand piano at the front of the room and picked up a photograph of a couple, himself and a woman who despite the decomposition, was undoubtedly the woman they had found.

'When did she go to Diane Whitfield's, sir?'

'I'm not sure.' His eyes flickered about the room as he spoke but his conversation was matter-of-fact. There was clearly little regret.

'You don't know when she went, nor when she was due back. It seems a bit strange, Mr Chell.'

Chris felt that the man was lying. They needed to get to the bottom of when Chell was expecting Susan home, and why he had done nothing about it when she failed to return. Or did he know perfectly well that there was no possibility of her coming home ever again? In spite of the situation, Chris felt his mood lighten. Now they knew who she was the investigation could begin.

'You didn't go to stay with your wife when she house-sat for these friends?'

He looked embarrassed. 'No. She's been going there for years. Long before she met me. I won't deny it was a useful arrangement for us though, Diane has occasionally come to house-sit for us too. My work takes me abroad and Sue used to come with me if Diane would pop over and house-sit for us.'

'You say *used to*. Does she not house-sit anymore?'

Chell paused, then 'Not really, no.'

'You didn't report Susan missing?'

'I told you. I thought I knew where she was. Look I could do with a cup of tea and I'm sure you could. Give me a minute will you?'

'Shall I go with him, sir?'

'No, leave him a minute to gather his thoughts.' They could hear the sounds of a kettle being filled and crockery put on a tray. After a few moments Chell reappeared and placed the loaded tray on the coffee table. He sat and looked at the officers.

'Sue and I were separating. I had asked her to move out.'

'When was this, sir?'

'Just over twelve months ago.'

'Twelve months! So do you know where she was living recently?' Hegarty's pen was poised. This didn't make sense.

'Well, here. She didn't move out. When I said

I wanted her to leave she told me she had just found out she was terminally ill. She had nine months to a year at most; that eventually she would need to go into a hospice but could she stay here till that had to happen? In the spare room of course.'

Hegarty looked up. 'And you agreed?'

'Yes, sergeant. I'm not a monster. I'm not quite hard enough to turn a dying woman out of the streets.' Again the puckish smile. Closer examination showed that the look was contrived, but Hegarty would have taken money that he had women beating their way to his door.

'And the nature of your relationship recently?' Chris said mildly.

'Just friends I suppose. Landlord and tenant.'

Which, wondered Chris. To his mind there was a deal of difference between the two.

'She paid rent?'

'Not really,' he said. 'Since that conversation she'd made her own arrangements about food. Sometimes she'd buy milk or bread or coffee and sometimes I would – nothing formal. She continued to pay the electricity bill and I the gas as we'd always done. I paid the rest of the bills. The house belonged to me long before I met Sue.' He waved a dismissive hand. 'The money wasn't an issue.'

'What was an issue, sir?' Hegarty wanted to know.

Again the hair was tousled; again it fell obligingly into attractive boyishness. Hegarty wondered whether he practised in front of the mirror.

'Relationships, sergeant.' He looked earnestly at her with the come-to-bed eyes. 'I'd already met Felicity, hence the showdown. It was Sue who introduced us actually. We were planning for her to move in here but as it is we've kept her place on and spend a lot of time there.'

I bet you do Chris thought.

'We'll need her name and address.'

He started to jot down details on a scrap of paper. 'It was difficult. Sue was often not at home, but we, that is Felicity, didn't feel comfortable staying here. We never quite knew when Sue might turn up.'

'How often was Mrs Chell away overnight? When she's not house-sitting that is.'

'It varied. Once, twice a week – sometimes more, sometimes she told me she had to have treatment and would be away for a few days, sometimes she didn't. Occasionally it was for a week or more. Of course I am often at Felicity's so wouldn't know whether she was here or not. I offered to visit her when she was in hospital but she said not.' Chris sensed his relief. Hegarty continued to scribble notes.

'What exactly was wrong with Mrs Chell?' Hegarty recalled almost verbatim the introductory words of Ben Hanchurch's report:

A healthy woman of approximately 35-40 years, having borne no children. One scar only is significant, a cicatrix measuring 3mm by 5mm situated 1.5 cm below the left shoulder blade.

''I'm not sure to be honest, sergeant. As I said by this time we were living pretty much separate lives and were on the verge of parting. Looking back of course, much of Sue's coldness and lack of interest in the preceding months may have been due to her illness. I don't know for how long prior to our discussion she had been feeling unwell. Like a lot of men I'm rather squeamish. I think women are definitely the stronger sex in many respects. I didn't ask for details.'

Again he favoured her with the seductive look but the sergeant remained unseduced. 'I assumed cancer of some sort.'

'Yet Mrs Chell seems to have remained in good health. You say she was given just nine to twelve months to live and had already survived in seemingly good health for the best part of a year.'

'These prognoses are notoriously unsound aren't they? Someone given six weeks lasts two years and vice versa.'

Chris admitted the truth of this, his own aunt had been just such a case.

'Can you have a look for us and see what clothes are missing? The body was naked when found.'

Chell closed his eyes briefly, as if in pain. 'I'll try but I'm not sure I can help. As I say we had been largely going our separate ways. And also ....'

Chris looked up, 'Mr Chell?'

'I may be totally wrong but I had an idea that she kept part of her life separate, not here, as if she had somewhere else to stay.'

'What makes you say that?'

'As I said, she went away occasionally for days, for treatment she said. She usually came back looking remarkably well, even sun-tanned. She joked that as skin cancer hardly mattered at this stage she had taken advantage of the clinic's spa facilities while she felt well enough. It boosted her morale she told me.'

'And her car, where's that?'

'I don't know, but then I often didn't. She had a Range Rover. She was passionate about it. Rather than leave it on the road to get damaged – with us being so near the pub and the school I suppose – she rented a garage from a chap just along the main road.'

'The scar on her back. Do you know what caused that?'

'Yes. It was just after the initial conversation I told you about. She looked a bit rough, and said that on her visit to the hospital that morning they had taken fluid from her lung, which along with the tablets she was taking, had eased her considerably. I was to get on with my life and not to worry about her.'

'Did you see the wound?'

'Unfortunately, yes. It needed the dressing changing daily for a week and she couldn't reach it herself. She asked if I could cope with doing it for her, otherwise she'd have to go to the surgery each day. I said I'd try and actually it wasn't too bad. It was about here.' He reached round and pointed out on his own back the site of the scar where Susan's cyst had been removed. So was it a cyst as Ben suspected, or pleural fluid as she had told her husband, Chris wondered.

'What did the wound look like?'

He scrunched up his nose. 'Horrible, to be honest I don't cope well with stuff like that. I just wiped it with the antiseptic pad like she explained, and stuck the new dressing on. It wasn't just a pinprick though, it was much bigger and sort of like a cross. As if someone had stuck a Phillips screwdriver into her lung.' The hand crept unconsciously to his hair again and he finished more quietly: 'except that would kill her wouldn't it, if someone did that?'

'We'll need the name of the person who rented

her the garage and the registration details of the car. Please try and find them. If you could also look through her clothes and see what's missing? We'll be back to talk to you again.'

As Chris returned to the car up the slippy incline he heard a tremendous crash. The crystal glassware, the phrenological head, or both had been thrown across the room. He wondered, not for the first time in his career, what was the question he should have been asking.

Chapter 11

Russell sucked the blood from his finger and gazed in despair at Sue's Dream smashed across the tiles. It had been her joke name for the head. All the markings were wrong she had told him, the Victorians knew nothing. She had traced a ghostly slender finger across the sections – this one is for contentment; and this for happiness. Here is freedom and this largest section here, is for love.

Damn her. Given time she would have come back to him – she would. And now there was no time.

The strident screech of the telephone interrupted his reverie, and he impatiently brushed away a tear as if embarrassed it would be detected. Felicity had promised she would ring him. Unable to ignore the clarion call at close quarters he opened the French doors and stepped into the frozen garden, striding swiftly to the boundary fence to be alone with his thoughts.

Hegarty had reached the car well in advance of the Inspector. 'He's very calm. He's taking all this in his stride isn't he? Do you think he's relieved? Whether he did it or not, her behaviour could mean that he was nearing the end of his tether.'

'Not as calmly as you might think, sergeant.' He told her about the crash of breaking pottery. 'Rather a cold fish I thought. Off with the old, on with the new.'

'He never even wanted to know what had happened to her until we told him.' Hegarty slipped the car into gear. 'I suppose he could have assumed nature had taken its course.'

'Unless he knew exactly what had killed her,' Chris mused, half to himself.

As they left the house a distinct chill had settled as the daylight relinquished its hold and surrendered to the twilight.

'What sort of illness remains concealed at post mortem?'

'None that I know of. I need to speak to Ben again.'

Hegarty swung the car out into the main road. 'Where too, sir?'

'Chell says he and his girlfriend were together, and no doubt she will confirm it. But they would, wouldn't they? Perhaps they had reckoned that by this time, over twelve months after her revelation, she should be dead or at least removed to a hospice and out of the way for them to get on with the rest of their lives. Maybe it was time to help her along.

'We need to speak to the girlfriend, see what she can tell us. I'll phone her now, before Chell can speak to her first, then Yorkie and I will need to go to these people where she should have been housesitting. It's on Stoke's patch. Give Pete a call and tell him what we're doing. On the way past we'll call at the rented garage. See if her car is there.'

* * *

A telephone call by DC Harris established beyond doubt that Ben's post mortem examination had found no trace of any disease, fatal or otherwise. Disappointingly it also confirmed that little more had been learned about the fragment of paint he had found. It was the type of paint used on plastics, matching nothing in the automotive range.'

DC Harris was more interested in the supposed illness. 'Why would she lie? It would be inevitable that she would be found out.'

'Yes, but it might buy her enough time to do ...what?' Chris's voice tailed away. He had the horrible feeling that already this case was getting away from him.

'To keep a roof over her head?' DC Harris suggested. 'While she decided what to do next, or found another meal ticket. Chell said money wasn't a problem but divorce nearly always leaves both parties worse off. They end up running two homes between them for one thing. It wasn't costing her much was it? And she was able to go her own way, short holidays maybe to acquire a tan, and no unwanted sexual advances from our Russell.'

'Mmm.' Chris was unconvinced. 'It was still inevitable that she would be found out.'

'Perhaps by the time that happened she was hoping to have moved on, created an alternative source of income for herself. In which case he would never have known how she had used him.'

'That makes more sense. We need to find out more about her. Make an appointment to talk to Chell again; he's had time to absorb the initial news. I want to know everything about her. Hegarty thinks she was at school locally. Check that out. She must have lived within the school catchment area too. Find out where. Where did she work? What family had she? And find out what clothes are missing. Get a current photo of her too.'

DC Harris noted it all down.

* * *

Hegarty spoke to Chris as he left for Milton, where the dead woman should have been house-sitting. 'Pete knows what we've got on, sir. He asked to be kept informed.'

'We've made a call to Russell Chell and we're going back there this evening. He's going to go through his wife's wardrobe, see what's missing. All that's come immediately to mind is a fancy denim jacket he had bought her a couple of years ago in a shop in Leek. He seemed surprised that we hadn't found the jacket, she wore it everywhere apparently.

'She generally carried a shoulder bag. Nothing unusual, just a black leather bag. She has a mobile and then there's the car. There must be keys to the car and the house somewhere.'

'The car isn't in the garage and the garage owner hasn't been paid October's rent. She normally puts a cheque through his letterbox on the last day of the month.'

'Get details of her car and get it into the computer. ANPR should be able to pick up its recent movements. Ask them to check back say, four weeks. Take an artist with you to mock up illustrations of the clothing items Chell can remember, especially that jacket, and the bag. I want them in the Sentinel tomorrow morning, and a description on local radio channels.'

Chapter 12

As she swept large arcs in the dust on the piano top, Diane Whitfield wondered why dusters were bright yellow. Playing the piano, like so many other short-lived enthusiasms, had soon exhausted its attraction for her stepson Dane, and the instrument had been standing untouched for several years now. She idly considered how best to spur her husband into getting rid of it.

Within minutes she found her mind straying to the topic that had dominated it all day, ever since she had received the phone call about the death – no, the possible murder – of Susan Chell. The chimes of the doorbell interrupted her thoughts. She glanced out of the window and saw that it was the police.

As head of the Newcastle Major Crimes Unit Chris and the Stoke teams often worked closely. Arbitrary lines of jurisdiction are written in the sand and in the balance sheets, but villains acknowledge no such boundaries and investigations often spilled over into adjacent policing areas.

In the village of Milton, part of the neighbouring policing area of Stoke on Trent, Chris and DS York sat in a living room very different from Russell Chell's.

The area bordered the Staffordshire Moorlands and the address they had found was part of a small development, probably for pit-workers, at the foot of Bagnall Heights, a steep hill rising from the valley of the River Trent below.

This enclave of houses had been built over a hundred years ago. The distinction was very evident between those who cared for their property and the others. At the end of the cul-de-sac had been an open area, the orchard at the back of a huge old pub. With an extensive car park to the front and side the site had been considerable. Over time it had been sold off for housing, the most recent some three years old.

The cul-de-sac's residents were divided about the new houses. Those with young families were pleased at playmates for their children and the addition of a small convenience store backing onto the far side of the plot. The older residents decried the loss of yet more green space, along with anything else that constituted change.

The Whitfields' own house had not been well maintained. There was peeling paintwork to wooden window frames, and several windows had obviously been replaced with double glazed units, a drainpipe was hanging drunkenly beside the front door, dripping onto a green algae-covered patch of concrete. Several of the roof slates were cracked, slipped or missing altogether.

Inside was not much better. No spectacular view here. The room was cluttered and functional, the owner having to move stuff off the sofa in order for the two detectives to sit down, and with, inexplicably, a large hole in the chimney breast wall. Cobwebs of ghost spiders with their invisible legs festooned the ceiling cornices.

Diane Whitfield's appearance matched the room. A large untidy woman, with impossibly dark hair showing grey at the roots, she was probably in her mid-forties, Chris surmised, but with the face and hands of a somewhat older woman. The voice was plummy. An unbecoming flush mottled her throat and neck. He was surprised to learn she was only thirty-eight – the same age as Caroline Fraser.

'This year we went away on the twenty-first of October,' she told them, 'which was a Saturday. We took my stepson with us. The school had ten days' holiday then two Inset days, so we came back on the first of November – All Saints' Day, and he went back on November the second, that was All Souls'. Seemed crazy to me going back so late in the week, but I expect there was a reason.'

DS York, a non-believer had no idea what she was talking about, but took assiduous notes nonetheless.

'I was exhausted I can tell you. Perhaps you think we couldn't have children of our own? This is my life, my choice. You have no idea how personal people get, even strangers assume you have a desire to procreate, and that's usually after you've met their own revolting brats.

'It wasn't till the Thursday morning after we got home that my neighbour came in asking if everything was okay. We were at cross-purposes for a while. I thought she meant with our holiday and I couldn't understand why she sounded so miffed.

'Then she told me she'd checked the house every day, watered the plants and so on, and she supposed that the house-sitter woman hadn't been able to stay for the whole ten days after all.'

Diane paused and, taking some laundry out of the basket, laid what was obviously a sundress across the ironing board.

'Have you changed the bedding on the bed

where Susan slept when she stayed?'

'Not yet, there's been so much of our own stuff from the holiday. I was going to do that next.'

'Leave it please,' he nodded to DS York, who left the room, 'We'll get it checked.'

As she applied the hot iron, Chris smelled a vague waft of suntan lotion, evocative of the beach.

'And was that the first you knew about Susan not having been here for the full ten days you were away?'

Diane nodded, then stood the iron up slowly, 'Except,' she paused, 'the house was not exactly as we left it, but it was a bit odd.'

'Odd in what way?'

'Some of the post had been brought in and put on the kitchen counter like Susan normally did, but there was some still left in the porch.'

'Can you work out on which day the post had last been brought in? It might help establish when she was last here.'

She shook her head. 'I'm sorry. It was mostly junk mail – it mostly is these days, isn't it? There's no way of knowing what came when, I just gathered it all up and put it on the counter.'

'Was that the only strange thing you noticed?' the sergeant asked her.

'Well, not much milk had been used but she may not have eaten here much; I didn't when I stayed at their house, just breakfast usually. I was a bit surprised though, Susan loved her coffee. I would have thought she'd have used more on that alone.'

She was talking more to herself than to the officers, 'I suppose she could have used loads of milk and got another one out of the freezer, but …' she looked up at them, 'I'm sorry. I sometimes have one, sometimes two bottles in the freezer. Seeing how much is there now wouldn't help.'

'Did you see her arrive, what she was wearing and what she brought with her?'

'Lord no! We left at the crack of dawn on the day we left – to beat the traffic you understand. We'd opened the curtains and everything. We wouldn't have expected her to come until that night at the earliest. Sometimes she would just pop in each day, but usually she stayed. Said it was a change from ...' she put her hand over her mouth, suddenly aghast at what she was telling them. 'The bed seems to have been slept in, but I've no idea how many times.'

Or by how many people, wondered Chris.

'Did you try to speak to her after your return, Mrs Whitfield? I know you weren't expecting her still to be here, but perhaps you'd phone to thank her? Maybe to query the post?'

'Of course I thanked her, but only in a text.' She got a phone from her bag and pressed a few buttons before showing Chris the message:

Thx v much. Lovely hols. Spk soon. D&A x

The text had been sent on the first of November, immediately Diane Whitfield arrived home, and received by Susan Chell's phone, wherever it was.

'We will need to search this house, Mrs Whitfield. I'll organise a team.' Chris reached for his phone.

'Need to search, but why? It's nothing to do with us. She was only house-sitting.' Diane Whitfield looked as if she might cry.

'I'm sorry, Mrs Whitfield, but this is the last location where we can place Mrs Chell. I will get a Court Order if necessary, but why would we need to?'

'I'll speak to Anthony, my husband,' she whispered and disappeared into the kitchen, from where they heard snatches of the conversation: '…says he'll get a Court Order.'

She gave Chris a tight smile as she returned, but said nothing more.

'DS York will wait here until the team arrive, and will direct their activities. Before I leave can you just confirm that the text was the last time you tried to contact Mrs Chell. You said in the text that you would speak soon.'

'Oh yes, I tried to. I phoned at the weekend, I can't remember now whether it was Saturday or Sunday, just really to follow up on the text. But there was no reply.'

'Was this mobile to mobile?' They would have to check the records.

'No, I used the landline, and phoned the house. I thought even if Susan was out Russell may answer.'

'Forgetful isn't she?' DS York whispered to Chris as they stepped into the hall before Chris left. 'Can't remember how much milk there should be, can't remember when she tried to phone the Chell house.'

'Some people are forgetful,' Chris tried to be fair, 'and the days do get confused when you're just back from your holidays, until you get back into your normal routine. It's a point well-made though. Perhaps her forgetfulness is just a useful tactic.

'I need the team to take this place apart,

Yorkie. We're looking for a handbag, a phone, anything that she can identify as Susan's or anything that seems out of place. I want forensics to look at the bathroom and take the sheets off the bed she slept in. Thank goodness Mrs Whitfield had not yet got round to washing them.

'I also want the junk mail and flyers that she says Susan had gathered up in their absence. We need the team to check what day each would have been delivered. Get on to the Post Office, and the neighbours. They may remember.'

* * *

Formal identification of his wife's body had been carried out by Russell Chell.

He remained calm but Chris could see that his hands began to shake as they left the mortuary and walked to Chris's car in a biting chill wind. There would be frost again before morning.

'Can I have her funeral now?' he asked in a small voice.

Chris shook his head, 'Not just yet, I'm sorry.' He spoke gently. 'We'll let you know as soon as we can.'

'Why does the funeral take so long?'

'It needs to wait until we have enough information to be sure. It would be much more upsetting to have to disinter your wife's body if new evidence came to light at a later date.'

He nodded, seeing the sense of this. 'And a disaster if she had been cremated.'

'Indeed.'

'Except perhaps for the murderer.'

Chris picked up a copy of the local paper on his way to the office. The Stoke Sentinel had dubbed Susan Chell *The Bride in the Bath* and in the edition printed on the following morning the front page published her name and a photograph provided by Russell Chell. On page five the artists' impression of her distinctive jacket, as well as her boots, and the black bag accompanied speculative text.

The inevitable rash of hoaxes was accumulating by the time Chris fought his way through the wind into the Guildhall. Some were from well-meaning members of the public, others from well-known exponents of the hobby who liked to feel important. All would need to be explored, and many would be a total waste of manpower and time.

Chapter 13

Tom Payne was a professor at Staffordshire University and his morning routine seldom varied.

He stepped into a morning blast of cold air with his dog, intending to walk Buster along the canal bank before going into work. There had been a heavy frost overnight, the first of the winter, but the temperature had risen after midnight as it started to rain, and he noticed that his windscreen would probably not need defrosting by the time he set off for work.

The wind was dropping but the sky was still heavy with rain clouds, and as he stepped out of the drive the rain began, striking his face like frozen needles. He had never been a fair-weather dog walker, believing that Buster needed daily exercise whatever the weather and certainly the dog showed no reluctance as they headed towards the pathway through the estate and thus down to the canal.

It was still dark, but Buster's coat had fluorescent strips and Tom wore a headband lantern, the rain sleeting almost horizontally now. He carried a hand torch and his phone in his jacket pocket.

A creature of habit as much as his dog, the pair crossed Baddeley Green Lane and he followed the dog down the well-known route, letting Buster have the full extension of his lead as they turned right down a narrow footpath.

To the left of this path a gully drained excess water. A steady stream just now after gentle overnight rainfall, it could soon become a torrent as it cleared water from the hills behind them, and would likely do so if this rain continued. These hills rose steeply up to Bagnall Heights and beyond them to the Staffordshire Moorlands.

The rain continued to pour down and there were few people about this early. The path was narrow, cindered and with no edging to the half metre or so drop to the gully's floor. At this time of year it was slippery with leaf drop from trees in the gardens backing onto it.

The path covered about a hundred metres, before debouching onto a small bottle-nosed cul-de-sac where the gully disappeared underground through a culvert protected by an iron grating. As they entered the path the street light on the main road went out, leaving a faint glow from the moon eerily illuminating the path.

Tom, like many who live alone, talked to himself and his dog. 'Come on lad, sooner we get the walk done sooner we can get dried off. I'll pop the fire on when we get home and you can lie there and dry out while I have my shower. You'll like that, won't you, hey?'

He switched off the headband lantern, redundant now that fingers of feeble daylight reached over his shoulder. The dog bounded ahead down the path rimed with frost. 'Steady boy, don't want to land in that gully. I don't fancy coming in to get you out.'

Buster, exploring the eight metres ahead of him that the lead would allow, was bent head down into the gully lapping water.

Something hard up against the side of the gulley where there was a slight dog-leg was acting as a dam, raising the water level alarmingly.

'That's not right,' Tom muttered to the dog, 'That needs clearing.'

Switching on the headband lantern again he directed the beam through the rain onto the blockage. A tumble of clothes, denim and leather with a flash of turquoise and yellow caught in the beam.

Gingerly Tom bent and hauled them out. This seemed odd. Occasionally one saw an odd shoe or a jumper perhaps, lost under who-knew-what circumstances, but someone had dumped a whole outfit. He pulled out the denim jacket, jeans and boots. These were quality boots, quite new but one with a damaged heel, and tucked into them was a t-shirt and lady's underwear and a garish handbag. He gazed some moments at the denim jacket and the boots. These looked like the items he had seen described on the Midlands news the previous evening.

'Something definitely not right,' he muttered to Buster who was eager to investigate the finds now lying sodden on the path.

Tom glanced at his phone, time was pressing. What to do? Sensing its significance he was loathe to leave this stuff here. Schoolchildren used this path, who knows how far this stuff could be dispersed by lunchtime. Not knowing the telephone number of the Bethesda Street police station in Hanley, for the first time in his life he dialled triple nine.

* * *

Pete Talbot, Chris's old team mate, and fiancé to Frances Hegarty, was on duty at Bethesda Street.

Letting the Guildhall in Newcastle know that the clothes had been found in their patch, was more than a matter of courtesy; the worlds of Stoke on Trent and Newcastle under Lyme often overlapped. There were residents of the latter who would prefer to distance themselves from the larger conurbation, but they fooled no-one except perhaps themselves.

This obligatory call received, Chris set off with Georgia Dearing to Baddeley Green Lane. Finding what could be Susan Chell's clothing not half a mile from the house where she should have been staying deferred the decision on which he had been pondering.

He needed to decide about Sunday working. The team members could not work at their best without a break, and also to be born in mind was the overtime budget. Pressure from above as to how he was using his manpower was always an issue. The situation in Baddeley Green would no doubt make the decision for him.

Whilst waiting for the whole investigation team to arrive, Chris examined the gully. Whoever dumped those clothes had a range of escape routes at both ends of the pathway. The safety gratings at each end were rusted and corroded in place, and evidently had not been moved for years, so the clothes must have been placed very close to where they had been pulled up onto the path, and continued to drip into the trickle of water. He spoke to the PC first on the scene and posted a uniformed officer at each end of the path to speak to would-be-users and divert them to the long way round.

The place had been carefully chosen. Half way approximately along the path the dog-leg meant that each end of the path was hidden from the other. At this point windowless garage walls backed onto the path, and to the other side of the gully fences and conifer trees shielded windows from intrusive eyes. Whoever had left the clothes here would have been unlucky indeed to have been seen.

Chris wanted to know when those clothes had been dumped, the names of those who used the path regularly, and whether they had used the path in the last twenty-four hours. If so, he wanted to know if they had noticed the clothing. The Sat Nav on his way here had shown a primary school on the other side of the main road, they should check whether there was a crossing patrol officer.

Glancing at his watch he looked down towards the bottom end of the gully. 'What's down there?'

'Housing estate sir, mostly bungalows; then a playing field; the River Trent and the A53.'

At a loss what to try next Chris wandered down the path and the cul-de-sac, and out into the estate. A few houses, then the road turned sharply to the right. There was no-one about at this early hour, except a recycling lorry reversing up the cul-de-sac and another elderly dog-walker.

Between two of the left-hand garden fences a narrow path led to a field. Chris followed the path and crossed the field to where two tributaries of the River Trent flowed swiftly towards the city. Although no outlet was visible, Chris decided that the underground culvert probably debouched into the nearest of these. With no particular aim in mind he crossed the bridges and found himself dropping down onto the towpath side of the canal.

No greasy strip of city centre water this. There

were reeds and willows aplenty and ducks bobbed hopefully towards him through the mist across the water. Another dog-walker was strolling in the direction of Leek and a cyclist heading for the city swerved by.

Opposite were a range of detached houses, all boasting canal moorings. Losing interest, mallards and coots went lazily about their business, ignoring him. He caught sight of a flash of brilliant blue, as a kingfisher stitched its way up the water, its colour matching that of the pattern on the reverse of the retrieved jacket.

His reverie was broken by a canal barge pushing a bow wave like a grubby moustache ahead of it … forging up from the city, the ducks moving indolently out of range as if they knew there was nothing to fear here.

This little detour had been of no use, he thought as he plodded back uphill, but there he was wrong.

Chapter 14

Returning to the gully as the Crime Scene vans arrived and the team started to cordon off the area and set up floodlights, Chris stood at top of the entry looking around. This was a side of the city little known to him. There were no street-mounted CCTV cameras in view but there may be some on individual properties. This would need to be checked and all the surrounding households questioned as to whether they had seen or heard anything. Across the road was a garage, its gate standing closed, its sign swinging in the wind, squeaking with each icy gust. Employees would need to be talked to and Chris watched as the wheels of the investigation began to take on their own momentum.

Tom Payne was incredibly interested. Being on the periphery of a serious crime, as long as it did not involve them or their loved ones, usually did bring out the curiosity in people. He stood beside Chris and asked 'Could you get fingerprints off the boots? They look like leather.'

'Hardly. The salts in perspiration are what creates fingerprints, and the gully water and the rain would eradicate them.'

If Tom Payne was correct and the clothes had been dumped very recently, why now? Surely because of the news coverage.

'Sir, you suggested that these things had been less than twenty-four hours in the gully. Are you quite sure?'

'Positive. Buster emptied his bowels around about here yesterday, very close to edge of the path. I had to go right across there to bag it up; definitely I would have noticed if they had been there then.'

Having made sure they had his contact details, Chris sent him on his way.

Officers were talking to local residents and the garage staff who were clocking on for work. All confirmed that they were sure there had been no clothes in the gully the previous morning. The school crossing officer was prepared to go further, as her nearest route home was down the gully. She was prepared to swear that the clothes had not been there when she went home at half past four the previous afternoon.

A car pulled up at the kerb and Pete Talbot, Chris's former partner stepped out.

'You were determined to get me involved in this, weren't you?' he grinned. 'I suppose now I'm going to have to step in with additional man power. We have no specific sub-aqua team in Stoke, but we have a contact in the Rivers Authority who should be here shortly. We'll get these gratings off at both ends of the gully and see if there's anything else to find. Your case Chris, but keep me informed.'

* * *

In detective fiction motive plays a key role. Often it is pivotal to the solving of a crime. In real life motive is of little importance to the police. They require evidence, and often Chris found that motive, if it were identified, was of such little consequence as to be almost risible. A woman looks at another man, so her husband kills her; a woman's cat is hit by a car so she goes and burns the driver's house down.

Where motive is useful is in helping the police to know what traits to look for in a suspect, and spotting behaviours outside of the norm. What they needed to establish was what was normal for this victim and what had happened recently to change it.

Half of the time in any enquiry was given over to paperwork, checking cross-checking reports and statements for details and anomalies. This was DS York's forté. He both enjoyed and excelled at it, far preferring the battle with technology to that out on the streets.

A DCI's deputy was always invaluable, and while he was out and about *chasing shadows and rainbows* as he put it, DS York could be left happily in charge of the Guildhall office. There he fielded telephone calls, and dealt with the day to day issues that fell to Chris when he was not involved in a major case. By lunchtime Chris was free to return to the Guildhall where he found DS York looking at the map in his office.

'This crime covers miles. Why take her clothes up to Baddeley Green? She was supposed to be in Milton and her body was found near Audley. The distance must be nine or ten miles.'

Chris joined him at the map. 'I wondered that. Milton and Baddeley Green are close though and something less than half an hour or so by car from Audley.' He blew out his cheeks,

'Ben has confirmed that the body was moved after death – perhaps trying to confuse the issue by placing her in water. She was drowned but not where she was found, nor where her clothes were dumped.

To that end the confusion succeeded. Not knowing how long she had been immersed nor the temperature of the water is complicating the investigation further.'

'So where have her clothes been since she was dumped at the Frasers' if they weren't put in that gully until last night?'

Chris shook his head. He began to wonder whether this case might never be solved.

'Focus on the car. We don't have the registration papers, Russel Chell couldn't find them, but he gave us what he thinks is the registration number. Follow it up with the DVLA and insurance companies. They're all computerised these days, they should be able to trace her from the name and Russell's address, even if she's since registered it elsewhere. Look at supermarket car parks locally – a lot of them have ANPR now. Anything you can get Yorkie.'

* * *

Frances Hegarty knew that Pete would not be finished at the Bethesda Street police station before eight o'clock. The final fitting for her wedding dress, and those of her bridesmaids had taken less time than she anticipated and, although strictly having taken an afternoon's leave she felt guilty about going home so early in the middle of a murder enquiry.

Excusing herself from the offer of afternoon tea with Pippa Timothy and Laura, she went instead to a small house on the outskirts of Nantwich. There she was in luck. The door was opened to her knock by one of the people she had wanted to interview. Having introduced herself, and shown her warrant to the understandably wary gentleman, she was admitted to the house.

Bob Jennings, Susan Chell's uncle, was formally dressed, particularly in view of the heat in the room. He wore a heavy-weight old-fashioned three-piece suit. In his left hand he clutched a snowy-white handkerchief, with which he frequently dabbed his eyes. Hegarty could not decide whether this was due to emotion or to an eye problem. There seemed to be a perpetual tear.

'I understand that you have been informed about the death of your niece,' she began gently, 'I'm sorry to trouble you at this time but are you able to tell us something about her? We need to be able to understand her life in order to establish why she died.'

'I don't know what use I can be, but I'll try,' he shuffled through to the living room, seemingly gathering his thoughts. Once there he plumped down on an orthopedic chair, and gestured Hegarty to the sofa.

The train of thought continued unbroken, 'although I hadn't seen her for years. She was a lot younger than Neil. He was the apple of his mother's eye as they say. Suzy was very much an afterthought. In fact her mother confided in my wife that she thought she was undergoing the menopause and was not best pleased to find out she was expecting Suzy.' He chuckled quietly and wielded the handkerchief, 'My sister-in-law was nothing if not blunt.'

'She must have been devastated after the accident.'

His face changed immediately, 'That is an understatement, my dear. She was distraught and I truly think she never recovered. Certainly she lost what little interest she ever had in Suzy. She was committed very shortly afterwards, and she never really lived full time out of care afterwards. She died nearly nine months ago in Holmedean Care Home.'

'What happened to Susan's father?'

'My brother kept going as best he could, the family moved away. In the early days Suzy went to stay with them some of the time when her mother was at home, but often he couldn't cope. Sometimes my sister-in-law would be at home, sometimes in institutions. It was very disturbing for the child.'

'So she spent a lot of time with you and your wife.' To Hegarty it made perfect sense.

'She did, but that wasn't ideal either. I am nearly sixteen years older than my brother. My wife and I had had our two boys and they were grown up. We weren't very good at starting all over again with a pre-pubescent girl.' He wiped his eyes, 'Suzy always seemed to have been one of life's victims. I feel in many ways we let her down. She left home as soon as possible and married when she was eighteen. Her father gave her away shortly before he died, but her mother was not well enough to attend the wedding. It was terrible for Suzy. What should have been the happiest day of her life was more like a wake.'

The sergeant felt they were straying from the point.

'Did Susan attend Neil's inquest? I understand she was possibly the last person to see her brother alive.'

'Good Lord, no! Suzy was eventually told that there had been an accident. She was only eight – just a child, and she wasn't there when he actually died. Neil was on the boat with his friend and that friend had to give evidence of course.'

'Did you go to the inquest, sir?'

'I did. According to Neil's friend – I wish I could remember his name – he didn't witness the accident at all. He had been reading in the cabin, then visited the lavatory and came back on deck only after a gap of about twenty minutes he said.

'Neil was crushed between the boat and the landing stage. By the time they got him out of the water, he couldn't be revived.'

'What were two kids doing messing about with the boat on their own, sir?'

'It's not as irresponsible as you make it sound, sergeant. Both Neil and Suzy were taught to swim from a very early age. They were not fancy swimmers either of them, but both were competent and Neil had a basic life-saving qualification. There were clear rules. Only friends who were able to swim were allowed unsupervised on the boat, and only with their parents' approval.

'Of course Neil and his friend were no longer children. They were both teenagers, Neil's friend a couple of years older than him, and they had several times taken the boat out by themselves, even overnight without mishap.' He wiped his eyes, 'My brother and sister-in-law were very careful, but it was all in vain. It was their own son who died.' He looked through the window into the past.

Uncertain where next to take the conversation Hegarty too gazed out at the view. The bare trees stood outlined against the darkening sky, creating a stunningly atmospheric background. It was beautiful when viewed from within, safe from November's icy blast, but promised to be deadly cold when she left the comfort of the fire.

Suddenly she turned to the old man and spoke again.

'Was Susan an attractive child?'

The promptness of her uncle's reply took her by surprise.

'Not really. Neither in appearance, nor in character. Even back in the time before Neil's death. Whether it was playing second fiddle to him, or perhaps she even then sensed her mother's rejection, I'm not sure. He was good-looking, lively, popular and bright – although not as bright as his mother would have everyone believe. He had lots of friends, always the hub of the group that went around together.

'He was a natural leader. The one who decided to go to the cinema and immediately half a dozen others wanted to go along too, or bowling or whatever. People gravitated towards him.'

'A hard act to follow then?' Hegarty was conscious that even in this explanation the uncle was focusing more on the boy than the sister about whom he had been asked.

After a while the old man seemed to notice this. 'But you asked about Suzy. She was very different, not at all clever, very shy and rather sneaky, devious. Not long after she came here, we caught her out in a number of lies; nothing very important, just ways of shifting responsibility from herself, denying her own involvement. Lies and being secretive just seemed to come naturally to her from an early age. It wasn't encouragement to put any trust in her, and she was lazy – reluctant to wash her hair or change into clean clothes. I expected a teenage girl to be always hogging the bathroom but personal hygiene became a real issue as she grew older.

'The inquest was dreadful, I shall never forget it. Susan's mother was led from the Coroner's Court shouting at the youth who was with him at the time: *'I'll sue you. It's your fault. How can Neil have fallen? You should have saved him.'*

Hegarty looked up, surprised at his vehemence.

'She had a point. There were grab rails all around the edge of the deck. Neil had been running all over that boat since he was a toddler.

'The youth's mother had turned on my sister-in-law. Shouted that it was wet, it had been frosty and the frost was melting, that anybody could have slipped and it wasn't her boy's fault. The boy looked terrible, white-faced. His mum put her arms round him and led him away. As she turned she said something about it all being over now.

'My sister-in-law screeched that it might be over for them, and over for Neil, whatever had been going on, but that for us – Neil's family – the nightmare was just beginning'

It was an unattractive picture he painted. Hegarty reflected on this young girl, unlovely and fundamentally unloved and now her life had ended by violence. Nobody deserved that, no matter what sort of person they were.

* * *

When Chris arrived home Frances Hegarty was there waiting for him.

'Frances.' The formality of her rank was left behind at the close of the working day. Off duty they were friends.

She related her conversation with Susan's uncle and the story of Neil's death.

'You're not going out again are you?' Pippa sounded resigned as she took the casserole from the oven. 'Pete will be here soon.'

'No need. Good work Frances.'

'I don't know if it's significant, but there is one more thing,' Hegarty told him, 'The Jennings' bungalow, where the accident happened, stood at the nearest point on the canal to where her clothes were found.'

'Now that's interesting.' Pete had heard her as he came in through the back door.

Pippa followed him through from the kitchen. 'If you three have finished sorting out the problems of the world for now, the casserole will be getting cold. Come to the table all of you.'

Chapter 15

Chris decided to visit Holmedean himself. This, according to her brother-in-law, was where Susan's mother had spent her last years and where she had died. Chris knew the manager there from a previous case and was shown directly into her office.

'Mr Timothy.' She indicated that he should sit down, making no reference to their previous connection.

Taking a surreptitious puff on an e-cigarette she turned her hooded eyes to him. Chris was fascinated. He had believed that these e-cigarettes were a kind of halfway house to stopping smoking, yet this woman seemed as addicted as ever. She blew noxious fumes at him, and he decided he preferred the smell of ordinary tobacco.

'Miss Cross, I understand Mrs Jennings lived here for some years, what can you tell me about the relationship between Susan Chell and her mother?'

Her first comment seemed irrelevant.

'Even if people are dreadful parents, a mother particularly still likes to see the kids from time to time to know they are okay. I think Mrs Jennings felt very let down by Susan. She had made it clear since Susan's childhood that the wrong child had died, and so there wasn't much affection on either side.

'To her credit though, Susan did visit occasionally, but I don't think the visits brought much joy or comfort to either of them.' She puffed on the noxious nicotine substitute again, filling the air with fumes of synthetic fruit. Chris resisted the temptation to back away.

'The family moved away soon after the boy's accident. They took a pub in central Wales and left their daughter with the uncle and aunt, in spite of their now having a home and some sort of life for her. Quite understandably I think, when she grew up she wanted little to do with them. Her mother needed a lot of treatment over the years.

'The old man died without ever really being reconciled to his only daughter, only he did soften enough to go to her wedding. It was as if he could never forgive her for being alive while his son was dead. After he died the mother came to live round here again, Audley I think. She had a stroke in 2014 then another from which she never recovered in early 2015. She was diabetic and diagnosed as schizophrenic. Hence Holmedean; she'd been here since just after her second stroke. I don't know if this is relevant, but she was a very unusual woman, in that she refused medical intervention.'

'Why?'

'She said that precious resources should be reserved for the more needy – the young and those with dependents relying on them. They should be entitled. That she was sixty-nine, and had never believed that she would make old bones. She felt that to all intents and purposes she had had her life. She believed that when she died she would go to be with her son. That she may also be with her husband didn't seem to interest her.

'I asked whether it had been a good life.' but she interrupted me,' Judith Cross looked at him levelly then drew on the artificial cigarette. 'She said that it had been what she made of it. If it hadn't been good, that was her own fault.'

'But she had a family, people who cared for her.' Chris interrupted. Judith raised her eyebrows.

'She said it was not much of a family really, no husband, no son, just a daughter who cared little for her, and who would mourn briefly and then move on with her life, as she should. She was totally intractable.'

* * *

At the Guildhall an excited DC Dearing was waiting impatiently for Chris's return.

'The Rivers Authority representative has removed the safety grating at each end of the gully, sir.' She failed to keep the thrill out of her voice.

'And?' Chris was in no mood for playing games.

'We have a phone. It may not be hers of course, but the likelihood…'

'Where was it?'

'In the top culvert sir, the one under Baddeley Green Road. Not far from the grating. Looked like it had probably been thrown.

'But the thrower of the phone had been unlucky. It had fallen clear of the bed of the culvert and was protected from the rain by the roof of the tunnel. It isn't saturated, just damp. Either they had not noticed it wasn't submerged, or hadn't been able to reach it and so it had to stay where it was.'

'They wouldn't have wanted to waste time. Someone could have come along at any moment and challenged his or her actions, or at least shown an interest. What's happening now?'

'It's been tested for prints sir, but nothing. Not surprising. It was so cold, they would have worn gloves.'

'Have the lab checked it out?'

'DS York thought it would be quicker if he did it, sir.'

'Okay. Have we texts? Calls?'

He's retrieved a number of incoming messages at around the time she died, 31st and then the first of November. Getting more and more annoyed that the recipient wasn't texting back, nor returning calls. Someone she has stored in her contacts as just 'A'. We have that number. DS York is on to the phone provider.'

'Is that it?'

'No, sir. There's one message that calls her Susan, and there's one that matches Diane Whitfield's Thank You text.'

'I think we can safely assume that this phone is hers.'

'Then,' she smiled up at him, 'There's one text outwards, back to this A, whoever he or she is, saying *Sorry about not meeting you; something came up – bit of a family crisis. I will contact you to rearrange soon. That one's dated 2nd November.* That's the last communication in or out sir. DS York's checking them all and going back through earlier calls and messages as well, also checking the contacts.'

Chris smiled, perhaps they were getting somewhere at last.

'Anything else?'

'I've spoken to Caroline Fraser's mother, sir. What a horror. She looked a real fright too, there is an age at which a woman really should not wear sleeveless tops.' DC Dearing took a bite from a lacklustre sandwich, and continued, 'She banged on about: *of course she had a key to her daughter's home, surely that wasn't a crime* and so on. Eventually I pinned her down to the fact that she hadn't visited the house all the time the family were away. She strongly dislikes Edward seemingly, and sees no reason to help her daughter out. Her daughter pressed her to have a key in case Sharon Welland was concerned about something, but I really doubt she went there. It may have been different if she'd known about the body. She might have gone then just out of curiosity. Perhaps that's an angle we should look at.'

Chris gave her a long look. Dearing's enthusiasm was to be commended, but sometimes she went too far. It was unlike him to chastise members of the team publicly, but now she was pushing the boundaries of acceptability.

'Confine yourself to the facts please, constable. We don't have time for flights of fancy about the woman's attire, nor supposition about an interviewee's motivation. Your job is to report your findings to your seniors so that the team may discuss and debate your findings. A senior officer will then decide on the necessary course of action. What about the dog walker?'

The constable had reddened, and offered a more suitable reply.

'The lady died three years ago. She was married, but only twelve months before her death. Her husband has no knowledge of her role as a dog walker, nor did she leave behind any keys other than to their own home. He said he had never heard of the

Chells, the Whitfields or the Frasers. I believed him, sir.'

'Thank you, Constable.' Chris moved on to DS York's exploration of Susan Chell's mobile phone.

'Triangulation of the signals, according to the phone provider, are only accurate within twenty yards or so. It's quite possible that the last text wasn't sent from the Frasers' house at all, and I don't believe Susan sent it, she was already dead.

'Anyone can reply to a text if there is no password on the phone or it's something obvious, as it often is to those who know someone well.'

'Yorkie was able to tell us Susan Chell's password. It's 1987.'

'The year of her brother's death.'

'So anyone could know the password who was involved with the family in 1987, or knew that it was a significant year for her.'

DS Hegarty reported her findings back to the team.

'The lad's death was a real tragedy. He died in 1987 when he was fifteen years old. It seems that there wasn't a lot of money in the Jennings family, but they had a boat – it was a day cruiser that Jennings senior had converted by putting bunks in it. They lived in a house where the garden backed onto the canal and moored the boat at the bottom of the garden.'

'Is that allowed?'

'If the house had a licensed berth then yes it is. One day the lad and his friend had stayed over on the boat. Mr Jennings had been working away and was not there overnight and when the two youngsters hadn't appeared by lunchtime, Mrs Jennings sent Susan out to call them in. They didn't appear and Mrs Jennings went down to the boat herself. Seemingly Neil had fallen between the boat and the landing stage and she and his friend couldn't get at him. By the time mother and the friend managed to move the boat and haul him out the boy was dead, drowned.'

'And what was Susan doing all this time?'

'She didn't know what was going on apparently. She was only a child of eight after all. According to the police reports at the time she seems to have blanked what had actually happened, and only repeated what she had been told by her parents.'

'Susan at eight years old must have been sheltered from it all. The family immediately sold up and moved. The house sold just a couple of months on from the newspaper report of the inquest.'

Chapter 16

Felicity Chadwick, Russell Chell's girlfriend, was heavy and overweight with a double chin, the antithesis of the body in the bath, but the impression was of luxuriant dark hair and beautiful smooth unblemished skin and a smile that seemed to stop just short of her eyes. She opened the door to a pristine white hallway with immaculate parquet floor. A blast of hot air hit the detectives as they wiped their feet in the porch.

'I prefer outdoor shoes to remain outdoors.' She enunciated clearly looking pointedly at their feet. For a mad moment DC Dearing wondered should they remove their shoes, as she followed Felicity over the threshold. Surely she must have been expecting them. Russell Chell would have been straight on the phone when they left him.

The flat was a jungle of damp-smelling foliage.

'I work at the big garden centre, Bloomers,' she said in explanation.

Chris looked around the flat, dominated by exotic and tropical plants, and with a temperature that must have been very expensive to maintain. He recognised the Swiss Cheese plant, Bird of Paradise and something that reminded him of a red firework from Pippa's television viewing and their holiday visits to the Abbotsbury Tropical Gardens in Dorset, but much of the dense foliage was unknown to him.

'This is not a social call, Ms Chadwick. If you would prefer your home to remain untainted we would be happy to talk to you at the Guildhall.'

Chris shot her a look, and she mouthed *Sorry!*

'Our call will be brief Ms Chadwick, he placated, 'and now we're here …?'

She glared at them both without a word and led the way to the inner sanctum. Expecting her to be clumsy and ungainly, the constable was surprised to find her so light on her feet.

The room reminded Chris of a museum or an art gallery. Ornaments were strategically placed and Dearing half expected each to be labelled with its name, creator and maybe a price. The fire surround on which she had displayed the small items of bric-a-brac was like part of a stage set, essential to convince her that this was a home.

But who was to say that her solitary and mundane existence was less fulfilling than one of restless travel and constant striving for the next adventure? Perhaps Russell Chell was ready for a life more pedestrian and less unpredictable than he had known with Susan.

Everywhere was a pristine white. No child or pet had evidently crossed this threshold. The elegant leather furniture looked hard and unyielding, yet was surprisingly comfortable.

Felicity indicated that they should sit on one of the sofas and took the adjacent matching chair. She perched on the edge of her chair, ankles and knees tightly together. Her outfit seemed over-formal for a morning at home alone, and Dearing wondered whether she had been on her way out when they arrived.

She wore a pencil skirt in candy pink along with, in a toning shade, a concoction that the constable believed was called a twin-set. Her hair was carefully piled up on her head in an elaborate confection of dark curls and she wore a string of pearls. Dearing had never before seen anyone so wearing pearls at this time of day. Evidently Felicity was taking them at their word that they would be brief, and offered no refreshment.

'I knew Susan Jennings at school, and the family. We were in the same class. It was she who introduced me to Russell. Poor man he was just looking for a little peace in his life I think.

'Russell told me she was supposed to be at someone's house over in Stoke.' Felicity turned up her nose slightly. 'I used to go and play at Susan's when we were little but her mother never got over the death of the older brother. I never visited after that. I don't think anyone was invited round any more, and then the family moved away.'

'It is strange that despite your relationship, Mr Chell continued to live with the woman he married five years ago.'

'I am not interested in analysing Russell's past, nor he mine. We agreed that early on in our relationship. What we planned together was the future.' He noticed the use of the past tense, but left it unremarked – for now.

* * *

DS York met Chris at the door, 'Information from the phone provider, sir. We know where we found the phone so the fact that their last trace of it was in Baddeley Green is no help. When the last texts were sent to and from 'A' on 2nd November, the phone was in Alsagers Bank. They've checked that last message first, as I asked them to. It's likely that it was sent while the phone was at the Frasers' house.'

'Really? Anything else?'

'Yes, I got a reply eventually from the number that last message was sent to,' he paused to build up the tension, until Chris snapped, 'Get on with it, sergeant.'

'It's Anthony Whitfield, sir.'

'And what did he have to say for himself?'

'Nothing yet. DS York told him who it was and that someone will be calling round to see him this afternoon at his place of work. He said that he was working away from home until tomorrow, then he would be going to offer moral support to his wife at a funeral in the afternoon.' She looked up, 'He confirmed that it will be Susan Chell's they're going to, so Yorkie told her somebody would be at the funeral and see him after the service.'

* * *

In the office Chris was cross-referencing reports. 'It doesn't hang together, Yorkie. Russell Chell says that he is dating Felicity. Felicity talks about them planning their future together, yet he was devastated when we told him about Susan. It sounded like he threw that pot head thing on the floor.'

He went back to talk further with Russell Chell. He opened the door and led them across the vast hall like an elderly man, barely acknowledging who they were. Chris noticed that, as he expected, the phrenological head had gone and there was a gouge on the tiled floor, along with a few shreds of white porcelain under the table. He had been correct, it was the head that had suffered from Chell's stress.

Russell had returned to the living room sofa where they found him looking through photos, evidently wallowing in a bout of nostalgia. There was no evidence of Felicity.

'This boxful was Susan's. I can't think that anyone would want it now.'

Chris looked more closely at the photos than on his first visit. One showed a garden view with Susan screwing up her eyes against the sun in front of a blue wooden shack, paint peeling off its window frames and verandah. He peered closely, this was a view he had seen, and recently. He gazed at the skyline, the trees, bridge to the right hand side and the pylon. Of course, the houses were new, one of them certainly replacing the tumbledown shack in the photograph, but this was undoubtedly the view across the Caldon canal he had gazed on when Susan's clothes were found, and he had wandered through the estate from the Baddeley Green footpath.

Dearing carried the evidence bags through to the living room, where the photograph albums were again laid out on the table. She wondered whether this was how Chell spent his time now, just reliving the past. She held out the evidence bag containing the jacket.

Russell Chell reached out to the clothes and boots,

'Don't touch them please, sir. They have to go to forensics.'

'Oh God yes. Her denim jacket. Hang on a

minute.' He extracted a photo album from the sideboard and a pile of loose photographs fell out. 'I had started sorted – you know, hers and mine, but lost heart.' He handed over the pile. Several of them showed Susan Chell wearing a denim jacket, but in all of them, the view was of the front, none showing the distinctive embroidery across the back. Then the boots caught Chris's eye. These were undoubtedly the ones they had found wedged in the culvert.

'And what about a bag? Did she carry a bag – yes, always.'

'Can you describe it, sir?'

'Not really. Just a bag, black I think. A shoulder bag?' he sounded uncertain.

Chris showed him the Cath Kidson bag.

'Did she have a bag like this?' but Russell Chell was already shaking his head. 'Not that I know of, but listen, she could have bought herself anything recently and I wouldn't be aware of it. Not her usual style though. Did you find her necklace? She always wore it?'

'No sir, is it one you gave her?'

'On no. Nothing I could give would match up to that bloody thing. She wore it all the time. It was ugly and clumsy but she'd never take it off. Her brother gave it to her for her birthday when she was a little girl, hideous thing.'

He scrabbled in a drawer and produced more photographs, 'Even as a youngster she wore it.' He sighed as he handed one of the prints over, 'Nobody prints off photos anymore do they, they're all stored on computers these days.'

Chris peered at the face in the photograph: a girl of about seven stared back. The image was not clear, but no doubt as Russell had said there were others of it stored in a computer file if, as Russell said, she wore this distinctive string of bead-like pebbles.

'I looked for the car documents. I know her car was about five years old, black with a beige interior, but what she's done with the papers I've no idea.'

'Had she made a will, sir?'

'No. At least I don't think so. We'd talked about it when we first got married, but never got round to doing anything about it. I hadn't discussed it with her since she became ill, it seemed a bit mercenary somehow, especially as I'd asked her to leave.'

Russell was still holding one of the photographs. 'Where were the clothes found?'

'The border of Milton village and Baddeley Green. Do you know it?'

'Not really, but Sue did. As a child her parents had a cottage on the side of the canal quite near there, they lived there until Sue's brother died.'

'Tell me about that. He must still have been a young man?'

'Younger than that. He was only a teenager – about fifteen I think. I never knew the boy, only what Sue told me.'

'And that was?'

'That it was some sort of boating accident. It upset her to talk about her brother so I didn't ever probe too deeply. Susan was always ambivalent about water, it had been her natural environment from a small girl. She was a very strong swimmer but after Neil's death she didn't really like being near water, like rivers or canals. She wouldn't go out to the seaside, not even for the day, and she would only swim in a proper pool.

'She told me that the Potteries was a good place for her to live because it's almost as far away from the coast as you can get in this country. I was surprised she kept that painting that her dad did. She kept a very distinctive 1950s Poole plate as well with a boat she said looked like theirs. It disappeared off the wall a while ago – I don't know where she's put it. That's one reason why I think she's got somewhere else – some permanent bolt hole.

'Apparently her dad threw all his paintings away when the boy died but Sue hid that one in her aunty's shed, and brought it here when we married. It's always hung in the hall. She loved that picture.'

He said sadly, 'She always liked boats – perhaps because they had one when she was growing up. She was a real enigma, and it's true, she was quick to fire up, but she'd not had it easy you know.'

Chapter 17

After ten minutes ruminating Chris had a lot of unanswered questions on his notepad.

Susan should have been at Milton. What was her body doing at Alsagers Bank? And what about her clothes? Had she been undressed at Audley and the clothes brought back to the pathway at Milton?

Or was she killed there and her body transported the ten or so miles to Alsagers Bank? And if so, why? He looked again at the photo of the little girl standing in front of the shack, and determined to go out there to the property that had replaced it.

'He told us he thought she had a separate place. Maybe her car documents are there, and the car too.'

'Yes, I wonder if it's her own place or does she go to stay with a man?'

'Who knows? And with Chell not able to give us the name of the supposed clinic she visited, we're getting nowhere fast.'

'We've asked him to think about the last week in October, where he went, who he saw. Hallowe'en may help him to focus on the dates. He'll no doubt talk to Felicity Chadwick. Goodness knows what story they'll cook up between them. We'll talk to him again.'

Hegarty held one of the evidence bags on her knee, 'The bag was unlikely to be a coincidence. Found with the clothes like that. It didn't sound like her style, if the husband was telling the truth and was used to seeing her with a black bag. Perhaps it was a present?'

'From an admirer maybe.' DS Hegarty mused, 'We need to find out.'

Chris answered the ring of his phone.

'DC Dearing, sir. We have spoken again to the Whitfields' neighbour. She called the station and said she may have something for us.'

* * *

'The bins go out for collection on Friday mornings. They usually come early so they would be put out the night before. According to Diane Whitfield, Susan was aware of this and would have put the recycling out for that Friday, if she had been there.

'The neighbour is, seemingly, a bit of a stickler for recycling everything so whatever is in her box now has come in since Thursday night.

'Comparing that stuff with the two piles of flyers and post in the Whitfields' – the pile on the kitchen counter that presumably Susan had brought in, and the pile in the porch that she hadn't – she stopped picking up the stuff after the postal delivery on the Tuesday morning,'

'The few days before Hallowe'en seems to be Ben Hanchurch's best guess at the time of death.'

'The earlier time, according to Ben, being the more likely. He says Hallowe'en would be the absolutely latest he would think.'

'Wouldn't the neighbour have expected to see Susan Chell's car in the drive?'

'Not necessarily, sir. She works full time. You

can't see their drive from her front windows. It was only when the post stopped being picked up that I began to look out for her, but there was no sign.'

'It's too far to walk from Russell Chell's, although maybe not from wherever else her bolt-hole is.. Her car must be somewhere.'

'We've got officers in the Guildhall going through CCTV around the area of the Whitfield house, but it's a slow job. They have to check every camera. One of our problems is that so much comes down to educated guesswork, given the passage of time. We could do with some help from Bethesda Street.'

'We need more manpower. I'll talk to Pete Talbot.'

* * *

'But it isn't a cold case, Chris. I'm not going to be popular adding cases onto that list when I'm supposed to be reducing it. It wasn't a suspicious death. There was no trial at the time and the Coroner brought in a verdict of Accidental Death.'

It was beginning to dawn on Chris how valuable had been his working partnership with Pete Talbot. At times they had almost intuited each other's thoughts and anticipated the next line of enquiry.

'I think it was, Pete, and now his younger sister's been murdered. I think the two are connected. I'm going to take you out for a drink and tell you why. There was something that girl saw or heard. Something that meant nothing to her at the time, she was only a child after all, but later – perhaps recently – something has made her realise its significance.'

'That's a lot of somethings'.

'Okay I know I'm hypothesising, but I feel I'm right. I'm not trying to reopen a cold case. But I need to establish whether Neil's death was murder in order to have a motive for his sister's. Could you at least have someone truffle out the Coroner's Report for me?'

'From thirty years ago!' Pete was horrified. 'God knows where they would have been archived by now. Even if we had a copy of the report I can't afford the manpower Chris, I'm sorry – I'm not being deliberately obstructive but …'

'But the clothes were found in Milton, on your patch. There could be a connection.'

'That's not what I'm saying. I'm saying it isn't a cold case because thirty years ago, there was no case. I've checked what few records we have and there's no reason even for us to have kept a copy of the Coroner's Report, or even to have seen it.'

Chris looked crestfallen until Pete slapped him on the back. 'This doesn't mean I won't help in any way I can, Chris.'

'You've lost me.'

'Switch off for a while, get your coat. The pub awaits.'

* * *

Computers were supposed to herald the advent of the paperless office Chris thought grimly, as he tackled the pile of memos haemorrhaging across the desk from his in-tray, but one such piece of paper proved to be worth following up.

A call had come in from a house that backed

onto the gully where Susan Chell's clothes had been recovered.

During house to house enquiries this woman had heard what she took to be the next-door son's motorbike. He felt the need to rev it up as he turned the key on parking it, and although that hadn't happened on the occasion in question, the bike had still woken her and she vaguely remembered wondering whether he was turning over a new leaf, She was just drifting back off to sleep then the bike revved up again and drove away. This was in the early hours of the day when the clothes were found.

She had been to the bathroom at ten past two and was just going back to sleep, so thought it could have been no later than three o'clock.

Talking to her neighbour about the findings in the gully next morning, she learned that the woman's son was on holiday for a fortnight and had gone on his motorbike, so it was not his that she had heard. That was when she called the police.

'A motorbike. She mistook it for a Norton 500, so a fairly powerful, throaty bike, being stopped nearby.' Chris was updating the team.

'SOCO's found no tyre tracks on the gully.'

'No but there had been some rain overnight, so if the biker pulled up on the main road, he could have walked down the gully with the clothes leaving no tracks at all.'

DS York spoke up from the computer terminal, 'No-one we've come across so far has a motor bike of any size.'

'So perhaps we're not looking in the right place.'

* * *

The inquest proceedings having been opened and adjourned, Susan Chell's body had been released to the family by the Coroner.

Although stretched for personnel, Chris decided some value could be gained from attendance at her funeral and he and DS Hegarty duly took their places at the back of the crematorium, from which he could best observe the protagonists. Chris silently gave thanks that the service was cremation and not interment; the cold weather would have made for an even more harrowing experience for loved ones.

Looking around they identified various other attendees: Russell Chell, with the victim's aunt and uncle, took the front pew. Felicity Chadwick sat alone at the rear of the congregation. He was pleased to see that Anthony and Diane Whitfield were also in attendance, sitting on the opposite side of the chapel from the Chell contingent, neither of them apparently acknowledging the existence of the other. Not surprisingly perhaps, Chris surmised, if as Russell Chell had said, he had never joined his wife during her visits to house-sit for them.

Chris was surprised at Anthony Whitfield's appearance. A body overdeveloped by exercise, his shirt, while generally the correct size, bulged at the biceps, and the bull neck stopped the top button from fastening. His thighs strained against the fabric of his suit, then tapered into petite feet, giving a strange, dancer-like appearance.

While Felicity Chadwick looked chic in a stylish wool coat with mock-fur collar and above-the-knee boots, Diane Whitfield had made no more effort over her appearance than when they had interviewed her at her home.

She wore a coat too lightweight for the time of year, and her boots were so scuffed and unkempt that Hegarty would have cleaned them once more then consigned them straight to the bin. The hem of her skirt hung below the coat in an asymmetrical way, which seemed not to be by design but because the hem was coming down. The gloves, knitted hat and scarf she wore mismatched in a seemingly inappropriate palette of colours.

What was even more surprising was the demeanour of Anthony. He appeared to be leaning heavily on his wife, to such an extent that at one point she staggered slightly and whispered something to him, whereon he took a deep breath and stood straighter. He looked around as if to see if this had been noticed, and, catching Chris's eye, he looked visibly shocked. Whispering something to his wife, she also allowed her eyes to stray to where the detectives were sitting. She gave Chris a baleful look and again whispered to her husband.

As soon as the service drew to a close, notwithstanding protocol, Anthony left the building in advance of the chief mourners, his wife scuttling to keep up beside him. Chris slipped after them, calling to him as they stepped to one side to allow the mourning cars to pull alongside the building: 'Mr Whitfield, may I have a word?'

He was ignored and it was only as they entered the car park that Chris caught up with Anthony.

'Mr Whitfield, you said you had no knowledge of Susan Chell, the woman who house-sits for you?' He put a question mark in the comment.

The couple paused, 'That's right,' he wiped his forehead with a snow white handkerchief. 'I don't – didn't. Why would I? I never even saw her,' as if washing his hands of it.'

Hegarty had caught them up, 'It seems strange to come to the funeral of a woman you didn't know.'

His wife turned and shot Anthony a look. 'This is hardly appropriate. Hounding mourners at a funeral. Obviously I knew Susan. I knew her well. I was upset and I asked my husband to accompany me, which he did. Now,' she took her husband's arm as if to turn him away, 'If you'll excuse us ...'

The sergeant interrupted her, 'Susan Jennings and I were at school at the same time as you, Mrs Whitfield.'

Diane peered at her, 'Good God, Frances something isn't it? How extraordinary.' Again she took her husband's arm and made to leave.

'Hegarty, Detective Sergeant Frances Hegarty.'

The sergeant turned to Anthony Whitfield, 'Could you explain why, sir, when we first talked to you, you said that you didn't know the drowned woman?'

Anthony glanced anxiously at his wife who had got into the driving seat, and he swallowed audibly.

Hegarty caught the look and persisted, 'Did you know her, sir? Susan Jennings?'

'No.' The voice sounded strangled in his throat. 'I didn't know her at all. Never seen her before' He looked close to tears, his knuckles clenched and white.

An interesting reaction Chris thought, for

someone who claimed not to know the deceased. Here was another slender thread to be woven into the cloth of their enquiries.

'Mr Whitfield, you seem inordinately upset. I believe you were involved in a relationship with Susan. Does your wife know about this?'

'A relationship? Who told you that?' Anthony blustered.

'Nobody, but I am not a stupid man.' The implication was clear and Anthony blushed and looked like a dog who expected a whipping.

'Get into the car, Anthony, I'll drive,' hurried his wife, gunning the car and leaving Chris and Hegarty standing alone in the car park as the remaining mourners began to file out of the building behind him.

'Shall we go after him?' Hegarty got into the driving seat.

'No need, sergeant. If I'm not very much mistaken Mr Whitfield will be coming after us before long.'

Chapter 18

As the next funeral party pulled up at the other side of the long porch entrance, Chris caught sight of a woman walking briskly down the drive. He recognised her but annoyingly, out of context, he could not put a name to the face. He was about to go after her and have a better look when one of the crematorium clerks approached him and Hegarty and said in a sepulchral voice, 'Excuse me sir, but are you the police?'

On receiving a nod he handed over a booklet.

'The funeral director asked us to pass on the book of attendees, sir. Not everyone signs it of course, but he thought it may be of some interest to you.'

With thanks Chris flicked down the pages of names. Someone he had missed during the service occurred halfway down the second page: Edward and Caroline Fraser.

He turned in time to see his mystery woman getting into a taxi on the main road, and being whisked away. He flicked through the attendees again, but there was no name there that rang the requisite bell. Tucking the booklet in his pocket, Chris followed Hegarty towards the car but his progress was stopped by Susan's uncle calling behind him.

Chris waited for Mr Jennings on the drive, and learning he was without transport he offered a lift into the town centre. Today he looked every day of his eighty years and Chris decided he needed a reviving cup of tea.

At the gates of the crematorium was a coffee shop, but Chris rejected this and went instead into the town centre, which he knew was on their companion's route home.

'I thought of this after your sergeant had gone. Of course after we'd talked I got to thinking back to when Neil died, the inquest and everything. I don't know if it means anything, but as you were at the funeral ...'

'Thank you, Mr Jennings. You share it with us, and we'll decide whether what you have to say is relevant, okay?'

The older man waited until a hot cup of tea was placed in front of him, then took a deep breath.

'The family, Susan's parents that is, wanted to bring a private prosecution against Neil's friend when Neil died, but they had no idea how to go about it. They blamed the young man who was on the boat with him for letting him die. All nonsense of course.'

Chris nodded. It had been another ten years before a private prosecution was brought in a murder case in this country. Surely Susan's parents were not thinking the young man had deliberately caused his friend's death.

'Susan's parents were not like the Lawrence family a decade later. They were ill-informed and ill-advised and with no funds. My sister-in-law was poorly educated and they had no idea how to go about drumming up support for a campaign. Poor Neil's death was marked with a whimper not a bang.

'The Coroner had commiserated with the family and closed his folder. We all moved in a daze out into what was a desultory sunshine to a small crowd of waiting onlookers.'

He took another slurp of his tea, warming his hands on the mug.

'The verdict was Accidental Death. None of us could speak. We were numb. Our solicitor told the group of poised journalists, that it was *the tragic end of a young life.*' I thought to myself that for them it was the end, the Coroner, the solicitor, the young man who was with Neil; even the press once their copy was filed, but it was not the end for us, it was just the beginning.'

* * *

Chris reflected as he drove back towards the Guildhall. In Newcastle death had long ago finished its work; had it now, thirty years later, headed for Milton?

He thought he understood what the old man meant. This second death, perhaps because of its currency, overshadowed that first cataclysmic demise. Perhaps the events of thirty years ago demanded further scrutiny. He would have to talk to Pete about it.

He had just taken off his coat and picked up the steaming coffee placed in front of him by DC Dearing, to be told that there was a telephone message from a woman. She has remembered something that the police should know about.

For a moment he had struggled to place the name, then he remembered – the Frasers' neighbour. He decided to go himself, and arrived just as a Range Rover drew into the Frasers' drive, with Edward alone at the wheel. The detective glanced at his watch and decided this was too good an opportunity to miss.

'A quick question if I may sir,' he said, approaching the car as the door was opened. 'When we identified the woman who was found in your bath, you intimated that you didn't know Susan Chell. Why was that?'

Fraser turned and entered the back door of his house, Chris close behind him. He went straight to the sink where he poured a glass of water and drank it straight off.

'It now transpires that she was a coeval of yours. She was in your school. Susan Jennings was her maiden name. Can you explain that, sir?'

His wife had entered the kitchen and spoke for him, an unbecoming blush spreading from her ample cleavage up her neck and settling on her cheeks. 'How could Edward know he was at school with her? He hadn't seen her for years, and of course we only had the slightest glance of her.' She pointed an accusatory finger. 'You wouldn't let us look again. Said we wouldn't be able to recognise her anyway.'

'That's right,' agreed Chris. He thought of that bloated face, peeling skin and the damage occurring after a week or more submerged in water. Even her closest family would have struggled to identify that face.

'That's right,' he said again, 'but we have reason to believe that you also knew her and knew her quite well in your youth, Mrs Fraser.'

Her eyes flicked from side to side, her hands clutched together till the skin shone white.

'We were friends to some extent, yes. But had lost touch long before we left school.' Caroline was shaking her head, 'That thing in our bath was Susan Jennings? I absolutely don't believe you. God, I haven't seen her for ...' She glanced at her husband, whose face was white, his fingers also clenched, 'It must be nearly twenty years. She was at our primary school but I've not seen her since we were about nine.'

'Sir?'

Edward Fraser seemed distracted. Slowly he unclenched his fists.

'Yes? What? Oh, yes the name Susan Jennings. It sounds vaguely familiar but I don't remember ...' He put his hands out hopelessly, looking at his wife.

She came to his rescue, 'So. Edward is younger than me. He wasn't in the same year at school as us. He would have been ...' She hesitated, her eyes never leaving his face, 'one or two years behind us.'

'I am more than a year younger than my wife. I knew none of her contemporaries. Except Diane, and I only met her later. I didn't even know Caroline at school. We met at college after we had both left.'

This seemed reasonable. Chris tried to remember school friends' names from primary school. He could barely recall the ones he had known well, never mind the children older or younger than him.

'You don't remember Susan Jennings at all sir? Haven't seen her more recently?'

'Not that I know of, I mean we haven't been introduced or it may have struck a chord, but ...' again he made the hopeless gesture with his hands, his eyes pleading to his wife who remained inscrutable.

She shrugged fleshy shoulders, looking sore where her suntan was beginning to peel.

Chris looked straight at Edward Fraser, 'I may

be needing to talk to you again sir. If you plan to travel away in the next few days, please let me know first.'

Eventually Chris was able to get across the road to the neighbour's house, where he learned of a violent altercation between Billy and Sharon Welland during the previous evening. Additionally he learned that this was a frequent occurrence and that Sharon had been twice hospitalised on this account. Whether or not this was relevant he had no idea, but he filed it away for future reference.

* * *

In Milton, Anthony Whitfield surreptitiously poured another tot from the whisky bottle before replacing it behind the gardening paraphernalia on the shelf. Slugging it back, he flopped back into the easy chair and closed his eyes, hand to his head. He remembered the day they had bought that chair. It had been at a flea market in the town and the two of them had struggled home with it, stopping the traffic at the zebra crossing and laughing so much they had to stop and sit down, only to kiss and set off again.

When they came to live here it had been immediately relegated to the shed by his wife. Not without humour she had bought him a pokerwork sign declaring his shed *The Dog House* and found an old patchwork blanket that she had thrown over the chair to disguise its weaker points.

'Your own little demesne, darling, for when the gardening gets too much.' She had raised her eyebrows quizzically and had rarely entered the shed since. Over the years it had become a bolt-hole for

Anthony whenever circumstances threatened the possibility of early divorce. Garden tools abounded of course – how else could he keep the plot looking immaculate, but increasingly it was his sanctuary with its little heater and the radio. Yes, and the whisky bottle, now alas empty.

'Susan,' he groaned, 'Suzy. What has happened to you, my love?' I will find whoever did this,' he vowed to himself, 'and deal with them.' Whatever Suzy was, and nobody knew better than Anthony, she never deserved such an ignominious end.

The Assistant Chief Constable wanted an update. The press were pushing for answers, and questions were being asked in high places in the Stoke on Trent police area.

It seemed to him that a lot of good policing was based on the instinct and experience of the investigating team; but neither of these could be taken to the Crime Prosecution Service and the ACC was looking for action. The CPS demanded *evidence beyond reasonable doubt,* which at the present time Chris could not produce.

'Who have we got as potential suspects?'

'Most obviously the Frasers. The woman was found in their bath and there was no sign of a break-in. Both denied knowing Susan, then it turns out she was at primary school with Edward, and at High School with his wife. That only came to light because DS Hegarty recognised the victim from the crime scene photographs and made the link. She too was at school with Susan and with Caroline Fraser.'

'But? I can sense there's a *But.*'

'They were in Vermont at the time Ben Hanchurch says she died.'

'But she didn't die where she was found. Could she have been kept somewhere else and then they moved her on their return?'

'Yes, but they still couldn't have killed her. The timing doesn't fit. They hadn't time to get the plane they did, drive home and get some sleep before moving her. I haven't questioned the children of course, but they were in the room and clearly the story their parents told is what they expected.

'Anyway why would you incriminate yourself by putting a body in your own bath, if you didn't kill her in the first place? If they had anything to do with the death, surely they'd have wanted the body as far away as possible.'

The Assistant Chief Constable drummed his fingertips on the desk, swinging his chair round to look out of the window. In the hush the sound of Christmas carols could be heard drifting up from the marketplace, a relentless backdrop no doubt for the next two months.

'And the husband? Chell?'

'Difficult to read. He has another woman; he seemed very uncaring, but explained that by saying they were going their separate ways. She only continued to live there because she was supposedly very ill, although Ben Hanchurch says not, but somehow I don't have him pegged as someone to kill her. He didn't care enough. Besides which, neither he nor Susan had access to keys to the Frasers' house.'

'So who did have access?'

'Her mother; the next door neighbour and possibly a woman who used to walk a dog they had years ago. She's dead now and nobody knows what became of the key. Edward has a vague memory that she never returned it, but I think it's a non-starter. The boy was allergic to the dog as a baby and he's eight now.

'Caroline thinks – only thinks, mind you – that there should have been another key to the back door. They leave the key in the lock day and night so a second one is never needed. She thinks there's one somewhere in the house with a little blue fob attached.

'I've asked her to look but it really doesn't get us any further forward.'

Chapter 19

DC Dearing asked, 'Is it just a coincidence that both these families, the Whitfields and the Frasers, have connections to Susan Chell, and were both away on holiday at the same time?'

'We'll have to ask them.'

A call came through to Chris's office. 'Mrs Fraser, sir. She won't speak to anyone else.' Chris took the call.

'What can I do for you, Mrs Fraser?'

The voice sounded shaken. 'Chief Inspector, I think you'd better come. There's something going on that I need to tell you.'

* * *

As he stood waiting for her to answer the bell, stomping his feet against the cold under a glowering sky, Chris gave more attention to the proportions of the house. It had an unusual layout, the result, so he had been told by PC Gregory, of its being started before the second World War, and not completed until 1947. Eventually Mrs Fraser appeared, looking more shocked if possible than she had on Sunday.

'What was it you wanted to tell me, Mrs Fraser?'

She glanced warily in the direction of the Welland house, then, surprisingly, led the way, not into the living room, but the kitchen.

'I really cannot abide gossip, and all this

business has upset me more than I can tell you. You go away for a nice relaxing holiday and come back to the most stressful events of your life.' She glared at him as if he were responsible.

Chris was beginning to wonder what she wanted when she leaned across the central island that separated them and grasped his wrist.

'I may have dragged you out on a wild-goose chase. I could have come to you, but the children ... normally I'd leave them with Sharon next door but I could hardly do that. She'd have wanted to know why I was going to see you. 'Yesterday evening, next door,' she inclined her head, there was this terrible argument.'

'What about?'

'I don't know, it started with something and nothing I expect. She hadn't got the baby to bed early enough or washed his socks, or she'd scorched his shirt with the iron. That's how rows usually start isn't it, about nothing much?'

Chris noted that in each example, it seemed someone was blaming Sharon for misdemeanors.

'Are you talking about Billy Welland, shouting at his wife?'

She nodded. 'It must have been. I saw Ryan go out about half an hour earlier.'

'So it started with nothing much? Tell me what happened.'

'I have to live next door to these people after all, and so do my children,' she paused, calculating he thought, how much more to tell.

'Then it escalated as usual, I could hear him hitting her. I went cold. I didn't want the children listening to that.'

'Mrs Fraser. We cannot jump to conclusions. How can you be sure that it was Billy Welland, and that it was his wife he was hitting. Perhaps she was hitting him? It's not unknown.'

'It is in that household. He's been in prison you know, for violence. I thought I'd better call you One of these days he's going to kill her.'

She put her hand to her mouth, suddenly realising the implication of what she had said.

'You did exactly the right thing, Mrs Fraser.' Chris decided that Billy Welland needed talking to. He rang the Family Liaison Officer and whilst awaiting their arrival he took the opportunity to question Caroline Fraser further.

'While I'm here, Mrs Fraser, does the name Diane Whitfield mean anything to you?'

She shook her head, 'I don't think so. Who is she?'

'Never mind,' he said, 'A shot in the dark, that's all.'

* * *

Newcastle was busy that morning, the market stalls doing a brisk trade. Sometimes it was beneficial to hold interviews at a person's home. The police may learn something from the place, and the witness would be more relaxed and therefore perhaps more forthcoming, but Billy Welland, interrupted from his diet of daytime television, was not pleased and had threatened Chris.

Future interviews would be held at Chris's convenience and at his choice of setting; he brought Billy Welland into Guildhall. Interviewing him with

DC Dearing in attendance yielded little however, other that the man was a bully and quite probably violent towards his wife and family.

'D'you know there's a murderer out there while you're talking to me?' he said ultimately, 'Two detectives, one an inspector taken up for hours on a wild goose chase and all the time someone is laughing at you.

'What are your combined salaries for the hours you've been shut in with me? You've provided lunch and I've never seen so much coffee. And all the time he must be laughing at you.'

'He?' Dearing pounced in self-defence, but the Chief Inspector's thoughts mirrored Billy's exactly. For ten minutes he continued to question him, then told Billy they were done for today and that he would organise a car to take him home. There was undoubtedly something he was not willing to share, but Chris had become increasingly convinced that he was no murderer.

* * *

The family liaison officer arrived at the Guildhall as Billy was leaving and spoke to him before joining Chris and DC Dearing in the interview room to discuss the case.

'You know mental abuse is harder to recognise, and therefore to deal with, than physical abuse, although I believe Sharon Welland has probably been the victim of both. I managed to get her alone. She's fairly extensively bruised and admits that Billy did it to her. She refused to go to hospital.'

Naïvely, DC Dearing asked, 'Will she leave

him now?'

'I doubt it.'

'But if he's violent, why on earth do people stay and put up with it?'

'It's a complex topic, constable. There's always more to it than seems on the surface. Maybe Sharon still loves him, although I'm not sure about that. What she said to me is, *How am I supposed to bring up the kid if I left him, tell me that?*'

It was unanswerable. Dearing was sure that it would be possible, there would be support available but she could not pretend it would be easy. Especially for a woman already browbeaten into believing herself worthless.

'So what did you do?'

'Gave her all the details of a refuge, helpline numbers, told her and him that I'd be calling in from time to time.' She sighed, 'It's a thankless job sometimes, but we have to keep chipping away.'

Chapter 20

On Sunday morning, the sixteenth of November, at the end of the second week of trading, Carly and Josie were alone in Bookends Café, the sign turned to *Closed*. Overnight there had been a change of wind direction, blowing away the previous day's fog and ruthlessly seeking out every crevice. The wind threw occasional handfuls of hailstones against the large picture window and Carly shivered and put on the overhead light.

It was truly ironic, Carly reflected as she scrubbed the two highchairs. The rail scheme that had forced her redundancy and led to the café opening had already provided a substantial number of customers, railway personnel amongst them. It was an ideal place for the contractors and surveyors to get a hot meal and warm themselves in the middle of the day.

Many local people of course knew the story of the shooting at Strawberry Fayre, and had come out of curiosity or to support Carly and Josie's new venture.

The work finished, she and Josie sat at the warmest of the tables by the radiator, to review the first couple of weeks, a plate of home-made cakes between them. Carly looked up from the accounts and sighed. She wondered at Josie's age, certainly she must be in her late seventies, she was remarkable really.

'Stop eating the stock,' Josie said as Carly gave her enthusiasm to a slab of millionaire's shortbread. She shook her finger at Carly playfully and removed the plate, emptying the remainder of the biscuits into a tin. 'What are you sighing about?' She set about making coffee for them both.

'As I expected, after the first flurry of activity the rush has died down, we could do with attracting more customers – ones who will come in on a regular basis. What did we do with those Golden Ticket ideas?'

Josie stowed the biscuit tin in the kitchen and, dusting sugar from her hands, brought Carly the pile of suggestion cards that they had left on the tables during the first week of trading, as well as the Golden Tickets they had attached to the flyers distributed in advance. All contained ideas of what local people would like to see happening at the café, and suggestions had come pouring in.

'I wondered,' Josie began tentatively, 'whether to offer pensioners a cut price lunch. Nothing fancy.' She gave a look towards the tiny kitchen, 'but Toasties, sandwiches, baked potatoes, soup – all the usual stuff, just a bit cheaper on a loyalty card.'

'Hmmm,' Carly was unsure about discounting prices so soon after opening. It may give the impression that they were desperate and they were operating on small enough margins as it was. 'Perhaps,' she temporised. 'Let's see what our punters have to say.'

Josie handed over the small stack of colourful cards and the stack of paper tickets. There were some good ideas – a reading group, a Knit and Natter session; a toddlers' book session one afternoon, and one suggestion similar to Josie's, but merely a loyalty card offering a free coffee for every ten visits, which would be more cost-effective.

As an additional incentive Carly had offered the Golden Tickets as a competition, with a lunch voucher for two people as prize for the best idea. She glanced down at the details on one of the last few tickets she had looked at. *Susan Chell,* it read, followed by a local address. Josie was taking them off her one by one and putting them to one side.

Susan's ticket fell onto the floor and Josie, in trying to retrieve it, trod it underfoot. She swooped it up, screwing it into a ball. Carly joked 'Hey, that's one of our competition entries. Don't put it in the bin.'

Josie looked down at it, 'Lor, I'd lose my own head if it wasn't fastened. I hope I don't forget to charge the customers for what they eat.' She still clutched the paper.

'Give it here, I'll put it with the others,' Carly held out her hand.

'It's wet and filthy now, I'll just throw it away – we've got lots of suggestions.'

'No,' Carly insisted, taking it from her, 'we should at least look at them all. Hang on a minute. That name sounds familiar.' Carly tried to recall where she had seen the name recently.

'I don't think so,' Josie went to take the ticket back from her, but Carly held firm, deep in thought. She looked up aghast, then stared again at the card she clutched in her hand.

'What's up?'

'Josie, what was the name of that woman they found dead in someone's bath – it was in the Sentinel?'

'Don't know, don't think I read it,' Josie told her.

'I'm sure it was Susan Chell, something like that. The paper will be under the sink for the recycling.'

It was the work of minutes to retrieve the relevant edition. Not a regular subscriber, Carly had bought that edition because it carried coverage of the café opening. They had been well-served by the press. A month before the opening a feature had appeared in the Sentinel newspaper on the new local enterprise. Then on the day of the opening itself was another double page spread with photographs and asking for locals to supply ideas of what they would like to see in the café.

The double page spread they had kept to frame, the rest still awaited collection by the council.

They looked at each other in horror.

'We probably shouldn't handle it any more,' Carly said as Josie picked it up for a look.

'Don't be daft. These have been lying around for the best part of two weeks. I gathered them up as they were filled in on the day and bunched them together. They're covered in my fingerprints and yours. As well as my footprints.' She pulled her cardigan tightly around her, a defensive gesture that was becoming habitual.

'All the same,' said Carly. 'Leave it there. I'll phone the police, or better still, I'll go and see them.'

*   *   *

Winter was Carly Broadbent's favourite time of the year. She could wear her beloved boots without garnering strange looks from the scantily-clad sun seekers of the summer months, and could scuffle in the fallen leaves like a child.

She walked through the market place to the Guildhall and asked if Chief Inspector Timothy was available. When Chris returned to the Guildhall late that afternoon a familiar figure was sitting in the foyer waiting to pounce as he came through the door.

'Carly Broadbent, from the new café,' reminded the desk sergeant, 'Says she's something for us.'

In Chris's office Carly explained about the Ticket idea, and then placed the pile of tickets, with Susan Chell's offering at the top, in front of him.

'So these are tickets you left out for people to put down comments. On the day of the opening is that?' Chris's heart fell.

'Yes. We did have some other stuff we sent out with promotional literature beforehand, but that was all paper flyers. These cards weren't used till the day of the opening.'

This blew the case wide open. If Susan Chell was still alive on the first Saturday of November, then all their hypotheses were incorrect. Alibis were nonsense and they would have to start again. The ACC would not be impressed, and as for the press ...

He could see that there were two different designs and asked for an explanation of the significance.

'The pink-edged ones were given out with flyers beforehand. I paid for some to be delivered locally, and we hoofed the rest to nearby villages – Madeley, Silverdale, Scot Hay and so on. Those bright blue ones were left on the tables in the café itself on the opening day. I've left more out since but kept them separate, so I know that this one,' she indicated the ticket with Susan Chell's name, 'was completed on café opening day, the first Saturday in November.'

'It's been in the wars,' he commented, 'compared with the others in the pile.'

'It was actually Josie who found it, she dropped it and stood on it.' Carly laughed, 'I only just stopped her from throwing it out, it wasn't as if we'd had no other suggestions but it seemed only fair to consider them all, seeing as it was a competition for the best idea. If she'd thrown it away I'd have been none the wiser.'

'And neither would we. I need to speak to her again.'

'Yes, she knows that. She said she'd call here when she's doing her shopping in town. We couldn't both come now because someone's got to mind the café –we were really busy this morning.'

'I'm glad it's doing well, Ms Broadbent.'
'It's Carly, please. Carly and Josie. After all that business at the fruit farm, I feel we've no need for formality.'

Chris picked up the ticket, 'May I photocopy this?'

'You can keep it.' Carly gathered up her gloves and scarf, 'If this was that dead woman, it's of no use to me now.'

Chapter 21

Typically for a British winter, the temperature had again risen sharply overnight and the rain set in once more. The wind had veered and now a north-easterly was blasting down from the Peak District across the Staffordshire Moorlands.

As Chris left the Guildhall the wind was blowing sheets of rain and hailstones over the town in successive waves. Leaves swirled in an angry vortex around the Guildhall, with huge puddles forming between mounds of sodden slush.

There had been some delay in getting a Court Order to gain access to the flat whose address Susan Chell had written on the Bookends Café Golden Ticket, a flat in a nineteen fifties block off Hanley's Regent Road.

Pete was standing at the doorway, blowing on his fingers and stamping his feet in the cold. 'Convenient for the city centre,' was Pete's comment as he followed Chris into the foyer.

'This is like old times,' Chris told him, 'Except not really, we're on your patch, you lead.'

After some challenges with his hearing aid, the caretaker eventually opened the door to Susan's flat for them, to their relief showing no more interest than that they shut the door firmly when they leave.

The flat had evidently been rented furnished and Susan had brought little of her previous life with her except for the Poole plate her husband had referenced, which hung on the chimney breast.

There were several changes of clothes in the bedroom and the bedside table held only a bottle of aspirin, and a paperback. There was an empty pack of birth control tablets in the bin, but no part-used pack that might have given an indication of the last night she spent in the flat.

In the living room again the furnishings were sparse. A daily paper for 30th October was on the coffee table along with a mug containing the dregs of a drink that looked like hot chocolate. In the kitchen sink they found a plate, wineglass and cutlery presumably from her last solitary meal.

A small cupboard in the corner yielded more promise and Pete produced a manila folder of paperwork. They were about to go through it when there was a gentle knock at the door.

There stood a middle aged lady wearing a mohair jumper and vivid red trousers, almost matched by her hair. She bore a tray containing two mugs and a sugar basin in arthritic fingers.

'I hope you don't think I'm just being nosey,' she began, placing the mugs on the coffee table. 'I saw you come. Actually I see most people come here, I spend a lot of time watching the world from my window. The caretaker said you were police about Susan and that you looked really cold. I thought maybe a hot drink?' She nodded towards the steaming mugs, 'Go on, get stuck in.'

Gratefully they did so as she continued, 'I have to go out shortly, and as I probably knew Susan best of the people here, I thought you might want to speak to me?'

She sounded hopeful and Chris wondered at

her lonely life living here watching the busy city from her window. They might find her useful.

Half an hour with Dorothy Sawyer, 'Call me Dotty', brought a few nuggets to ponder over and as she went off to her appointment, having topped up their treacly coffee, and told them to leave the cups outside Susan's door, they sat together on the sofa to consider what they had learned.

Dotty had confirmed their suspicions that Susan had lived alone at the flat, which she had taken about eight months previously. She had occasional overnight gentleman visitors but none that Dotty ever met or could name. There had been one man who she had noticed several times recently, a big blond-haired fellow with a smart grey overcoat, but more than that she was unable to say.

Dotty told them that Susan's mother had died in a home, about the same time as she had moved to the flat. Susan had told her that she had not seen much of the old lady up until a couple of years ago but then, she told Dotty, she realised that her mother was her only link with the past, and particularly with her beloved brother who had tragically died very young.

'And did she learn a lot from her mother about her past and her brother?' Chris had asked. Dotty thought not. The old lady was declining quite quickly and would became very upset when Susan delved.

Chris had wondered whether Susan actually lived at the flat – there seemed so little of her personality about it. It took Dotty some time to process this, but she was confident that Susan lived there.

Of course her job took her away a lot, she had qualified, *so there were long periods when the flat was empty.*

When Chris had asked what sort of work her neighbour had done, Dotty was less sure.

She confirmed that Susan had owned a large dark car when she first came to the flats, but she had said at about the end of September that she was getting rid of it. Said you didn't need a car living so near to the city. Dotty had thought it strange. In her experience most car-owners would fight tooth and nail to keep the independence it brought them, no matter how inconvenient or expensive.

'I'd like you to look around her flat and tell me if anything strikes you as out of place or missing. Will you do that?'

The older woman stood in the small living room looking at the decorative plate with a canal boat scene, over the gas fire.

'That was the first thing I saw Susan bring into the flat. There were other things she went back for over the weeks, and no doubt would have been more, a divorce settlement, dividing the spoils and all that, but at the time she said that was all she wanted from there.'

Left to their own devices the detectives' first find of significance was a jewellery box on the bedroom dressing table. It contained nothing of commercial value, these were trinkets, probably gathered over Susan's lifetime, and having little meaning for anyone else.

Chris decided to take them, log them and then return them to Susan's husband, suggesting that he pass them on to her aunt. There was no wedding ring, nor was there the much-photographed necklace.

They took the two handbags they found in the

flat, but there was no evidence of the black leather item described by Russell Chell. The wedding ring and necklace were small enough to be easily disposable, the bag less so, but the local refuse collections had been taken at least once since the murder so both could be long gone. Still unexplained was the brightly coloured bag found with Susan's clothes.

Having considered all this information Chris and Pete turned their attention again to the file they had found in Susan's kitchen.

There was a pile of letters rubber-banded together along with a passport. The handwritten envelopes suggested that these were from various people. These and a large brown envelope containing bank statements Chris passed over to Pete, but there was no sign of a will.

Pete exhaled on a whistle. The statements covered the eighteen months Susan had been at the flat and showed a salary being paid monthly by the council for the first twelve months only. This coincided with Russell saying that she had given up work when she fell ill, but Dotty seemed to think she was still working.

'Worth a chat to her employer. See what reason she gave for leaving. I'll get someone on that,' Pete made a note, 'perhaps talk to some of her colleagues. Did she still see any of them? What was she like?'

What he found more surprising were the large cash sums paid into the bank, one fixed amount on the fifteenth of each month, and other smaller amounts at irregular intervals. All the statements showed these sums, right back to when Susan had first taken the flat. There was also a cash sum paid in of two thousand pounds paid in four weeks before she died.

'Where's all this money from?'

'Dotty thought she had a job that took her away a lot, perhaps she did.'

'Working for the council. Payment in cash?' Pete was sceptical, 'Something shady then. I wonder what?'

Chris was idly flicking through the passport.

'How many border stamps have you in your passport?'

'Hardly any,' Pete said, 'they mostly just glance at the picture and wave you through.'

'Hmmm, me too, yet she's got four, no five stamps the six years she's had this. Suggests she's probably been abroad a good many more times even than that doesn't it?'

'What for?' Pete considered, 'Exotic holidays, or something more sinister – drug smuggling, people smuggling. It would explain cash payments but it just doesn't fit in with what we've learned about her. She worked for the council, she went house-sitting for people she knew. It might explain perhaps how she ended up dead though. Come on. Let's take the paperwork back to the office and read them in comfort.'

* * *

Chris still had to debrief the team before he could call an end to the day.

'So, what have we got? DS Hegarty?'

She straightened her thoughts for a moment, 'The victim should have been housesitting in Milton between October twenty-first and the second of November. Not necessarily sleeping there but at least visiting daily. We now know she did stay, the lab says the bedding had been slept in since it was last washed, but probably only by her. There was certainly no sign of sexual activity in that bed, and judging by the post it looks like she stayed or called in each day until the Tuesday.'

DC Dearing took up the tale, 'But then why isn't her car here somewhere? A search of the garages and outbuildings has produced nothing. And where are the registration documents? They are not at Russell Chell's house, and they're not at her flat. She can't have yet another place surely?'

'It's stretching credibility a bit certainly. Her neighbour at the flat said she was planning to get rid of the car. Perhaps she did.'

Hegarty went to the map on the incident room wall. 'If she was planning to go house-sitting out in Milton from Russell Chell's she would need transport. Surely she'd have kept the car at least until the house-sitting was done.'

'If she was going there from the flat she could possibly have walked.'

'More likely hopped on a bus.'

'None of the drivers on that route have come forward. We've tried taking a photograph to the depot to see if that jogged any memories. It was a long shot though. We don't know what day, what time or whether she used the bus at all.'

'So maybe a lift. Chell?'

'Possibly. What about the man who has been seen at her flat?'

'We need to trace him, sir.'

'I'm not sure – I suspect he is already in the frame.'

The team were used to Chris's occasional intuitions,

'By the pricking of my thumbs, sir?' Yorkie was ever the sceptical pragmatist.

Chris allowed the laughter for a few moments, then: 'Back to business. How did she leave the Whitfields' place, Yorkie?'

'No signs of a struggle so probably she was alive but whether of her own free will?'

'And again we come to transport?' He looked round the room for ideas.

'If a friend took her, or her husband, she could have left in the same way.'

'Or on a bus.'

'Or maybe by taxi.'

Chris's phone rang. He spoke for a minute then held up his hand to stop Hegarty leaving the room.

'By the pricking of my thumbs, eh? DS Hegarty I want you to come with me. That was Anthony Whitfield. He would like to talk to me, away from his home preferably. He'll meet us at The Pitman's Lamp in half an hour. Bring that fancy bag we found with the clothes. We'll see if he's seen it before.'

Chapter 22

It was forty-five minutes short of closing time when they arrived at the local pub and Chris had to wait for several vehicles to nose carefully out of the car park before he could pull in. As he showed his identification to the barman, all but two of the remaining patrons hastily left.

At the bar sat a thin-faced consumptive-looking man of middle years, and a younger man was sitting at one of the tables. As Chris looked his way he raised his whisky glass in mock salute before emptying it in one gulp. By the smart coat and his blond hair, this could be Dotty's visitor to Susan's flat. Chris ordered him another and carried it over to the table.

'Mr Whitfield. I believe you wanted to see me?'

Whitfield looked significantly sleep-deprived. His recently holiday seemed to have done him no good. He looked deep into the glass, then rubbed his hand tiredly through his thinning hair.

'That's right. You see,' he paused, 'I knew her, I knew her quite well.' He started on the whisky Chris had brought, and his slightly mis-focused eyes made the detective wonder how many he had already consumed. Hegarty sat at an adjacent table, primed to take notes.

'You'll have to explain that, sir.'

Without being asked the barman put two further small whiskies on the table between them.

When they were alone again Chris pointedly moved his to one side, whilst Anthony grabbed his current glass and clutched it tightly.

'I met Susan Chell through my wife,' he said, 'We got along really well and after a while we exchanged mobile phone numbers and talked a few times.

'I had in fact known her at school vaguely, but I had no idea that she was the Susan Jennings I used to know.'

The man at the bar coughed noisily.

Whitfield looked deep into his glass, 'I couldn't tell you before, but I came home that day, the thirty first.'

Chris was inscrutable, denying himself a look of triumph at DS Hegarty.

'We were only on holiday in the Lake District, but I missed her. We were only able to grab time between my wife and her... he paused, 'commitments, but this way I reckoned I could see her in the afternoon, and stay overnight. Then go back to the Lake District next morning.'

'What did you tell your wife? Where did Diane think you were?'

Clearly this was a line he had not expected, 'She ...er... she thought I was at home. I told her when I got up that I had been awake all night with toothache, I was going to phone the dentist. I pretended I had got an appointment for that afternoon, that I didn't want to go to a strange dentist and it was less than two and half hours home from Kendal. I didn't want to spoil the holiday for her and my daughter.' Chris raised his eyebrows as Anthony said, 'She never questioned it.'

'Honest people don't.'

He had the grace to look away, embarrassed.

'I know, I know. I'm not proud of myself. Then I phoned Susan, and told her I would pick her up in time to take her for lunch. She wouldn't let me collect her, but she said she would meet me in Leek.'

'We spent the morning browsing the shops, then went to Primo Piano for lunch. Susan's handbag strap had broken as she was on her way to meet me. She had caught the handle on something and the stitching pulled apart. There's a shop a couple of doors away from the restaurant and I got her a new one before we went in for lunch, but you don't want to know about that.'

'On the contrary, before you go on sir, I'd like you to describe the bag you bought.'

Anthony looked puzzled, 'It's a designer sort of thing – purple sort of butterflies and a label on the outside – Cath something or other. I don't remember.'

'Kidson?' DS Hegarty suggested.

'That's it, Kidson.'

The sergeant produced the evidence bag containing the brightly-coloured bag. 'Is this the bag?'

He frowned at it, and then at the detective, 'Yes, that's it. Where did you...?'

A glance passed between the detectives.

'When did you last see Susan with it?'

He thought for a moment, 'That afternoon. That was the last time I saw her.'

'Before that day – Hallowe'en afternoon – when was the previous time you saw her?'

'On the Thursday night before our holiday. It was a regular...er...'

'Rendezvous?' Hegarty suggested, 'How did

you manage that?'

'Meet regularly? My wife knows – thought – I play snooker every Thursday. Pub league.'

'The league's loss was Susan's gain then?'

Whitfield flushed, 'You make it sound so sordid,' he said.

Both detectives looked at him blandly.

'So Susan had the new bag with her that afternoon. Where did you go by the way?'

'We didn't go anywhere. After lunch we went home. In the restaurant she had taken all the stuff out of her old bag and transferred it to this one. The broken one she put in a refuse bin in the car park before we left Leek.'

'You took her home?' Chris was surprised, thinking of Russell Chell.

'She lived in a flat in Hanley. We spent a couple of hours together. Then I went back to my house. I was planning to spend the night with Susan, but my wife thought I was going to sleep at home, so I had to ... make it look like I had, pick post up and so on.' He looked at the floor.

'And where were your regular Thursday rendezvous, sir?'

'I don't see that that has anything to do with it.'

'Answer the question please,' Chris was insistent.

'At her flat. We – I – couldn't afford to be seen out and about with her.'

'Was she a married woman, sir?'

'She had been. She and her husband had been separated for several years.'

'Did she tell you that?' Hegarty sat back in her

chair. Chris's face remained inscrutable. Whitfield looked from one to the other, 'Yes. Why?'

'Did you not think it strange that her husband was chief mourner at her funeral?'

'I suppose I just thought ... they were still married technically. I expect he paid.' He must have seen how callous this sounded. 'Why? What are you saying?'

'Mr and Mrs Chell continued to live together *technically*. We understand that she would have regular evenings – Thursdays no doubt – away, as well as an occasional week or fortnight her or there. Did the two of you holiday routinely, sir?'

Whitfield was wringing his hands now and looking at the floor.

'No. Of course not,' he said in a small voice. 'How could we go away on holiday? I'm married.'

DS Hegarty turned to Chris, 'I wonder who she went on holiday with, sir. Mr Chell said she often returned looking tanned and refreshed.' The sergeant was overstepping the mark but Chris was disinclined to rein her in.

'Indeed,' he added, 'and there were all those stamps in her passport.' He saw no reason why Anthony Whitfield should be spared the truth.

'We were to meet up again in the pub here at seven o'clock that evening.'

'Just to clarify sir, this would be October 31st?' Chris sought to clarify.

'Would it? I suppose so, yes.'

Just about the time Ben suggested she had died.

He again looked at the floor, 'But she never came.' Again there was an expectorant cough from the bar's sole remaining other customer.

'She didn't come,' he looked shamefaced. 'She stood me up.'

There was a harrumph from the death's head figure at the bar.

'I could understand it to some extent. She had been fine earlier, when I was spending money on her, but then she wouldn't well ... we had a bit of a dispute when I left the flat in the afternoon.

'I said I'd see her here later, and she said maybe I would, maybe I wouldn't, she'd see how she felt. Then she just didn't show. I was damned annoyed I can tell you. I'd dreamed up some cock and bull story that had only half convinced my wife, and driven all the way down from Kendal.' He took a deep draught from the glass.

'Didn't you go round, have it out with Susan?'

The man ran his hand over his jaw. 'I – no. I thought something must have come up – some reason why she couldn't come. Then I became so cross I thought *sod her, I don't care.*' He paused, 'I'd had quite a lot to drink.

'How cross exactly?' Hegarty's voice was quiet.

'Oh, no! No. I'm nothing to do with whatever happened to her. You have to understand that a relationship with Susan was very much on her terms. I had agreed. She'd said several times, right from the start of us seeing each other, that if I ever just turned up unannounced, that was it, we would be finished between us. She had to have her own space. She wouldn't turn up at my home, and I wasn't to do it to her. What could I do? I didn't want to risk losing her.' He put his head in his hands, 'and now I've lost her anyway, haven't I?' He sounded near to tears.

Chris was appalled. This man was married, he was disgusted at the idea of a married man treating his own wife so callously but he had to admit that the man seemed genuinely distressed, he must have been very fond of Susan. He probed on for a while, but all he gained from Anthony Whitfield was that he had subsequently telephoned and texted Susan, but received no reply from her until the following Saturday. He showed Chris the phone and its message.

'The rest you know.'

'Hardly, Mr Whitfield. There's a great deal we don't know. What did you do when you left here? Did you sleep at home as you had planned?'

'No. I drove back to the Lake District that night. I left here at closing time and got on the motorway. I had to stop for about twenty minutes at Tebay services I was so tired, but I got back to the holiday cottage at about two o'clock.'

Chris considered this. It would mean that Anthony was about a hundred miles just before the window cleaner noticed the steamy bathroom in the Fraser's home. It looked like he was off the hook, but Chris was not letting him know that just yet.

'We'll leave it for now Mr Whitfield, but I want you to give some thought to what else you may have to tell me. I'll see you at my office tomorrow morning at nine o'clock to make a statement. Before then you may feel it wise to explain all this to your wife.'

* * *

The landlord had listened silently to this

exchange. Once Chris and Anthony Whitfield had left he continued with the routine already established in his six-month tenure of the pub. He locked the optics and collected the remaining glasses before stationing himself behind the bar.

He watched from the corner of his eye as his remaining customer downed the last of his drink and shot the glass along the bar like a character in a western. The landlord caught the glass deftly and looked at Jim, an unreadable look. Jim merely gave him a toothy grin before turning for the door. The landlord reflected on his choice of career, that it was not a balanced relationship he had with his customers. They felt they were socialising with him, but for him they were just business profits, his livelihood.

'Tomorrow, Jim?' the landlord said, hating to hear the slight crack of panic in his voice. Jim's retreating figure simply raised a hand in acknowledgement.

As he disappeared the landlady appeared in the doorway. 'Quiet tonight,' she stated the obvious.

'It'll buck up when we get nearer to Christmas. I hope Anthony isn't scared off by that policeman – Jim neither. He only drinks bitter but by God he drinks plenty of it, and every night. There are plenty of other pubs he could take his patronage to, and his cronies would follow.'

He need not have worried. Jim had enjoyed himself far too much that evening to change his drinking allegiance. He was looking forward to what future visits might bring.

Before he dropped Hegarty back at her car Chris stretched back in his seat, tapping the steering wheel with his fingers.

'Anthony Whitfield's a weak, feeble, downtrodden man, but this has a ring of truth about it. He says he kept phoning over the next couple of days and received a text from her on the second saying that something had come up, she would be in touch.'

'But she never was?'

'No, because she was dead.'

'That message wasn't even from her. By then her killer could have the phone, her bag, keys everything.'

Chris nodded. 'I'd thought of that, but it doesn't get us any nearer to finding out who it was. Nor does it explain the ticket in her name left at the café by someone who knew the address of her flat.'

He looked at his watch, 'I'm off home. I'll be working this evening.'

Hegarty was surprised. Chris had not previously mentioned this. 'Sir?'

'I'm going to go through the paperwork from Susan Chell's flat. There were cuttings confirming what Chell told us, and so I've asked Harris to order up a copy of the Coroner's report and also the Post Mortem report on Susan Chell's brother. Tomorrow evening I'm going back to the Pitman's Lamp. I want to track down our noisy-throated friend from the bar. I have a feeling he wouldn't take much persuading to have a little chat.

* * *

'Her did come.' Chris was once again in the lounge bar of the Pitman's Lamp. He had ordered a whisky, whilst he sorted out his questions.

He turned to the cadaverous man who was

staring into his empty glass, and who offered nothing more.

'Here.' Chris pushed his untouched whisky towards him.

The man drank it up without thanks, then said again, 'Her did come – that woman. He might not have seen her but I did.'

'When was this?'

'Dunno, but I reckon it were the night he told you 'bout.'

'What makes you think that, Mr...?'

'Jim. Jim Townsend. He were mad 'bout summat, and he were all done up, jacket and that. Never seen Anthony Whitfield that dressed up afore.'

'So you thought he was waiting for someone?'

His informant gazed gloomily into the empty glass and shrugged his shoulders, but the towels were now over the pumps and the landlord busy washing glasses at a sink at the far end of the bar.

'Di'n't think nothing. Not then. Only when I saw her picture in the paper, see? I knew I'd seen her.'

'Where did you see her exactly?'

He swivelled on the stool and indicated the rear door. This, Chris knew, led through to the kitchen, past the toilets and eventually to the rear car park.

'How come Anthony didn't see her if she came in from the back?'

'Mebbe she didn't come in. He kept looking round, watching the main door at the front, then looking at his watch. Mebbe she got in the doorway and looked around, then went straight back out again, like a bat out of hell it were. I only saw her 'cos I went out for a smoke. I thought *now the fun'll start,* but he never said nowt.'

'What time was it?'

'Dunno. Early, I gen'lly comes in earlier than this.' He looked again at the covered pumps.

'You're sure it was her? You recognised her from the photograph in the Sentinel?'

'And the name Susan – only she were Susan Jennings when we all knew her.'

'You knew her? When was that?'

'School. We all went to school together.'

Chris thought a moment, 'Who do you mean when you say *when we all knew her*? Who else was there at the same time?'

'About eight hundred of us, Mr Policeman.' He cackled at his own joke, leading to a fit of phlegmy coughing. When he was quiet once more, Chris tried again: 'You weren't talking about all eight hundred though, were you? Who did you mean? Mr Whitfield?' But, the whisky finished and with the towels over the pumps, nothing more was going to be shared.

Chapter 23

'*Cui bono?*' Hegarty threw the pebble into the pond.

'Hmm?' Chris was scrutinising the crime scene photographs.

'Who stands to benefit?' Georgia Dearing grabbed a pen and started a list.

'Let's have a brainstorming session.'

'Offensive.' This from DC Lyle, fresh from a psychology course, 'Brainstorm is a potentially offensive term to people who suffer from brain disorders,' he explained. 'It's a genuine issue for them and an unpleasant situation,' then more quietly, 'my sister has a brain disorder.'

'Sorry. No offence meant. Now – Russell Chell. He wouldn't benefit financially to any great degree and his business is doing fine. Money isn't an issue.'

'But he gets to be the grieving widower, rather than the heartless marriage wrecker, going after another woman. Especially if his wife has been telling other people that she isn't well.'

'Or the cuckolded husband if he found out she was seeing someone else.'

'Her death gave him freedom to pursue the fair Felicity. Maybe she's a wealthy woman.'

'Make some discreet enquiries about that, although it doesn't get us very far.'

'What about the bag?'

'The shop recognised Anthony's photograph.

He was in there when he says, with a woman, and he bought a Cath Kidson bag.'

'What if Anthony's wife found out about the affair? She would be glad to see the other woman eliminated.'

'But she was in the Lake District, wasn't she?'

'So the stepson confirms. They were in a rented cottage so she could theoretically have sneaked out after he was asleep, and be back before he woke, but they were staying at Crossthwaite. It's over six miles to Kendal station, and Anthony had the car, remember. He would still be driving up the M6 if he's telling the truth.'

'He is, sir. Confirmed by CCTV cameras at Tebay Services.'

'Then I agree it's unlikely she could have done it, but get on to car rentals in the Kendal area. We can't afford to leave anything unchecked. I think we can discount the Frasers. They were abroad. What checks were done?'

DS York nodded, 'Airport, their passports, boarding passes and the park and ride all confirm the timings. They were in America over the period of Ben's reckoning.'

'Diane Whitfield was in Crossthwaite. Supported by the step-son, the distance from the station and the lack of a car.

'So we have Anthony Whitfield who was in a relationship, seemingly happily, with Susan Chell and we've found no reason for him to wish her harm.'

'On the contrary. I'd say he was gutted that she is dead.'

'Quite, so we're left with Russell and Felicity, both of whom would be free to get together. They have no alibis except each other. I think we need to have them in.'

As he finished speaking DC Harris came in to the room. 'That was interesting, sir. The clerk to the Coroner's Court says this is the second time in six months that someone has ordered a copy of the Neil Jennings report. He remembered because he had to go into the archive.'

'Don't tell me. Susan Chell!'

* * *

DC Lyle was updating himself in front of the the time line in the incident room.

'The completion of the card by the victim at the café opening on the first Saturday in November, threw into question Ben Hanchurch's conclusions about the date of death, sir.'

Chris agreed, 'So, she may have been alive on the first Saturday in November, although Ben Hanchurch is very surprised at that, and it looks as though she left the Whitfields' during the night of Hallowe'en. Did she go and stay at her flat? If so, why wasn't she responding to Anthony Whitfield's texts and calls, and where's her car?'

'She did reply to one of the texts. That suggests she was alive after Hallowe'en.'

'What about her car?'

Lyle shrugged. 'It's a Range Rover. Not at Russell Chell's, nor the flat. The Frasers each have a car, but both are on their drive. The neighbours confirm that his was absent while they were on holiday and that checks out with the airport parking and valet service. The Whitfields have one car – the one Anthony drove back from the Lake District.'

'So she's either driven off herself voluntarily or left at someone else's instigation, possibly her murderer, and we've no idea of knowing whether she was held somewhere or taken straight to the Frasers', except that Ben's certain she didn't die there.'

Chris sighed and rubbed his head. The hair still refused to grow across the now-healed scar, and always would. A constant reminder of the attack he had sustained on a previous case. The headaches too were a result of that attack and he felt the pain beginning to develop.

Lyle considered, 'but Ben did say he could be wrong. The length of time before he saw the dead woman, the temperature of the water, how long she had been submerged. It's not as if he's seen a lot of drownings.'

'That could explain why there was no sign of a drowning at the Whitfields'. There's no sign of anything in the bathroom or kitchen. Yorkie's been over it.'

Hegarty raised her eyebrows but said nothing.

'She must have been alive still on the Saturday, she went to the café opening.'

'Are we sure that was her?'

'Her denim jacket, the description of her hair and her boots. I think it was.'

'And she was there during the afternoon?'

'About three-thirty to four. It wasn't Carly who noticed her but the other woman, Josie, who's usually in the kitchen. They were so busy that both of them were backwards and forwards all day. Josie thinks she may have been with a man but she's not sure, it's possible they were just sitting at the same table.

'And this man's not come forward?'

'No, but it was ...'

'Busy – yeah I know.'

They seemed to be going round in circles. Chris decided it was time to finish for the day. His sister-in-law was arriving for the weekend.

'Yorkie and Georgia Dearing are visiting everyone who completed one of the tickets on the café opening day to see if anyone remembers seeing Susan Chell there, and who she was with.' The team would tackle the case fresh in the morning.

* * *

Chris arrived home from the Guildhall to hear laughter and conversation in the living room. He took a moment to make the gear shift from work to domesticity as Pippa directed him to an open bottle of wine on the table.

His mother-in-law Maxine, who worked as a translator, was talking into her phone and sounding exasperated.

'It really isn't my strength, I usually work with the Scandinavian languages; with Brexit I have a lot of European work coming up.' She paused and listened, 'I'm not saying I couldn't, I'm saying the timing would have to fit in with my other commitments. I can hardly expect the EU to shift its summit date to accommodate your client, no matter how high he is in the Saudi pecking order.

'I'm also sure that you must be able to find someone more experienced with Arabic languages.'

She smiled at Chris, listening to more

expostulations from her caller. Raising her eyebrows she lifted her empty wine glass, which Chris filled for her. 'Of course. If I can, but please try the university first.' Closing the call she thanked her son-in-law.

'You didn't tell your caller that you have a private commitment due to the wedding of the century?'

She laughed, 'I should have, shouldn't I? He would have thought I had an invite to the wedding of Prince Harry and Meghan. Far more important than Brexit shenanegins or the whims of a Saudi prince.'

Florence's voice came from the region of the floor behind the table, 'He wouldn't have thought you were scheduled to babysit Rachel, while Laura was bridesmaid to Pete and Frances, that's for sure.'

Chris's sister-in-law lay stretched on the rug, Laura beside her whilst his younger daughter Rachel climbed over first one then the other and back again, causing a great amount of tickling and giggling.

'Hi, Chris. I can't get up, I'm busy just now.'

'So I see, Florence. How long have you been down there?'

'Long enough,' decided the teenager, getting to her knees and swinging Rachel up into the air, to her squeals of laughter.

She was still holding the toddler when the doorbell trilled.

'I'll go.'

Chris raised his eyebrows to his wife behind Florence's back and received a thumbs-up in response. This seemed an altogether more cheerful Florence than they had seen on her last visit. Perhaps she was coming to terms with her mother's alcoholism. It boded well for the future.

* * *

When the desk officer told Chris on the phone that a Wilf Baldwin wanted to speak to him, he expected some sprightly octogenarian, and was therefore surprised when a young man of thirty-something years was shown into the office. The rain was once again driving down, several degrees warmer than overnight, but none the less unpleasant for that. The young man placed a sodden umbrella to drip onto the carpet in the corner of Chris's office.

'Named for my grandad,' he explained as he removed and shook the sodden raincoat. 'There, that's better.' He threw the coat on the floor and gave Chris his full attention.

He explained that he worked out of small garage just off the A34 to the north of Newcastle under Lyme.

He had been working on the previous month's returns – VAT, Hire Purchase plans and so on when something had rung a bell. He fiddled in his briefcase, and brought out a pile of documents. He had come across the name he had seen in the papers – Susan Chell. She had been in the garage the previous month and sold her car.

'Trade-in?' Chris asked.

No, a straight sale he was told. She had said she would no longer be needing a vehicle of her own.

He found it odd because people don't normally put a Range Rover, even an old one like that, in for a straight cash sale.

'She'd have done better selling it privately, but not my job to tell her. I asked if she would be getting a firm's vehicle, and she just gave me this funny little smile and said, *Something like that*. Then she opened up a bit and said her boyfriend was going to buy her a new car. She laughed and said he didn't know it yet, but he was.'

'How much did you pay her?'

'I don't know that I have to tell you.'

'Of course, Mr Baldwin.' Chris stood up, surprising DC Dearing, who took his cue, 'Our team will be back this afternoon with a warrant.' Chris smiled broadly at him, 'They'll want to see your accounts and VAT records, and of course the warrant will give them authority to look at and impound anything they feel may be relevant. Good morning.'

'Oh, hang on a minute. You don't need to go to all that trouble,' Wilf sat down and waved Chris back to his seat.

'No? That's very accommodating of you, Mr Baldwin,' Chris waved Dearing back to her corner seat, where she ostentatiously began noting down what the salesman said.

'It was two thousand pounds, not very much I know,' he seemed very defensive, but Chris was not interested in his selling techniques. 'But it was an old model, the bodywork needed a lot of touching up and these are expensive motors you know.' He gave an oily smile, less confident now. Chris half-expected him to rub his hands together, Uriah Heep fashion.

'How did you pay her?'

'She insisted on cash, very unusual but she had all the paperwork and the signatures tallied, so not a problem.'

'And did you have two thousand pounds on the premises, sir?'

'Yes, officer, I deal in cars. You can't get much of a Range Rover for a couple of grand.'

Chapter 24

It was so cold the following morning, Chris opted to wear his heavy overcoat. He normally avoided wearing it for work, finding it cumbersome to drive in, and over-hot when he was going indoors – say to interview people. He had not worn it since the day of Susan Chell's funeral, and in the pocket he found the list of attendees given to him on the day.

This he had examined on his arrival at the Guildhall, when he suddenly remembered that the woman whose identity he had been able to place was Josie from the café. He had telephoned to remind her that she needed to come into the Guildhall and she was now on her way in to speak to him. As he waited, he perused the Golden Ticket Carly had brought in from the café, wondering at its significance. He and DC Harris would be interviewing the woman together.

Josie was fuming inside. The weather had turned colder again. She hated these winter mornings, the cold, rising from bed in the dark to wet leaves outside and steamed-up windows within. Coughs and sniffles of passers by threatening who-knew-what awful diseases. She really disliked going to work in the dark and it was dark again before it was time to go home. She wondered whether she suffered from that Seasonal Affected Disorder that people were talking about these days.

And now she was trekking across the Market Place because Carly had told the police about her finding the ticket that damned woman had completed.

She was unaware of the changing displays in the shop windows, Hallowe'en and Bonfire Night giving way to fairy lights and tinsel. In the window of the television retailers, multiple images of the same ski-jumper filled the window.

She was shown into the smarter of the two interview rooms and immediately Chris saw her, he knew that he was right – the woman who sat opposite him now was the woman at the funeral – the one whose name had escaped him.

'I'm sorry to have kept you waiting. We are having central heating problems and the interview room is freezing. At least you are well wrapped up and we have found a couple of electric heaters. It should warm up quickly enough.'

Chris and Harris had joined Josie at the table, noticing that her eyes seemed drawn to the ticket on the top of the folder Harris had placed on the desk. It was clearly unsettling her. Not sure why she seemed so concerned about the police having this, but sure that it was in some way significant, Chris deliberately drummed his fingers lightly on it as he spoke. She looked anxious, swallowing loudly, watching the mesmeric beating.

'Tell me about this ticket.'

Her voice cracked as she spoke, 'It's just one of the suggestion cards. Carly thought it would be a good idea to get people's thoughts from day one. There were some good ideas.'

'And this one?'

'I can't remember what it said, Carly got sidetracked by the name and once we found the article in the paper about the body being found.'

'So it was Carly who singled out the ticket?

You didn't know the name?'

'That's right, I dropped it off the pile and stood on it by accident. It was barely legible. To be honest with you I'd have put it in the bin, but it was a competition you see for the best idea. Carly insisted it wasn't fair not to consider them all, so she picked it up and straightened it out. That's when she spotted the name.' She was visibly relaxing now – the worst seemed to be over.

The team had already compared the signature with papers they had found in Susan Chell's flat, and on the documents resultant from the sale of her car. The signature was clearly not hers.

Keeping this information to himself for the moment, Chris moved the conversation back to the script he had agreed with the DC Harris, who remained inscrutable.

'Did you see her at the café on the opening event? Would you have recognised her?'

Josie gave a forced laugh. 'Of course not. She was just a name on a card.'

'So you didn't know Susan Chell yourself?'

'No, of course not. I told you Carly recognised the name from the papers.'

'Then why did you go to her funeral?'

Josie had blanched.

'I...er, knew her mum.'

'Oh yes? Is that what made you realise it was her, when you saw the ticket?'

'I expect so.'

'Yet you told me a moment ago that it was Carly who recognised the name from the papers. Which was it, did you recognise her, or did Carly?'

'You're trying to confuse me.'

'Quite the opposite. I'm trying to clarify what happened to a young woman who turned up *dead!*' He banged the flat of his hand on the table, and almost shouted the final word. DC Harris wondered momentarily whether he should intervene, but Chris sat back in his chair.

'Now. The truth please.'

Josie noted the shift to formality.

Thankfully in spite of the glut of supposedly true-crime programmes offered by the television, few interviewees had the skill of refusing to answer questions or remembered to ask for legal support.

'I told you. I knew her mother. I went to the funeral as a gesture of…I don't know what. It just felt right to go.'

'How did you know that Susan was your friend's daughter? You didn't recognise the name Chell when you saw it on the ticket. Her mother's name would have been Jennings.'

'She must have told me, once when I was visiting her.'

'And you remembered it enough to go to her funeral, but didn't remember it when you saw it written down?'

'That's right,' she said brazenly, but she was unable to meet his eyes, 'and that's all I can tell you. I'm going now, you can't keep me here. I'm phoning my grandson to pick me up – it's inhuman keeping people here in this temperature, inhuman.

Chris took a moment. He was far from satisfied with this explanation but he needed more evidence in order to hold her. In any event she seemed an unlikely suspect to drown someone, even someone as slightly built as Susan, and then move the inert body upstairs into a stranger's bathroom.

He decided that for the time being he would have to release her, but he was unhappy. There were too many tenuous links between her and the dead woman. He left her with the desk sergeant to sort out her transport.

'I'll try calling my grandson. You've met him I believe, your lot.'

'Have we? I don't think I have.'

Josie looked at him strangely, 'Of course you have. He lives near to where that woman's body was found.'

Suddenly Josie caught sight of the expression on the desk sergeant's face and put her hand up to her mouth.

'Oh, he didn't know her. She was years older.'

The door flew open and a woman entered, a child in her arms clearly in a state of some distress. This totally distracted the sergeant from Josie's comment, and so the snippet of information about her grandson was never shared upstairs. Josie turned up her collar against the wind and forced cold hands into inadequate gloves. She made her way across the marketplace and to the entrance of the Midway car park, where Ryan Lee was waiting in his taxi.

* * *

Chris Timothy stood at the window of the Guildhall office overlooking the market square. He had been pleased at the move a few years ago from the previous premises on Merrial Street, where he had always felt a little out of things.

Here was the hub of the town and he felt he

could look out over honest stallholders, and the less salubrious clientele that were his bread and butter.

There was, as he saw it, just one disadvantage to the move. There was no immediately adjacent parking and he watched as DC Dearing, damp already only half way through the working day, struggled through the market stalls holding an umbrella up in defiance of the raging wind.

Had the move to a pedestrian area in the town not been made, the Chief Inspector would perhaps have seen Josie's chosen mode of transport.

Pete Talbot arrived at the Guildhall just as Chris had decided on lunch at the Roebuck café and the two made their way across the square together.

After relating the events of the morning to Pete, Chris waited in turn for information from Susan Chell's erstwhile employer and her old colleagues. Only one of these had shown any interest in remaining in contact, and Pete felt that the relationship, such as it was, had been driven by Susan herself. The colleague would not have called herself a friend.

She did have one snippet of information however. Susan had had a boyfriend until about twelve months before. This was someone she used to go away with occasionally. She had seen photographs from Spain on one occasion, the Algarve on another.

'And what happened to him?' Chris asked as a sandwich was placed in front of him.

'He died.' Pete saw the look of surprise on his friend's face. 'Nothing suspicious, at least not according to what this colleague said. He had cancer and he died. His phone number is in her contacts book, crossed out and the number is unobtainable. I've got a PC chasing phone records and St

Catherine's house. I feel sure we'll find a death certificate.'

'They are all interconnected aren't they?' They started off at school – Susan, Diane, Felicity and Edward Fraser. Susan introduced Felicity to her husband Russell and she herself got involved with Diane's husband.'

'All we need is Diane involved with Edward Fraser and we've got the full set. Like a card game.'

'Happy Families!'

'So what *is* the Fraser involvement? The school connection, then the body being found at their house?'

'Nobody seems to benefit from her death. Certainly not financially. She didn't have a lot of money to leave. She'd effectively chosen to leave Russell, so he was already free to carry on his affair with Felicity.' Pete attacked his lunch enthusiastically, smiling at the waitress.

'Cramps his style though doesn't it? That break not being complete. He's paying the bills, majority of them anyway.'

'It would cost him though if the split was a legal separation or divorce. He'd probably have to sell his home with that lovely view. She'd be entitled to perhaps a third.'

'She wouldn't have wanted to formalise it. If she was asked to prove she couldn't work and support herself she'd have been in difficulties, we know now that she wasn't terminally ill.'

'What about Felicity? Perhaps she got fed up with waiting for him, suspected maybe he was stalling. She thought Susan was dying, should have died already from the information Susan had given to

Russell.' Chris pushed his plate away and reached for his mug of tea.

'Or was it something Russell made up? We only have his word that she told him she was ill. Perhaps that was his story to keep Felicity at arms' length. After all we know definitely from the PM that Susan wasn't ill.'

'And the aunt and uncle said Susan had made no mention of it.'

'I know we now have some confusion over the dates, but Ben Hanchurch is adamant that she cannot have been alive into November, no matter the temperature of the water in the bath or any other confusing factors.' Several years previously Ben had made an error giving evidence in a murder trial, which had made him doubly careful about committing himself to detail. Chris was thus inclined to put a lot of faith in his judgement.

'I'm inclined to believe Ben. Also the post at the Whitfields' suggested that someone had been there regularly until the thirty-first of October, but not after. So for the moment, let's consider that date only, and have another look at Russell and Felicity's alibi. He said they were together but he had plenty of opportunity to talk to her on the phone before we even discovered her existence.

'After the initial shock Russell Chell was not particularly moved by Susan's death. Perhaps now he's seeing the benefits of being free to go to Felicity. Perhaps that's understandable.' Pete finished the last of his sandwich.

'Or has he made sure he's free by drowning Susan. They say they were together, but they would, wouldn't they? He may have known that Susan hadn't made a will, everything would go to him.'

'Yes but the flat is rented, she had a fairly run-of-the-mill job. He wouldn't have thought there was much.'

'Cheaper than divorce though. The girlfriend, you said, seemed rattled. I'll get Frances to go and see her again, get the detail from her, minute by minute from lunchtime on the thirty first, for the next twenty-four hours. She told the same story but she's not as adept as him at lying.'

'I'll get one of my PCs to check the CCTV footage near to where Russell Chell lives,' Pete offered, 'There was no sign of her car on the A34, but why did they meet at Chell's house? He's already said she wasn't comfortable going there. Susan was only supposed to be in Milton, she could easily have come home and interrupted them at any time.'

Chris summed up what they were both thinking, 'Unless one or both of them knew that was impossible because she was dead.'

Chapter 25

DS Hegarty met Georgia Dearing at her car and they went together to speak again to Susan's husband. 'About the evening you told us Felicity came to your house,' the sergeant paused, 'you told us when we first spoke to you that Felicity didn't like to come here – felt awkward about it still being Susan's home. So why did she come here on that occasion?'

'I don't know. No particular reason. I don't remember.'

'Do you have a poor memory, Mr Chell?' DC Dearing wanted to know, 'It's not so very long ago is it? Remind me, was that the Monday or the Tuesday?'

He gave her a long look, 'It was Hallowe'en that you asked about.'

'So it was. Did she often come here, Mr Chell?'

'Often? Sometimes she came here, sometimes I went to her home, sometimes we met elsewhere. What is all this?' He was suspicious now. 'This is nothing to do with Felicity.'

'Just trying to clarify the details. Now we need to establish what happened in the run-up to your wife's death. Can you talk me through the previous few days?'

''I don't know that I can...I can look in the diary but I'm always here there and everywhere. Also as I told you, we lived separate lives. I work you know. I'm not always local.'

'Oh yes, work for yourself don't you, Mr

Chell? I expect being the boss you can come and go as you please. Don't have to ask permission to pop home from time to time if you want to.'

'Now look here ...'

'When Felicity comes to visit you here how does she get here?'

'What do you mean how does she get here? She drives of course. She's not likely to come on the bus is she?'

'Does she park in your drive? No, I suppose your car will be in the drive. On the road then?'

'I suppose.' He sounded wary.

The two detectives exchanged looks, 'So I expect some of your neighbours would know when she's here. They'll remember I expect, it being Hallowe'en.' DC Dearing closed her notebook, preparatory to leaving.

His eyes flickered to the window and the house across the road where the windows were shrouded with nets. The defeated look in Chell's eyes spoke volumes as he watched the detectives knock on the door of the house opposite.

'Yes, of course I remember Hallowe'en,' in answer to DS Hegarty's question. 'Come on in by the fire, girls. It's freezing out there. I won't be surprised if we have snow overnight.

'I always buy a tin of Cadbury's Roses so I have something for the Trick or Treaters, then what's left I put away for Christmas.' She considered, 'Well, I always intend to put it away for Christmas but I'm partial to chocolate and once the tin's open it's very hard isn't it?'

Hegarty smiled her agreement.

'This year there weren't many callers, only

two lots if I remember rightly, and they weren't little children, quite teenage. I suppose it could even have been the same lot twice because you can't tell behind those masks, can you?

'I stayed by the window because one year someone threw an egg, even though I hadn't refused them a treat. I keep an eye out now, and I definitely saw that posh woman arrive over the road. Now, I'm forgetting my manners. Would you like a cup of tea?'

Hegarty could see Russell Chell standing looking out of his window. He had no doubt observed them coming straight over here. Let him wonder what was happening, they would take their time. Turning to the older woman she said: 'That would be lovely, thank you.'

'Susan had disappeared some weeks before and Russell Chell had not reported her missing, would you have any idea why not?' She waited until her hostess was again seated.

'He probably thought she'd left him again.'

'Again?'

'Oh yes, she made quite a habit of it over the years. Quite a turbulent relationship they had by all accounts.'

'Recently?'

'She looked thoughtful, 'No, not so much recently.'

'Did she work?'

'Yes. A clerical job I believe. At the council, but fairly low-powered. She was a bit … challenged.'

'Challenged how?'

'Just temperamental, threw a hissy fit on their wedding day because some confetti went down her dress I remember, and that set the tone for the next five years. She stopped work recently, saying she couldn't cope. No intention of doing another day's work in her life she told me. I suppose she'd got the meal ticket she wanted in Russell,' she looked slyly to one side, 'or in her new man?'

'Is this gossip, or are you aware that she definitely had someone else?'

'I know what she *said*, also she told me she wouldn't be living around here much longer.'

'Do you have any idea who this man is?'

She shook her head. 'I can tell you one thing though, Russell Chell would never have killed his wife.'

'I'm sure it's a thought difficult for most people to accept.'

'No I didn't mean that. I mean he just didn't care enough.'

DC Dearing looked up from her notes, 'What accounts?'

The woman looked blankly at the constable. 'I beg your pardon?'

'You said their relationship was turbulent *by all accounts*. Whose accounts?'

'Why, hers. I would hardly speak to him about what she said would I?'

As they walked to the car Hegarty asked, 'Do you think that could be right? That Chell didn't care enough?'

'Not about Susan maybe, but about his pride?'

'We'll go and talk to the other woman again to check on his story although by now he will probably have been on the phone to her.'

Felicity Chadwick opened the door with a towel fastened, turban-style, round her head. She wore a grubby housecoat and had a second towel draped across her shoulders. Evidently she had been washing her hair.

'Washing your hair, Ms Chadwick. Going out tonight are you?'

'Why would I be? I like to keep looking nice all the time.'

'We won't keep you long. We want to talk to you about Hallowe'en, an evening that you spent at Mr Chell's house. Why did you go there, why did he not come to your place?'

'No reason, he just rang and invited me, round.'

'Did you know Susan was house-sitting?'

'No. Yes. I think Russell had mentioned it'

'Had he or hadn't he?'

'He had, because generally he came to me. When he invited me to Alsagers Bank I said *What about Susan,* and he told me that she wouldn't be coming home. Then he said she was house-sitting for a friend.'

'Did he say where?'

'I don't think so.'

'So you didn't know she was only in Milton, and that half an hour's drive would have brought her home, yet he invited you round instead of coming to you?'

Felicity was losing her composure now 'Yes. Yes. Yes. You're trying to trick me. I'm not saying anything else. I don't have to answer your questions.'

Hegarty answered by closing her notebook and standing up. 'That's all for now,' she smiled at Felicity, 'but we may need to talk to you again. Don't go away anywhere without letting us know, will you?'

The way it was said suggested more than the words themselves.

As they were leaving Felicity's, a familiar car pulled up two spaces away and Hegarty watched as Anthony Whitfield went to the door of Felicity Chadwick's block. The sergeant signalled Dearing to stay where she was and got back out of her car. She waited in the doorway of the adjacent block, stepping forward in time to see him press Felicity Chadwick's entry-phone button.

'Good afternoon, visiting Ms Chadwick are you? Why would that be?'

'Why not, she's my sister.'

Hegarty was taken aback. She supposed there was no reason for the police to have been given that information, but felt that somehow they had been kept in the dark.

DC Dearing had joined them, 'I thought it was your wife who knew Ms Chadwick?'

'She does – did. They were at school together. As were you I understand.' He looked steadily at the sergeant. 'Just because my sister knew my now-wife doesn't mean I knew her. I didn't meet Diane until years later. They weren't even friends.'

'How do you know that, sir?'

'Oh for God's sake, she told me, Diane told me. Ask her.'

It made sense, but nonetheless Hegarty wondered whether he was not protesting just a little too much.

* * *

Pippa told Chris she was going to Bloomers,

the garden centre, next day with the children, to make a start on buying Christmas presents.

'Who are we buying plants for?'

'Not plants, silly. Garden Centres sell everything these days; food, cookware, clothes. You can buy anything at Bloomers from toys to Koi carp.'

'Can you? That's interesting.'

Chris made his own detour to the garden centre at lunchtime. As he wandered around he saw Felicity Chadwick in the restaurant. Other garden centres he believed had cafés, but this was far too smart to be designated as such.

She was evidently enjoying a solitary lunch. Collecting a cup of coffee, he went to stand beside her and indicated a vacant chair, 'May I?'

'Don't you lot ever give anyone any peace? This is harassment.'

'Nonsense. Have a look around. Yours appears to be one of the few tables with available seats.'

'You can have it. I'm finished.'

Clearly she was flustered; just as clearly her meal was far from finished.

'Just a couple of questions before you leave – you said you were departmental manager here?'

'That's right. I manage one of the clothes franchises. Now I really have finished. She stalked out of the restaurant leaving a plate half full of fish pie.

Chris eyed the fish thoughtfully, then went outside. He found the open-sided area where they sold rigid pools, flexible liner by the metre and mock waterfalls in all shapes and sizes. There was an array of ornamental fountains and associated statuary and large raised troughs, at this time of year filled only with water. He fingered the plastic edges of these but all were smooth and bright yellow, positioned at waist-height, presumably the better to show off the range of water lilies depicted on the accompanying signage.

He shivered in the cold and gave himself a mental shake *Don't be ridiculous, you can't kill someone with a dormant water lily.*

* * *

They discussed the interview back at the Guildhall.

'There are no money worries for Felicity Chadwick. She has a senior post at Bloomers Garden Centre. The clothes she wears, even at work, are expensive and good quality,' he told the team.

'Hmm. Not a fashion plate, but certainly her hair is well cut and those shoes she wore when we round there cost a bit. Her home is lovely too. I think you're right. I've been wondering about something else though. Where's Susan's necklace? Russell said she always wore a necklace her brother had given her.'

DC Harris was uncertain, 'Mmm, does any woman *always* wear the same piece of jewellery? My girlfriend seems to need as many necklaces as she has outfits.'

Chris was thoughtful, 'You may be right, but she doesn't seem to have been particularly fashion-conscious and there would be particular sentimentality attached to this one. She was wearing it on all the photos Russell showed us. So where did it end up?'

DS York joined her, 'Down a drain? In the canal? In the river? What's that pool a mile or so down the A53 – Holden Pool? Could be anywhere. She didn't die in situ so someone had transport to move the body, so they could have dumped the necklace miles away.'

DC Harris sighed. 'Our killer could probably tell there was no commercial value so just got rid of it.'

'Or maybe decided there was no value and so kept it.'

More reports were coming in, one that was to make a significant difference to the enquiry, but first DS Hegarty updated the team.

'A neighbour of Russell Chell reports that Felicity Chadwick was definitely there that evening – she was watching for Trick or Treaters in the window. She didn't see her leave, but went to bed at 11 o'clock.'

'We've got the reports back from the death of Susan Chell's brother,' Chris scanned the paperwork, 'Coroner's inquest *Accidental Death;* PM report *death by drowning, contributory factor – a skull fracture.*'

He looked up, 'It was assumed that he hit his head when he fell off the boat and that was why he couldn't get out in time. His friend was in the cabin at the time, in the loo actually. He dashed out as soon as he could when he heard the splash, but couldn't get at Neil, seems he'd slithered down between the boat and the side of the canal. It wasn't until the friend got the engine started and moved the boat, that he could reach his friend properly. He wasn't experienced at handling the boat and got in a bit of a panic, which cost valuable time. He was only a lad.'

'How old was he, this friend?'

'He was, let me see ... he was seventeen. He's

never come across our radar since then.'

Chapter 26

Chris was replacing the telephone as DS York entered the office.

'Across the road from the Whitfields' lives an anxious new mother. That night she was pacing the floor with her fretful teething bundle, and saw the Whitfields' security light come on at 2.45am in the morning after Hallowe'en. The automatic garage doors had opened and a big black car had tiptoed, as she put it, out and down the drive with its lights off. At the gate it turned towards the D road, gathering speed into the distance and out of sight. A terrible noise it made once it got to the road she said.'

'Terrible noise? Possibly a diesel, maybe a Chelsea taxi, but there are enough of those around, they're a useful vehicle round the Moorlands. Not Susan Chell driving her Range Rover; by then it was in the possession of Wilf Baldwin.'

'No, she thinks it might have been a taxi – there was some sort of logo on the driver's door.'

'Better go back and talk to her, but first check with the Whitfields, have another look round. See if they have any idea who it may have been.'

DS York, along with DC Dearing was once again visiting the Whitfields' house – the door had been opened by a round shouldered teenager with long hair and acne, who left them and went off to find his mother. At first the sergeant thought it was the lad who lived next door to the Frasers', he had the same long dirty hair, slouching walk and grubby jeans, but a closer look revealed that this youth had a stockier frame and was at least five years younger.

Before the detectives embarked on a further search of the house, they went into the living room where an animated discussion involved a man in overalls. He turned to the officer despairingly and raised his eyebrows, nodding in the direction of the kitchen.

'This really isn't very convenient officers, we're having trouble with the television. Seems our wall is wrong or something.' The comment, caustically made, preceded Diane Whitfield into the room.

'Murder seldom is convenient I find, Mrs Whitfield.'

The television engineer was becoming exasperated at the diversion. 'This hole is huge. I've got a lot of work to do here. It's a bigger job than you suggested on the phone Mrs Whitfield.'

She was becoming quite pink in the face. 'But it's a fifty inch screen – we got one that big especially to cover it.'

'It's not a matter of covering the hole, Madam, it's that there's nothing to fix the brackets to.' He tapped the wall at intervals and sucked on his teeth. 'This is a stud wall, I'm going to need to put strengthening beams across here to take the weight and then face it with plaster, otherwise you could get soot and all sorts falling down the chimney. Or the whole lot crashing to the floor. What sort of television was here before?'

'Oh it wasn't a television. I was hoping the big screen would hide the mess from when we took the fish tank out; neon tetras and guppies and stuff – one of the whims of Dane years ago.' She looked across at the unprepossessing youth, who ignored her.

'Every so often you had to take all the gubbins out and give the tank a good clean, and of course that falls to mum after the novelty has worn off – about a month wasn't it, Dane? I'd been looking after the fish for about two years and enough was enough. And anyway the works are so ugly,' she added as an afterthought.

'Ugly, how's that? I thought they were supposed to be restful.' The television engineer was measuring up.

'Yes they are in a way, when they are just swimming about and they were, but there's a filtration system and it has a thing called a power head circulation pump with a tap thing that sticks out at the top, and made disconcerting noises, so we just took it all out and stuck it in the cellar.'

DC Dearing interrupted, 'Mrs Whitfield, you mentioned a cellar, and the *"gubbins"* as you call it?'

'That's right.'

'And is this stuff still down there?' she glanced at DS York, 'and the tank?'

Diane Whitfield nodded, looking worried now.

'How long has it been down there, Mrs Whitfield?'

'It's all still there. Tank, filter, pipes and tubes, everything. It's been there since just before we went away. Dane wanted the television for his birthday so we got that in the middle of October.'

'Where is the cellar, Mrs Whitfield? We have seen no cellar.' DS York was horrified that this had been missed. He and a constable from Stoke had searched the house. Human error was the cause of the oversight, but he knew that blame would be attributed – the officer from Stoke had searched the downstairs and looked in everywhere, but under Yorkie's direction. He puffed out his cheeks. They had really needed a bigger team but understaffing in the service was a perennial problem and there were so many potential leads to be followed up. In hindsight he should have asked for the SOCOs to continue looking, but on his say-so this had been stopped once Susan Chell's clothes had been found.

Leaving the engineer to his planning, Mrs Whitfield led them through the kitchen and to a small room at the back of the house. It contained the central heating boiler, and the keypad for a sophisticated burglar alarm. On the far wall a door opened into the garage, but what the search had not revealed was a further doorway, concealed behind a pile of garden furniture – not a full-size door but a hatch about sixty centimetres off the floor and perhaps a metre and a half square. Mrs Whitfield flicked a switch and, opening the hatch, revealed steps leading down.

DS York led the way gingerly down the steep stairs ahead of DC Dearing. He was annoyed with himself, he really should not have missed this. But it was what they found inside the cellar that truly shocked them both.

* * *

For the sake of protocol Chris had taken one of the Stoke on Trent constables with him down to the canal-side. They visited the property where he estimated the Jennings family home had been during the nineteen eighties.

'My wife was upset when that land was bought by a developer.'

'Upset? I was livid and so were you, darling. Imagine! We paid a premium for this plot, the location, the view, easy access to the motorway ...'

She was sounding like an estate agents' brochure, 'and then to be living cheek by jowl with ... an estate.' She spat the word out like it was poisonous. Chris was beginning to dislike Mrs Poole quite strongly.

'Yours was bought as a single plot then, Mrs Poole?' Chris steered the conversation, 'from whom?'

'The people who lived here before in the shack. Honestly at first I couldn't believe they actually lived there. It was more like a sort of beach hut.'

'Not quite, darling,' Mr Poole managed to get a word in. The interjection earned him a glare.

'You can see where it was if you wish, Chief Inspector. We got rid of it, of course. There's a summerhouse there now, to keep the deckchairs there and so on.'

Chris saw no value in this, and shook his head. 'And their name?'

'No idea,' Mrs Poole took up the reins again, 'It is over twenty years agor.'

'Do you know whether the deeds to the property are registered with the land registry?'

'I'm afraid I've no idea. I know we threw out everything about the move a long time ago and I cannot recall their name.'

Her husband, mute, shook his head.

'They had children,' she offered, 'I remember that – I saw a whey-faced little girl once when I came to check the exact position of that pylon. It was very clever of dear Jeff, our architect to keep that monstrosity out of our sight line from the house.'

To one side of the Poole's garden bloomed the new estate. Chris wandered under the echoing bridge towards Leek and looked at the bank beyond. Here too were new houses – much newer, and he was about to turn away disappointed, when he noticed a woman's face at one of the windows of the first of these. She waved at him, indicating that he should join her.

The route was convoluted. Once he had crossed the A53 he walked towards the city centre, then took the first turning. Eventually, through a series of twists and turns, and once going completely wrong and having to retrace his steps, he found the correct property. By this time his would-be interviewee was standing on the doorstep, wearing a coat against the cold and leaning heavily on a walking stick.

This was a small house but cozily warm and both Chris and the constable were glad to get in out of the chill.

'Saw you were a policeman,' she told the younger uniformed officer. 'Is this your boss?' Without waiting for a reply she led the way into a tiny living room, which wore a shawl of dust; a room barely large enough to contain a three-piece suite was thus furnished, with the addition of a wall unit and a table with matching chairs and the biggest television Chris had ever seen.

'The kettle's on to boil. My husband was on the force, spent years of his life standing about in the cold, I know what it's like. What's going on over there? Someone fall in?'

Throughout she had spoken to the uniformed

constable, and Chris nodded for him to take the initiative.

'I'm not sure you'll be able to help us Mrs...?'

'Jones,' she answered, 'Cherry Jones. My husband was Ken Jones, did you know him?'

This last she addressed to Chris, evidently deciding that the constable would be far too young to remember a time when her husband was a serving officer.

'I'm afraid not,' Chris told her, trying not to smile, 'I'm actually with Newcastle, not Stoke, so it's unlikely that our paths would have crossed.'

'No, never mind. What's going on then?'

I think our problem probably goes back before your time here, Mrs Jones. How long have these houses been built?'

She laughed at him then. 'Bless you, the houses have been here five years, but I've been here a lot longer than that. My father owned all the land here on this side of the bridge. We were farmers and the family sold it to the developers five years ago. Before that the farmhouse was just out at the back here – that's how I come to have the biggest garden of them all.'

'Did you know the people who lived on the other side of the bridge from here in the late eighties?'

'Of course I did, lovey. They were called Jennings. It was a tiny little place, much smaller than this.'

The constable looked round the room in surprise, but fortunately Mrs Jones failed to notice.

'She was second generation canal people. That probably helped them cope with living in such a small space.'

'Did they keep a boat on the canal?'

She laughed, 'They did. It was barely watertight but the children used to play in it, before the accident of course. You heard about that?'

The constable caught Chris's eye. 'Tell us.'

'I will, but I'm making that tea first, you look frozen to the bone. This weather is not fit for a dog to be out.'

After she had made sure Chris and the constable were near the fire and were both primed with a cup of builders' strength tea she continued, 'The boat would barely move but of course they didn't want to keep it after their boy died. My husband offered to buy it from them and we promised not to keep it on the water where it would have been a constant reminder, but we moved it to the side garden. It proved to be useful additional space for us over the years, and the children used to play in it for hours when they were little.'

'So you lived here while the Jennings family were next door?'

'Not quite next door lovey, with that busy road in between, but close enough.'

'Were you here at the time of the family tragedy?'

She sighed deeply, 'No, we were away on holiday. It was a dreadful thing.'

'So you won't remember when it was?'

She paused, 'Not exactly no, but I've always kept a diary.'

Chris's heart lifted.

'When did you say? Late eighties? Let me go back through my old diaries. It may not help but worth a try.'

She was rummaging in the sideboard and produced a pile of diaries.

Chris stood and drained his tea, ready to leave.

'I'm going to leave this constable here, Mrs Jones while you search for that date.'

'No, no, no. Just fill the teacups young man, while I have a look through these. It won't take a minute.'

The constable hid his smile.

'I distinctly remember that we came back from the Peak District to the news, not our main summer holiday on the south coast. So it would either be Easter, Whit or the October half term. In August every year we went to the West Country. My dad had inherited a small cottage in the Peak District – long gone now, but the income from letting that cottage all summer paid for our holiday down south. Always two weeks. Then what we called *the little holidays* we'd go to the Peak District cottage ourselves.' Chris watched fascinated at the tracery of veins mapping the back of her hands as she flicked through the pages.

In fact it was all of ten minutes before she sat back in the chair, 'Aha. Here we are. It was October half term, 1987. 23rd October we went away to the cottage, then I've written on 31st October *Neil Jennings died.*'

It fitted with the Coroner's Report. Was it a coincidence that Susan Chell had died on the anniversary of her brother's death? Chris thought it unlikely. 'Thank you Mrs Jones. You've been very helpful. We won't take up any more of your time.'

'But don't you want to see the boat?'

'You've still got it?'

'It's in the garden, a bit overgrown now but

you can still get at it, what's left of it.

'When Neil died they couldn't bear to look at it, his mother in particular. Although we live virtually next door as far as the canal goes, there's no access with the towpath being on the far side of the canal as you've found out, and as far as roads go, this road comes off the A53 to one side, whereas to get to their house you go off the other side of the main road, and round through the new estate now.

'Before the estate was built this side of the bridge was all our farmland and there was just a rough track. What I'm saying is that it was quite a way round on foot. I'd see Susan's mother in the village from time to time, but we weren't neighbours in a conventional sense. We bought the boat off Susan's dad and moved it while they were all out at the funeral. I think he wanted to see the last of it as soon as possible.'

She smiled at the constable, 'Drink up and I'll show you.'

She led the way out of the front of the house and, complete with walking stick, limped after them across the frost-encrusted grass, dotted with ducks who, unlike the humans were oblivious to the weather. Under the side shrubbery, virtually hidden from view was a ramshackle wooden hull about eighteen feet in length.

'Go aboard if you want, have a good look round, it's propped up quite safely. My grandchildren play in it now.'

The constable enthusiastically crawled into the tiny galley while Chris circled the boat as best he could for the overgrown branches. His knee joints complained their protest at his activity as they occasionally did in the cold weather.

'It was made in an evening class according to Susan's dad. Some chap asked the teacher if it could be done, and the teacher did a lot of the basic work himself, then the students did the trimmings and embellishments and so on. Later, after Susan's father bought it, he made adaptations so the four of them could sleep on it. Put bunks in and the little cooker, fancy ship's wheel that he made himself, it was a real labour of love.'

Chris was running his finger across what was left of the nameplate – *Susan Ellen*.

'They named it for the girl. I'm sure they'd have called it *Neil* only boats tend usually to be given girls' names aren't they? They had a berth at bottom of garden, all properly licensed, they were allowed to keep it moored there. There were always youngsters round. You can imagine how popular it made young Neil.'

Chapter 27

It had taken only minutes for the detectives to explore the cellar and return to Mrs Whitfield's kitchen. The musty, damp smell had assailed DS York as soon as the door was opened; there was just one room, probably beneath the kitchen area, and it had been constructed with a drainage gully around two of the edges of the floor, where any water would run into a covered drain opening in one corner.

There was the usual detritus of a forgotten childhood dumped in the room – a broken trampoline, bicycles of various sizes and degrees of rust and, propped against the wall, a fish tank, complete with circulation pump of the type Diane Whitfield had described. There were filaments of green weed clinging to the inside of the tank.

'What's the betting those are Cladophora, the weed Ben found on the body?'

DC Dearing was examining the wall and the plastic pump. There's some paint missing off this sir, and this looks like blood. We need to get the team in here.'

Mrs Whitfield stood, aghast as the sergeant spoke to DC Dearing then got on the phone.

'Seal that door, constable. Sir, I'm at Mrs Whitfield's. We need SOCO over here again. I think we may have found our murder weapon.'

* * *

By the time Chris and the team arrived Mrs Whitfield had telephoned for her husband to come home and he had sent her off to the living room.

Photographs and fingerprinting complete, Anthony Whitfield explained the fish tank accessories to Chris. Picking up a peculiar looking motor with attachments, now encased in an evidence bag, he showed how it fitted into the edge of the rectangular tank, with the adjuster projecting above the water level. The inside of the tank contained remnants of moisture – it had obviously contained water a lot more recently than the middle of October. The scraps of pond life clinging to its inside were now also bagged and labelled. Chris spoke to the SOCOs.

'So there would be a sharp edge of glass at the corner and this narrow protruding pipe with a tap at a ninety degree angle?'

'Yes and there's a paint fragment or fragments missing from the adjuster tap. We need to check that against the sample on the body. We need to try for DNA as well, on the tap, the tank and take swabs from the tap near the drain, handles on the cellar door, and door to the cupboard, prints too, and check for blood. Then Ben can try matching this against the wound.'

'Okay. Give it all we've got. But I think you could be right.'

Chris turned to DS York, who was still smarting at the earlier oversight.

'Never mind. We got there in the end. Good work Yorkie, you too constable.'

* * *

Chris found Pete Talbot waiting for him at the

Guildhall. Once he had updated him on progress with the fish tank, Pete explained his presence.

'I've found someone you might like to talk to. Noel Coates worked on Neil Jennings' death at the time. He's retired now but I met him again by chance in town and he asked was I involved in this enquiry. We got talking about the current case and he said he had been one of the first officers called out to the brother when he died in 1987. He remembered it quite well.'

Chris was inclined to dismiss the historic happenings, now that he had firmer evidence about his current case, and he was abrupt, 'Really? Does he remember all his cases from thirty years ago?'

'Of course not, he said it made a big impression because as well as being so harrowing, it was his first case in CID. Also he had a boy the same age, a boy also called Neil, so there was a lot to make it memorable. It really hit home for him as you can understand. His lad is grown up now with teenage children of his own.'

'As this boy should have been.'

Chris thought it would probably be a waste of time, but Pete had come in specially to speak to him.

'I'd like to talk to Coates. Do you think he would see me?'

'Certainly. He asked me to get you to call him if he could be of any help. He was a good officer. I don't think you'd be wasting your time.'

As Chris made his way home that evening, he was pleased to see that the rain had stopped, although the clarity of the stars suggested the possibility of another heavy frost. He crossed to his car with a lighter heart. Strands were starting to come together.

Murder is murder, unique, the file may gather a film of dust, but it is never closed. The investigation is never permanently abandoned, and rightly so. Many crimes have been solved years after the event through developments such as DNA matching, and improvements in fingerprint data. On reflection he was glad he had agreed to talk to Noel Coates.

* * *

The nuptials of Pete Talbot and Frances Hegarty was not the only upcoming celebration.

At the Bookends Café Carly Broadbent had been secretly planning a party to celebrate Josie's birthday. The café had thankfully been too busy to spare the time on the day itself but Josie had seemed a little depressed during the past couple of weeks, and Carly was intent on cheering her up.

Having invited her family and regular customers Carly spent the morning putting the finishing touches to a special birthday cake, and ticked off the menu on her fingers.

She had decided on a hot meal with a choice of fish pie, vegetarian quiche or a mild curry with rice or baked potatoes. These would be cooked in advance in her own kitchen then heated through on the limited facilities at the café. For dessert she had decided on ice cream, chocolate-filled meringues and the now completed cake.

* * *

In the Pitman's Lamp pub Ray threw his newspaper down in disgust. It was the girl's fault, all her fault. If she hadn't been hanging around him, haunting him, he wouldn't be in this mess now. Why had he got involved with this bloody, bloody family?

He knew his disingenuousness for what it was of course. He knew exactly why he had got involved with them, he coveted their lifestyle; he was envious and he saw an opportunity to be with the person he thought he loved.

Throughout primary school he had mixed only with children and families like his own: living mostly in rented housing, the few who owned their own modest terraced houses struggling to pay the mortgage. Children with parents who were tradesmen like his father, or unemployed.

High school had changed all that. He had met children who routinely holidayed abroad, who lived in large country houses with Jacuzzi baths and even swimming pools. Most of all he mixed with children whose parents loved them, like Neil. The contrast bred discontent and a growing contempt for his downtrodden mother and his feckless father; and all the time the confusion about who and what he really was.

He reach out for a swig of his beer and found the glass empty. During his ruminations he had been drinking steadily and he called for another pint. He had to decide what to do next, and he had to decide today.

The nightmares, never banished entirely over the years, had at least abated in frequency. Now they were as frequent and as terrifying as ever. Back *with a vengeance* his mother would say. He had never quite understood the expression, but he did now.

* * *

It happened again on Wednesday, the nightmare that had been haunting him for nearly three decades; especially at times of stress, and this was certainly one of those times.

In this most recent incarnation of the dream the boat was transformed into a prison cell with a small, high window. The act of private sodomy was observed by a crowd of interested spectators, viewing from a gallery like in the operating theatre in an America drama series.

The embarrassment was acute but he was too far-gone to stop and the rape continued to its inevitable conclusion, Neil crying out in pain and terror.

As his breathing slowed he withdrew from the younger boy. The spectators had melted away, all but one serious little face, a small child, the younger sister, whose face crumpled as she screamed, 'Neil, Neil!'

He woke from the dream, a cry dying on his lips. The sheets were a tangled heap and his torso was slick with sweat and smelled rank. His heart raced wildly. Moisture beaded his hair-line as he wiped his sweaty hands on the bedsheets.

Locking himself in the bathroom he emptied his bladder, drank a glassful of cold water and was starting on a second when a grumpy male voice from the adjacent room called to him, 'Shuddup can't yer, I'm tryin' to sleep.'

He sat on the edge of the bath and held his pounding head. What had he been drinking the previous night, and how much? The headache tablets he had retrieved from the cupboard slipped out into the basin with a clatter that brought further expletives from the old man in the bedroom next door, followed by female giggles.

He lay awake for a long time and listened to the sounds of the night: a siren wailing as an ambulance rushed to the Royal Stoke Hospital, a barking dog and its echo, and the chime of the church clock. Somewhere nearby a car engine was reluctant to embark on its cold journey, at last spluttering into life and the sound fading in the distance.

He groaned inwardly as he counted pints and chasers, it would be mid-afternoon before he felt human again and he had so much to do. He turned his face into the pillow, what a mess he had made of everything.

* * *

That between mother and son was supposed to be the perfect relationship. Josie seriously doubted it, and her son would have been horrified, but at the moment he seemed unable to keep away.

'Hi, Mum. How are you?'

'Fine, and you?'

'Yes everything's good.'

Both recognised the other's lie, the hurt behind the eyes giving them away.

Now he had come to see her there seemed little to say. The telephone cut through their silence, a relief to both of them.

'Now?' he heard his mother's incredulous voice, 'Yes, but it's gone … Yes, yes, calm down. Give me five minutes. My son is here. No of course he doesn't.' The phone was replaced quietly and it was a full half minute before Josie rejoined him in the living room.

'That was the police. They want to talk to me again. What is going on? Is there some sort of trouble? Do you know?'

'Sit down Mum. There's something I need to tell you.'

Chapter 28

Josie again sat in the interview room, a uniformed constable standing behind her, which unnerved her as much as was no doubt intended. She had a sudden feeling of vomit in the back of her throat — a phenomenon she had read about in books, always in relation to a woman. Was it then gender specific, something that just never troubled the male of the species? What a stupid thing to be thinking about now.

She pressed her fingers to her eyes in an effort to stave off an incipient migraine. Her throat was tight and she would have found it difficult to speak in a normal voice.

She listened sadly to the melodious strains of a ubiquitous Salvation Army band playing carols in the marketplace and thought she had only ever noticed them in the run-up to Christmas, wondering idly where they went and what they played for the rest of the year.

Shifting in the chair, she thought that the problem with the Guildhall heating must have been solved, the room was much warmer now, and she turned to watch as rain once again coursed down the steamed-up window panes, for the radiator blasted hot dry air across the room.

She caught sight of the constable and wondered how much longer she would have to wait. Even her eyelids ached under the relentless fluorescent lighting. Would this never end?

She was beginning to wonder what would happen if she just got up and left, when Chris and DS Hegarty entered the room. After the introductions and preliminaries with the recording device, the sergeant began: 'Tell us again about how you came to find Susan Chell's ticket, Mrs Ashmore.'

'Oh, for Goodness' sake! I've been through all this already,' nodding at Chris, 'with him.'

Hegarty smiled brightly, 'but not with me. What happened?'

Josie, visibly riled, ran through the story again. It was broadly what she had said in the previous interview but varied in one particular.

Chris held up his hand to stop her, 'So you're saying that she was at the café that day, and that you saw her?'

'Well, of course she was there. She couldn't have filled in the card if she wasn't, could she?' she spoke as to a child.

'And you saw her?'

'Yes, I think so. I've thought of little else, this has really upset me.'

Chris considered this. She seemed more angry than upset. Previously she had been adamant that she would not have known Susan Chell.

What time would that have been?'

'I don't know,' she hesitated. 'Some time in the afternoon?'

Chris turned to Hegarty: 'My notebook, Sergeant – could I please have a look at it?'

Quick on the uptake, she handed across her own notebook, which Chris made a pretence of scrutinising.

'Yes, here we are, I quote from our last

interview: *'So it was Carly who recognised the ticket? You didn't know the name?'*

'That's right, I dropped it off the pile and stood on it. It was barely legible.'

He snapped the book shut and Josie jumped.

'I remember now, I saw this woman there and I'm pretty sure it was her – her picture was in the Sentinel after she died. The boots and the jacket. As I said I've been thinking about it a lot.'

It hung together – just, but Chris was very sceptical and her body language showed that the sergeant felt the same way.

Beads of sweat had formed across Josie's top lip and she was becoming red in the face.

'Are you allowed to do this – it's like torture. Calling me in here twice. I'd barely had time to get home.'

'Really? That must have been a very slow taxi journey...' Hegarty began, but Josie was still speaking.

'First time it's cold enough to freeze and now it's so hot.' The room was pleasantly warm for a November day. Chris suspected a tactic to abbreviate the interview, but he was not finished yet. He opened the door and spoke to a passing officer.

'Constable, fetch us each a cold drink would you please? Or would you prefer tea?'

Josie agreed to a cup of tea and made much of removing her coat.

As she took the scarf from her neck and placed it on top of her bag on the table between them, DS Hegarty had to suppress a gasp.

Instead she wrote two words on her notepad and placed it where Chris could clearly see it.

Susan's necklace

'That's an unusual necklace.'

'Josie fingered it, 'Yes, it was a birthday present. My birthday was this week. Why?'

'Nice present. Who from? May I have a closer look?'

Josie was nervous now. 'Yes, I suppose.'

'Who did you say gave it to you?'

'I didn't.' Her hands fumbled on the clasp, then she handed it over.

'Don't you want to tell us who gave it you? Why would that be?'

She stared at the officers, who remained implacable. 'It was from my grandson,' she said finally as she handed it over. Chris studied it closely then handed it to DS Dearing, who gave it a closer look, nodded her head and left the room.'

'Hey! That's mine!' Josie said to her disappearing figure.

'We'll give you a receipt for it.' Chris was brisk. 'What would your grandson's name be?'

He was becoming more and more confident that before long the details of the case would bit by bit come together sufficiently clearly to serve to the CPS.

Hegarty had recognised the necklace from the photograph now posted on the incident room wall, along with crime-scene photos, but Chris's luck was running out. Josie sat back in her chair, 'I don't have to tell you that.'

Chris considered all the things people say by not saying anything at all.

'No, but when someone refuses to answer a

straightforward question, it does make us wonder why.'

The silence lengthened.

Eventually Chris decided to let her go home, and for the team to regroup. 'For the tape this interview is ended at ...'

'I just can't see any motive, sir, and Josie – she's an elderly woman. I can't see her on her feet all day in a café and then up in the middle of the night lugging a woman's dead or unconscious body upstairs to some stranger's bathroom. It doesn't make sense.'

Checking the time, he told Hegarty that he would call once again on the Frasers and update them on progress. He had paled gradually throughout the interview with Josie, and although he would not complain, DS Hegarty suspected he was suffering from a headache.

'I'm going that way, sir. Pete's mum and mine are both coming to Corbett's Cottages tonight for a meal. I virtually pass the door to the Frasers. Shall I look in on them? I can always call you if there's anything important.'

Chris stretched his aching shoulders. 'You might as well. So many dead ends. That necklace was probably ten a penny in the nineteen eighties, there could be thousands of them out there. I feel it is significant, but have no way of proving anything. This case is going nowhere.'

There, he was quite wrong. Something was to happen before the end of the day that would blow the case wide open.

* * *

Frances Hegarty was still concerned, about the injuries Sharon Welland had received, she suspected at the hands of her husband Billy, and decided that, as she was going to update the Frasers, she had time to call next door before going home.

It was not really her role since the matter had been handed over to the Family Liaison Officer, but she would feel happier if she could reassure herself that the woman had suffered no further abuse.

The old-fashioned pram was in the garden, and as the sergeant approached the Frasers' door she could hear the child gurgling.

In the pram the infant's contented noises had soon become a grumble, then a wail of distress. Sharon Welland hurried from the house and extracted the child impatiently from the pram, then startled, she stopped and looked at Frances Hegarty, whilst the baby hung suspended over one arm. In the wintry light her face looked haggard and Hegarty thought a reassuring word may be welcome, but Sharon hurried inside, slamming the door.

The sergeant rang the doorbell but no-one answered and she turned away.

The Fraser family were just pulling into the drive and Caroline guessed at the reason for her call.

'We've heard nothing more from next door,' she told the sergeant, 'I think the message has got through. Even young Ryan seems to be settling down, he's still working.'

'We have a bit of an update for you, Mrs Fraser. May I come in?'

Once settled in the living room, children dispatched to play elsewhere, Hegarty shared what she knew with Caroline and Edward.

'We now know that Susan Chell's body was moved from the Whitfield home in Milton, where she almost certainly died, on 31st October – Hallowe'en, and was brought here in a large dark vehicle, possibly black, possibly a 4x4. This would be either the early hours of 1st November, or in the following few days. Do you know of anyone with such a vehicle?'

They shook their heads.

'We don't, do we?' Caroline was keen to seek her husband's support. 'I can't think of anyone with a four by four can you?'

'No.' He was dismissive.

'No,' she was happy that they had sorted that out.

'Oh God!' she suddenly said aloud, 'It's not really a four by four,' she hesitated, 'No, it can't be, except perhaps ... Ryan's job. Next door. He drives a taxi.'

'Are you sure? I thought he was driving for a friend.'

'Of course I'm sure. He's often got the taxi here overnight. He offered to take us to the airport when we went on holiday but Edward prefers the park and ride. That way he can get the car valeted while we're away.'

It seemed that Hegarty's working day was not over yet.

Chapter 29

Having been out of the office for most of the day DC Dearing was unaware that Josie had been in the police station until Chris was summing up the afternoon team meeting. All but DS Hegarty, busy with the Frasers, were present.

'DNA and fingerprints had been found in the Whitfields' cellar, and the benzidine test done in situ shows that there is blood on the filter, and splattered across part of one wall and one side of the floor of the cellar. An attempt has been made to clean it up but I don't expect the perpetrator ever thought it would come into the picture, and the clean-up was fairly superficial.'

'Perhaps there wasn't time.'

'Maybe. The lab will do what they can, and hope to be able to tell us whether it is Susan Chell's by the end of tomorrow, but it seems fairly certain that we've found where she died.'

'We also have some fingerprints.'

So far there had been no match in the records, but Chris said was hoping that Josie would cooperate. Even as he wished for this he knew that this elderly woman could not have committed this crime and dealt with the body by herself – someone else had to be involved, it seemed very far-fetched. Tensions within the team were running high. This was not conducive to an effective investigation, but the constable was about to change things.

DC Harris took up the story, 'We've checked

all the local taxi firms already sir, but no-one had booked a taxi to or from the Whitfields' address.

'I've spoken to John Stuart, the owner of the only taxi company that has a logo anything like the neighbour described. I'd say he's hiding something. He sounded decidedly shaken. More likely to be about his accounts or the lax way he carries out his business than anything to do with the murder though. Eventually he admitted to illegally employing casual drivers, but claimed he couldn't tell me any of their names. They just turn up when they can, and if he's any work for them it's cash in hand.

The constable checked his notes, 'He went through his log for October and says there were no bookings from the Fraser's area on Hallowe'en night, nor in the few days either side come to that, but eventually he admitted that he sometimes let the drivers use the cabs for their private purposes.'

'I don't suppose he keeps records of those occasions?'

'No, of course not. I suspect he just lets genuine customers absorb the additional fuel costs and fiddles the books to cover it.'

'How old is John Stuart?'

'Don't know sir. He sounds fairly young. I can get onto the census and find out.'

Chris took over, 'Never mind. I want to talk to the woman from the café again first. Then we'll go and see what young Stuart has to say for himself, and have a quick look at his records while we're there.'

DC Dearing was listening intently to the conversation. 'It's all circumstantial, isn't it, sir? I doubt the CPS would consider prosecuting on this.'

'Me neither. That's why I want to speak to

Josie some more.'

'Josie? The woman from the café, sir, have you talked to her already? In here before lunch?'

'What of it, Dearing?' Once again a headache was threatening Chris and he was keen to get home.

'I must have seen her, sir – just after she left here. I'd gone to the Court and was on my way to meet DS Hegarty at her car.'

'Yes, yes.' Chris remembered the troublesome umbrella, 'She said her grandson was picking her up.'

'Really? I saw her get into a taxi.'

DS York butted in, keen to move the meeting along, 'Perhaps her grandson couldn't come.'

DC Dearing looked shocked, 'Or ...'

Chris looked up, questioningly.

It's probably nothing, only I hadn't realised. I thought she'd just got in a taxi, sir. Only if the driver was her grandson, I've seen him before. So has DS York.'

Chris nodded her to continue.

'The grandson is Ryan Lee, sir. He lives with his sister, next door to the Fraser family.'

Chris's phone rang. It was clear to the team that Hegarty was phoning in, with the news that Ryan Lee was moonlighting as a taxi driver for Stuart's Taxis. Bingo!

'He's cropping up a lot in this investigation.' Get him down to the Guildhall.'

Dearing nodded, 'The taxi the café woman got into had a coloured logo on the side. I noted down the plates, it's one of Stuart's taxis.'

Chris was thoughtful, 'I don't like those sort of coincidences. We'll speak to his grandmother again tomorrow. Meantime go down to Stuart's and get

Ryan Lee in here. Have them radio him if he's working to return to their premises, and then bring him in, I think it's time we had a chat with young Mr Lee.'

* * *

Chris spent the first part of his morning planning the crucial interview ahead, trying to anticipate possible obstacles, to decide how to counter possible lines of obstruction. He was in no mood for wasting time. He challenged Ryan Lee across the table.

'Tell me about the necklace you gave your grandmother for her birthday.' He indicated the evidence bag on the table.

Ryan rocked back on the chair, and too late Chris saw that he was underprepared for the coming interview. If Ryan insisted that he had bought the jewellery at one of the many town-centre charity shops, then his story would be impossible to disprove.

Ryan, however, was not such a quick thinker. 'Er...it was left, left in the back of my cab. Not worth trying to track down who'd left it.' He warmed to his story, 'You'd be surprised at what some folk...'

Chris glared at his stonily, 'and now the truth?'

'God's honour it was.' Ryan went to move out of his chair, but the burly constable behind him moved forward and he thought better of it.

'Honestly, it was left in the car. I can't tell you anything more. I hung on to it for a few days in case someone asked about it, then I give it my gran.'

It was a good performance but his eyes told

Chris that it was all bluster. He failed to look Chris in the face, eyes flicking side to side. His leg was jiggling and he kept cracking his knuckles until Chris told him to stop.

'I don't think so, Ryan. I think you took it off Susan Chell's body.'

The colour had drained from Ryan's face and for a moment Chris thought he might faint. He turned and nodded to the constable by the door, who left the room, returning almost immediately with a glass of water, which he placed on the table.

Meanwhile Ryan was silent, evidently weighing up what had been said.

Chris changed his approach, 'Did you go to the opening of the Bookends Café, the place where your grandmother works?'

'Course not. Working wasn't I?'

'Had you met Susan Chell before?'

'No,' this was emphatic with the ring of truth, but there was something not right here, Chris was sure of it.

'Yet she must have been in the café to fill this in.' He showed Ryan a photocopy of the blue card completed in Susan Chell's name.

'I told you I didn't go to the café on the first day.' It was said with great conviction.

'Okay Ryan, I believe you. Now let's talk about your taxi-driving job and where you were in the early hours of the morning following Hallowe'en... at about two o'clock.'

* * *

In Audley the Bookends Café was closed for

the day. Carly came through from the kitchen to where Josie was wiping down the tables and chairs, prior to sweeping and washing the floor.

'Josie, I'm so sorry, that was the police on the phone. They want to talk to you again. They say they have sent a car, which will be here directly.'

As she finished speaking a police car pulled up at the front door, and Josie hung her head. 'I'll get my coat.'

'Josie, is there anything I can do to help? Should I let your son know?' Carly asked as the two police officers came through the door.

'My son won't be contactable, he'll be at work. Get my grandson please, Carly.'

Carly tried, but the phone simply rang out, without even a voicemail to leave a message. She was deciding what to do when the café door opened again. The police car had driven away, bearing Josie back to the police station, but the detective sergeant had remained behind, and came back into the café.

'I'd like another word, Ms Broadbent. May I sit down?'

* * *

With all the activity about Josie and Ryan, Chris had totally forgotten his arrangement to go and talk to Noel Coates until reminded by DC Dearing, and he had to think for a moment before remembering that this was Pete's old colleague.

The old man now had failing eyesight and manoeuvred his way carefully around the familiar kitchen as he assembled the wherewithal for making coffee. He took his time and Chris let him. He doubtless had few visitors these days, and the chance to talk about old times must be a rare luxury.

Eventually, with them both settled in front of a cosy gas fire, with coffee and biscuits to hand, he turned to Chris.

'I kept all my notebooks. Not supposed to of course. All that confidential information, but I had a dream that I might write down my most interesting cases, make my fortune preaching to the next generation of officers like young Pete Talbot.' He paused to lift his coffee mug with a shaking hand, 'Never happen now of course. I can barely write a note for the milkman.'

Chris smiled and wished Pete could hear himself described as young – it would make his day.

'And would the Neil Jennings case be one featured in your memoir?'

The old grey head shook sadly, 'Tragic of course, absolutely tragic. Young man, his whole future ahead of him. It was a very strange case but not enough to start any alarm bells ringing. Pathologist thought the same as me. Lads fooling about on a boat, one fell, banging his head and drowned before his mate could get him out. There was only the one odd thing really.'

'The sodomy?'

'There is that, it was illegal of course. Neil was only fifteen, no matter how old his partner, but what I really meant was the nature of the attack.'

'Attack?' Chris didn't remember reading of any attack, just the bang to the head.

'I think it was an attack, yes. The sodomy you see was quite violent. There was, not to be too graphic over coffee and biscuits, a fair degree of damage. Of course it could have been consensual – perhaps they both liked their sex rough. But I did wonder at the time whether it was rape.'

'But you didn't take that any further?'

'Of course we did, tried anyway, but there was no way of knowing exactly who was with him.

'The Coroner questioned one lad who denied it was him. If he had used a condom and chucked it in the canal then the DNA would be lost. He gave evidence at the Coroner's Court, saying that a gang of lads had been round there during the morning, three or four of them he thought.

'He claimed not to know who they were, nor could he give a description, not that that would have been much use. He said one of them must have sodomised Neil. He himself only arrived shortly before Neil fell. He could tell Neil was upset. He told the Coroner that he saw these boys, but only their back view as they walked off up the garden and onto on the A53. From there he had no idea where they went.

'The girl who found him, your victim, spoke of two voices but she was hysterical, incoherent. We really got no useful information out of her. Nor would I have wanted to push it, she was only what? Seven or eight?'

Chris nodded his agreement, but wondered if there was some significance now to what the girl had said. Did it in some way impact on her own murder thirty years later? He decided to speak again to Susan's aunt, and set off for Telford, taking with him a letter they had found in Susan's flat.

Chapter 30

Vivien Jennings, Susan's aunt, read in silence, then folded the letter she had sent to her sister-in-law relating to Neil's death, and passed it back to Chris.

'And she kept it? All these years?' She looked bewildered. 'It turned her mind you know, his death. Help for mental illness wasn't what it is now. There was a terrific stigma attached. Her doctor wasn't helpful at all, his attitude was *pull yourself together, count your blessings. You have a loving husband and daughter.* Nowadays of course we know that the mind doesn't respond to that sort of bullying. I think she would have coped better if someone had been found guilty of killing Neil. She couldn't accept that it was an accident. Some people suggested that he had killed himself.

'There were always youngsters on the boat. I don't think Neil and Susan's mother had a strong mental constitution even before he died; she didn't like the noise of the children and their friends playing in the house, so the boat was like a playhouse for them.

'The police wanted to talk to whoever was there, and they talked to one lad for a long time – I'm afraid I've forgotten his name – perhaps my mind has done that deliberately. Anyway, other than him there was only Susan. She'd heard voices earlier, at about half past ten, her brother's and that of one of his friend's.'

She shrugged her shoulders. 'Neil had a bash

to the head and they couldn't match the wound to anything he might have hit falling off the boat.'

She took a moment to blink away tears. I think the police held some information back from us. I would have preferred to know the truth, but Susan's mother couldn't have handled any more. Do you know anything?'

Chris bit his lip, 'There was something else. There's no nice way to put this. Neil had been sodomised.'

'Good God, how dreadful. I wasn't able to go to the inquest. I was at home looking after Suzy. My ex-husband never said. Was my sister-in-law ever told this?'

'I suspect not. The police would have tried to spare the family's feelings. They would have tried to gather as much information as they could, but not told the family why.'

'God is good,' she said, 'that is a relief. Susan came to stay with us, in fact she lived with us for several years, transferred schools, and everything. It was as if my sister couldn't stand Susan around her. And the poor child couldn't understand what she had done wrong. She must have been bewildered, poor mite. She wasn't an easy child to love, but she'd lost a big brother she idolised, then her mother rejected her. No wonder she ended up like she did.'

'Your ex-husband said she was difficult.'

'She wasn't likeable, people never knew quite where they were with her. She pushed as hard as she could against everything. She was a liar, I would almost say compulsive liar if there is such a thing. It started in childhood to get herself out of trouble, or avoid getting into trouble.

'She played truant. She made no secret of the fact that she hated me. She stole from me and my husband, told him I had men round when he was out at work – all sorts of things.

'It was as if she couldn't let barriers down and trust people. Our relationship wasn't strong enough to withstand Suzy. I've often thought since, that she was just a confused child, we should have tried harder to help her. My ex-husband told me you had spoken to him. We separated years ago but we still speak fairly often on the phone.

'It wasn't entirely Suzy that broke us up of course, we married too young, our two children were virtually grown and off our hands when she came to us. I think we'd have gone our separate ways anyway but having her arrive certainly wasn't easy.

'Even Russell who loved her devotedly from what I could see, she kept him at arms' length, never really let him in, and then, as I heard, she left him. When bad things happen early on in life, Inspector, a child thinking they are to blame, is especially sensitive.'

'And was Susan a sensitive girl?'

'At the time I'd have said she wasn't, no; that it was her brother Neil who was the sensitive one, far too sensitive for a boy. Looking back now I'm not so sure. She didn't speak for three months after she came to us. I used to wonder what on earth was going on in her head. Of course there wasn't the psychotherapy that would be available now, not back then. Chris snapped Then later, when she might have been able to talk about it, Bob and I decided it was better to leave it be. We would never discuss it with her, maybe that was wrong on our part – I think now that it was, but of course we were thrust into this as suddenly as everyone else. It was a nightmare time for us all.

'I met Susan once again recently when she was on one of her rare visits to her mother in Holmedean. Not by design, it was coincidence that our visits overlapped and we went for a cup of coffee. Her mother wasn't going to come out of there, we both knew that. It was heartbreaking to watch someone we knew well going through a steady decline.

'Susan had lost touch pretty much with her mother – she rarely visited. She knew she wasn't wanted. Her mother never wanted her, and she didn't want anyone else either after Susan's father died. I pleaded for her to see some purpose and tried to interest her in Susan, but Susan wouldn't cooperate, resented the neglect and lack of warmth I suppose, or was warped and unsettled because of what she had seen, without understanding why. It was like all the life was sucked out of the woman the day her son drowned.

'Susan rang me a couple of weeks after her mother died, devastated and in tears. She had read the Coroner's Report. I wasn't surprised at the state she was in. I never saw the report but it wouldn't have made for comfortable reading – the things that had been done to Neil.' She balled a handkerchief, twisting it so hard Chris feared it would rip, and shook her head.

'There was something else,' she added. 'Susan told me that she had found letters. I knew about my letter of course, but she definitely said letters, in the plural. She said she couldn't tell me what was in the other letter but suggested I'd be horrified at the contents. That didn't make sense if she was talking about the letter I'd written to her mother, but I wondered if she was just being dramatic. I told you she had a tendency to lie when she was younger. Anyway,' she dismissed the thought, 'there can't be another letter if you've found nothing.'

Chris shook his head.

'Or, if there was, she must have thrown it away. I'm sorry. I can't bear to talk about this anymore. My ex-husband may be able to tell you more.'

* * *

Chris was walking across to the Guildhall from where he had parked the car, when he heard a shout, and Neil Coates caught up with him.

'Glad I caught you.' He fell into step alongside Chris. 'I've remembered something. I've been thinking a lot about that business of young Neil Jennings's death. I recalled my first visit to the boat after the call came in. Of course I was just a rookie – Inspector in charge was a dour old bugger – sent me out to look around.

'There was no-one on the towpath at the time, so no corroboration of what might have happened. It was not as well used then – more overgrown than now and difficult to access. The Inspector talked to Susan, but she was not aware then, nor was she told for some time afterwards, that Neil was dead.

'I remember something of the inquest too. Susan's mother shouting at someone in public gallery, that it was his fault. He should have helped Neil; how could Neil have fallen? Gut-wrenching stuff to listen to. I stopped afterwards and spoke to the woman who was with the youth because she was still very shaken. I patted her down, organised a car to take her and her son home.'

'Why are you telling me this?'

'Because I came across her again recently. If you'd asked me two months ago what her name was, I wouldn't have been able to remember, but I saw her name in the Sentinel, something about a café opening?'

'Carly Broadbent?'

'No, that's not her. Josie, Josie Ashmore.

* * *

After talking to Carly Broadbent at the café, Frances Hegarty had joined Chris in the interview room. They had kept Josie waiting for some time.

'You said that Susan Chell was in the café that day, during the afternoon you think, yet no-one else seems to remember seeing her. The interviewer from the local paper didn't, and Ms Broadbent has no recollection of Susan Chell being at the café opening.'

'We've checked the photographs she took,' Hegarty offered, 'from the café opening, but Susan Chell's not on any of them.'

'Not surprising,' Josie responded, 'they were all taken earlier, I reckon Carly put the camera away about lunchtime. It was so busy and she was worried that someone might pick it up if she left it lying around.'

'We have been able to show Ms Broadbent several recent photographs of the dead woman and she is sure that she was not there. She did however see your son at about lunchtime. You didn't mention that.'

'Why should I? You didn't ask, and why shouldn't my son come? He called to support me in this new venture. He's a good lad, always thoughtful. He came and supported me, why shouldn't he? We've not really been close, but he was always good to his mum.'

'But if he saw you in the café at lunchtime why did he call round again at...' Hegarty checked the time that Carly Broadbent had given to her, 'four o'clock in the afternoon?'

'That wasn't to wish us well with the new café, more to see how the first day had gone, more like a celebration.'

'The café was already closed by 4 o'clock?' Chris looked pointedly at the flyer which clearly indicated that it would be open till five on weekday evenings.

Josie's eyes flickered, 'No, but he wasn't sure what time we would shut, he hadn't seen the flyers.'

'But he had come into the café earlier that day hadn't he? Strange that he got in touch again so soon, especially as you say you aren't close.'

He let the statement hang in the air, aware of the usefulness of a silence, but in this case he was to be disappointed.

'He said he wanted to chat about something – something personal – but we were clearly too busy at lunchtime, so he called back and brought the bubbly.' A thought seemed to occur to her and she stood up.

'I've answered your questions, which I needn't have done. I took advice after I last spoke to you, and I was told not to say anything.'

'And who told you that? Never mind. We'll show the photographs of Susan Chell to your son –

see if he remembers seeing her that afternoon. What is it you're not telling us?'

There was a further silence.

'Murder brings a loss of privacy for all concerned.'

Chris had read her correctly, this garrulous woman had to fill a silence.

'But I'm not concerned.'

'Then there's no reason not to tell us what you know.'

'I don't know anything, I didn't know her but I had heard of her. She was evil.'

'Susan Chell?'

'Who else? I have a friend works in Holmedean and she said Susan Chell hardly bothered with her mother when she was alive, then swooped quickly enough on her will and paperwork as soon as she died.'

Her face was closed, the burst of confidences over, as she shook her head slightly, looking at the floor. Chris stopped the tape.

'We'll take you home.'

'No!' Josie almost shouted, 'No thanks, the old biddies will be twitching behind their curtains as it is. If it was a bit warmer they'd be out in their gardens – front gardens of course. I'll make my own way.'

Chris thought of his own cul-de sac and Doreen Heeley standing sentinel at her window. He felt that Josie was right, but was her reputation merely the first piece of collateral damage endemic to any murder enquiry, or was she an accessory?

* * *

Chris reflected with Hegarty that where two people have been involved in a crime it could often be effective to drive a wedge between the two, and wondered whether this would be possible between Ryan Lee and Josie Ashmore.

DS York was beavering away at the computer and suddenly looked up. 'Sir, I've got something. I was feeding in all the information we have about Josie Ashmore and about her grandson.

'Ryan Lee is the son of Josie's son. He's Lee because his parents never married and he was given his mother's surname when he was born, but look at this.'

Chris peered over his shoulder at the screen.

'Ryan Lee's father is Raymond Ashmore.'

The sergeant opened another file, the transcript of the Coroner's Report of the inquest on Susan Chell's brother in 1987.

DS York sat back in his chair, 'The teenager with Neil Jennings when he died was Andrew Raymond Ashmore. When you think about it, it could be the same MO, hit on the head, then forced under water and held there till they drowned. The woman at the inquest with her son was Josie.'

Chris was contemplative. Here was the connection. The pieces were at last beginning to fall into place. Ryan's father was Andrew Ray Ashmore, whose mother was Josie Ashmore. But why now? All this had happened thirty years ago.

'Sir,' DC Harris put his head round the door. 'We have confirmation from the lab. The blood in the cellar is Susan Chell's.'

* * *

The door to Stuart's Taxis opened to the furious onslaught of rain and wind. The owner looked at his watch. 'Why are you so late?'

'Go' held up, mate. Helping the police with their enquiries do they call it? A violent crime.'

'Oh, yeah?' John Stuart was sceptical.

'Yeah, but they told me to say nothing about it to anyone. They'll *issue a press release* when the victim's family have been told.'

'A murder?'

'Why do you say that?'

'I don't know, violent crime sounds so prissy. Do tell.'

'I've told you mate, all I'm allowed to say'

'That's convenient.'

'What?' Ryan was incredulous.

'An hour and a half late for work, and today of all days, but you're, he made inverted commas around the words, "*not allowed to tell me why.*" Very convenient.'

He stormed into his office, slamming the door.

He would be lucky to keep his operating licence after this. The SOCO's were going over his vehicles now, and wanted to see all his records.

Chapter 31

DC Dearing took a call at the back of the incident room. As she put down the phone, she was clearly excited about the conversation, 'Thank goodness for the media coverage, sir. Someone's tried to use Susan Chell's debit card. This was at the Dagfields Antiques Centre. Two youngsters had been for lunch and they have a strange system there. If you want to pay on card for something in the café area you have to take the bill to the front desk, whereas the café is at the back of the complex. I'm surprised loads of people don't just do a runner.'

'Is that what they tried?'

'No, they'd have been better off if they had. One of the staff thought they might, they seemed very young to have a card. It was quiet in the café so she followed them to the front, and saw the card rejected. The bank must have blocked it immediately they were told of Susan Chell's death. She waited to see what would happen next. They did do a runner then, dropped the card and dashed.

The member of staff dashed out after them in time to see their car drive off. She got the car number, then came back to speak to the manager about what action she wanted to take. The bill was less than twenty pounds. The manager was just going to hand all the details over to the locals in Crewe when she noticed the name on the card and recognised it from the Sentinel, so she called here instead.'

'The young couple?'

'Local to Dagfields. Incidentally the car is his older brother's; the lad, Noah Bennett, is too young to drive. He and the girl,' DC Dearing checked her notes, 'Tammy Powell, are both fifteen. She'd presented the card at the till, as it was clearly signed by a woman.'

'Fifteen? We'll need a responsible adult in there before we can even ask a question.'

'They're both in the interview rooms downstairs, we've sent for the parents.'

* * *

Tammy Powell sat back in the chair, legs crossed and one foot beating an air tattoo. She was trying for insouciance but the rapid jiggling of her foot gave her away, as did her anxious looks at the detectives.

Her mother had joined them, still dressed for her work in a school canteen, and the older woman's presence was obviously not having a calming effect. When they entered the room she slumped forward, allowing her hair to hide her face.

Chris took Tammy through the preliminaries, then asked for her side of the story.

'Noah just handed the card to me and said that I was to pay using it. He asked if I could copy the signature if I needed to. I said I didn't know, I thought I could.' She glanced at mother, who was looking at her lap. 'Then he said that it didn't matter. It was less than thirty quid so it would be contactless, no signature would be needed, and no pin would be needed.' She smiled vacantly.

Noah Bennett looked grubby, his hair unwashed and an outbreak of acne across his chin, nose and forehead. He picked constantly at ragged fingernails and began to bluster as soon as the officers were seated.

'Let me tell you what happened.' He had clearly decided on the sanitised version he was most comfortable with in front of his mother.

Chris was sharp. 'No. Your girlfriend's told us what happened. You tell us where you got that card.'

He continued to bluster for a while, giving various explanations. He had not known it was stolen, he was doing what a friend asked him to, then that a friend owed him a favour and said to take Tammy out for lunch as a treat, and he had given Noah his card to pay with.

Chris remained impassive in the face of the lies. 'He?' he said eventually, 'His name is Susan is it? Strange sort of name for a male friend. I see from the till receipt his surname is Chell, so if I contact Susan Chell she will confirm that it was her intention for her card to be used to treat Tammy and you to a meal?'

'Yeah. Well, no.' He sighed, 'Okay, I bought it in a pub. Twenty quid. The bloke says everyone does it, this new contactless makes it easy. Bloody brilliant.' He spoke impatiently as if his pronouncements should be unnecessary to anyone with half a brain.

Chris ignored this last, 'Except of course you know that I can't ask Susan Chell that, don't you Noah? Because Susan is dead. Susan was murdered. I wonder how much you know about that.'

Mrs Bennett moved in her chair and breathed in sharply, her eyes never leaving Chris's face.

Chris was determined to puncture the

arrogance bubble, 'And what did you do with the body?'

White-faced now, Noah's eyes darkened, darting from one to another of the detectives. His mother swallowed deeply and groaned.

'The body?' Hegarty picked up the thread, 'When you'd killed her and stolen her cards what did you do with the body?'

'I don't know ... body?' he looked like he was about to faint. His mother groaned again.

'You don't know what you did with it?'

'What do you mean? I bought that card in the pub like I said – legit.'

Chris gave him a cold look, 'Hardly, lad.' They left him to his thoughts and a tin of Cola, and went next door.

* * *

Twenty minutes later Chris returned to the interview room.

'Tell me again about how you say you got the card.'

'I've told you, I bought it in a pub.' An idea occurred to him, 'Can I have a solicitor?'

'You can, son. Yes. The constable will go and get you a phone book.' He nodded towards PC Harris, who knew he would be expected to take his time and headed first for the kettle.

'You can call a solicitor unless you already have the number of one handy, perhaps you often need the services of a solicitor?' He glanced at Noah's mother, who shook her head, 'but that takes time and it makes it all very official doesn't it? A lot of extra paperwork for us, just for the price of your lunch.' The tone was placatory.

'We'll pay it back,' his mother was quicker on the uptake than her offspring.

'I'm sure you will, Mrs Bennett, but Noah, I'm more interested at the moment in this card. Where did you buy it, and from whom?'

* * *

Towards the end of the afternoon, the team met again at the Guildhall, Pete Talbot along with them.

Chris glanced at his watch. 'I think young Mr Bennett has had long enough with his solicitor. Let's see what more he has to say. Pete, do you want to sit in on this?'

The empty cola can, crushed now, lay on the table in front of Noah Bennett and his solicitor. His mother had gone, and the solicitor looked as if he would rather be anywhere else. Introductions made for the tape, Chris began: 'Which pub?'

'The Pitman's Lamp, up Newcastle.'

'Someone you'd seen in there before?'

Noah gave his solicitor a covert glance. 'I'd never been in there before.'

'Describe this person who sold you the card, and tell me exactly what happened.'

Noah pursed his lips as if thinking was a real effort until Chris decided they could be there all day, waiting for inspiration, 'Was it a man,' and to the affirmative nod, 'How old?'

'Dunno.'

'Older than you?' Again the nod.

'Older than me?' Chris's head was beginning to ache. He thought to himself that he probably looked about a hundred. Noah looked at him closely for the first time. 'Nah, I reckon prob'ly about twenty four or five.'

'Okay, and what did he look like? How tall? What was he wearing? How long was his hair and what colour?'

The questions went on and on, but at the end of it all Chris had was a description of someone in their mid-twenties with unremarkable looks, no noteworthy clothes and no distinguishing features.

'Early to mid-twenties?' Hegarty tapped her pen on her front teeth at the update, Noah and his solicitor having been seen off the premises for the time being. 'Too young then for Edward Fraser, Anthony Whitfield or Russell Chell. Could be Ryan Lee.'

Chris nodded. 'If Bennett remembers accurately, and if he's telling the truth. For what it's worth, I'll go to the pub, they'll co-operate if they don't want their trading licence revoked. Under-aged drinkers for starters. If the landlord knows we are also looking into allegations of stolen goods being sold on the premises he's likely to cooperate. If I need to jog his memory I'll tell him these goods seem to have been stolen from a murder victim. My guess is that he'll fall over himself to help. I can have a chat to the regulars too, see if any of them can give me an idea of who this individual was. There's a character called Jim Townsend spends a lot of time propping up the bar. I fancy another chat with him. Hallowe'en may jog a memory.

'You call at the Wellands' and see if there's a

photo of young Lee. I don't want him and Bennett to meet face to face at this stage.'

*   *   *

Chris went to the Pitman's Lamp and spoke to the publican, who was non-committal. The officer guessed that he would not wish to alienate customers, and ergo had nothing of substance to say. As the conversation came to an end, a man at a nearby table drained his pint.

He placed his empty glass on the bar and looked at the clock: 'Gotta go,' he said to the publican. 'My old dad's on his own. I have to put him to bed.'

Chris missed the expression on the landlord's face, the raised eyebrows showing surprise. He did however, hear the comment of Townsend, the man he had spoken to on his previous visit.

'What's come over him? I never knowed Ray Ashmore worry hisself about his old dad.'

'Was Ray Ashmore one of the eight hundred?' Chris asked, 'the eight hundred that were at school with you?'

Again came the phlegmy cough from the character at the bar, 'Ray is a lot older than us. He had already left school afore we started. He was friendly with Susan's brother though,' he gave a leer, 'Very friendly.' Chris phoned the Guildhall and asked Frances Hegarty to pass Noel Bennett and Tammy Powell over to Juvenile Division.

He glanced at his watch. The man was only a couple of minutes ahead of Chris. Surely he would not yet have dealt with his father's needs and retired the night?

* * *

It took Chris only minutes to reach the address given to him by the publican, but it seemed that neither Ray nor his father were there. The doorbell gave the hollow sound of an impotent cry in an empty house.

Criminal investigation raises a similar dilemma for a detective, to that of a research scientist. Has he got enough information to satisfy the Crime Prosecution Service? Does he have to ask his suspect more questions in order to satisfy the CPS? If so, this could alarm the suspect enough to destroy evidence, or concoct an alibi. Also Chris reflected, the police have to keep to the letter of the law. Often he thought that the cards were unfairly stacked. He wanted to avoid alerting Ryan Lee to their interest in his father, thus giving him chance to talk to the older man, so he phoned and arranged for DS Lyle to have Lee brought to the Guildhall for questioning and let him wait.

Chris sat in his car, the engine turned on to keep the heater blowing against the frosty weather. He was pondering his next move as a taxi pulled up and disgorged two people onto the footpath, an older man with a much younger woman, slightly unsteady on her feet. They headed for the empty house, opening the front door with a crash and shushing each other, the woman giggling like a teenager.

About to follow them Chris noticed that the taxi driver was still parked at the kerbside. He tapped on the window and showed his ID as the driver completed a call on his mobile phone. Seeing the warrant the young driver looked concerned. Chris was quick to put him at ease.

'Good evening. Nothing to worry about, sir. I wonder could you tell me where you collected the fare you have just dropped off?'

'That couple?' He glanced in the rear view mirror, where the couple had now closed the door behind them.

'Stoke Station. Last train from London. They were lucky to catch it they said, been to see a show.'

Waving the taxi driver on his way, Chris again rang the doorbell as his phone rang.

'Ryan Lee's at work, sir.'

'Damn.' Chris cursed watched the taxi disappear round the corner, 'I could have asked that guy if he knew Lee. Never mind – get on to Stuart's. I want him brought in for questioning.'

Although it was only moments later that Chris knocked on the door of the house, already the woman who opened it was wearing a tatty housecoat and slippers. Her breath misted in the cold air as she called: 'Bob! Bobby, it's the police.'

The man came through from what was evidently the kitchen, carrying two steaming mugs. He was an unprepossessing sight, with excessive nose and ear hair, and a yellowing fringe of dandruff at his receding hairline. Prominent eyebrows, heavy and almost conjoined gave him a malevolent appearance.

'Police?' his face looked stricken, 'It's not Ray is it? An accident?'

Chris was quick to reassure him that Ray had been fine and seemingly on his way home when the Chief Inspector had seen him leave the Pitman's Lamp not fifteen minutes earlier.

He decided his tactics, 'I need to speak to him

again as a matter of urgency. Please get him to call into the Guildhall first thing tomorrow morning. If he hasn't presented himself there by eight thirty I shall send a car for him. Have you had a pleasant evening? I saw the taxi drop you off.'

'Pleasant day, duck.' It was the woman who answered, 'my birthday tomorrow – a big birthday,' she shushed conspiratorially. 'But I'm not telling you which one. Bobby took me up to London to a show.'

Chris could see that on the coffee table lay a programme for Les Miserables, plus a couple of train tickets and various receipts.

'Do you mind me asking which taxi firm you used?'

'Stuart's always. Bobby's grandson works with John Stuart. It was Ryan collected us at the station.' Chris saw too late that he had just waved on his way one of the two people he wanted to talk to.

'Happy Birthday,' He turned on his heel and left them in the doorway, the woman waving as if to a departing guest. Chris reached for his phone, and gave instructions; Ryan Lee had just left his father's address in one of Stuart's taxis, all traffic patrols were to look out for him and someone was to get over to the taxi firm's premises. Chris wanted him brought in for questioning.

As his father closed the door behind Chris, Ray appeared in the kitchen doorway.

'I heard,' he pre-empted his father's outburst.

'What's going on? We need to get this sorted out. Police coming round here, it ain't right. This is a respectable house.'

The young woman went quietly up the stairs, 'I'll say goodnight then.'

The old man patted her buttocks in a familiar gesture Ray thought disgusting at his age, then waited for the bedroom door to close.

'Respectable house! You horny old toad. You just want me out. You're planning to throw me out of my house. Out of my home.'

'It's my house.' Bob said, squinting through the cigarette smoke. 'Bought and paid for with my own money.'

'But the new windows, the conservatory,' Ray gestured to a small lean-to at the back of the kitchen. 'The upstairs loo that I plumbed in.'

'I know, I know. I'm not throwing you out on the streets with nothing. We'll come to ...' he struggled to find the right expression, 'an arrangement.' His father's face was implacable.

'An arrangement? What arrangement are you going to come to with only your pension coming in? You stupid old man.'

'You don't know everything,' his father shot back, 'and Gayle has a bit put by.'

Feeling he had the upper hand now, the older man blew smoke at the nicotine-stained ceiling. 'I've had enough. You're out drinking and coming in half pissed, then cavorting rowdily round the house half the night. It's time you left home, I've had enough I tell you.

'We had this conversation six months ago. I mean it, Ray. Out by the end of the month.'

'You're just a dirty old man, can't wait to move your bit of skirt in permanently. And what's she after with an old toad like you?' he sneered, 'Perhaps it's your startling good looks, or perhaps your immense wealth or your charm. You run-down old has-been. You're pathetic.'

Ray glared at the old man, then without a word turned away – he had no time for this now.

The old man's voice followed him out of the room, 'I think you're jealous. If you got a woman of your own you'd leave me here on my own without a thought, but that's not likely is, it? Poof!' He had to shout the last bit as Ray stomped out of the door and upstairs.

Chris opened the back door on the tail end of this conversation, letting in a blast of frosty air.

'Just a moment Mr Ashmore. I have some questions for your son.' He followed the old man to the bottom of the stairs,

'Mr Ashmore? Mr Raymond Ashmore? I have some questions for you.' As Ray appeared at the top of the stairs, the older man asked,

'How did you know he was here? I thought you'd gone.'

'Obviously.' Chris added, 'Difficult though, isn't it, to come in quietly on a motorbike?'

* * *

For the whole of the night the rain had continued heavy and unremitting, though it now gave way to grey, heavy clouds and a biting wind.

Ben Hanchurch joined the team meeting.

'Her head was smashed down on the corner of the fish tank, the wound matches exactly. As does the scrap of paint found on the body. We've just had the report through from the lab, and the plant fragments from the tank are definitely Cladophora.' Ben beamed at them all.

'So, after her head was bashed – probably knocking her out, the tank was filled with water and she was held under until her killer was sure she was dead. There is a convenient water tap and hose connection in the cellar.'

'Why move the body?'

'Good question. Why bash her head and then drown her? I think the body was moved to confuse. Perhaps she had told her killer that Anthony Whitfield was back in the area and would likely be coming to his home that night to sleep. She may have thought this would keep her safe, but it probably put her killer in a panic. This would be his only chance.

'Of course when Anthony didn't arrive home he would assume he was safe as long as he disposed of the body before morning. He didn't know when the rest of the Whitfield family would be back, perhaps only a day or two. It was lucky for him that he caught up with her whilst she was looking after their house. It meant he could drown her somewhere where there was apparently no opportunity and no connection to him at all.'

'Moving her body to a bath over in Audley caused us a lot of confusion for a while, so that worked.' Chris turned to DS York, 'It was lucky you stumbled across the conversation where Mrs Whitfield told the television engineer there was a cellar. You did well.'

'I should have found it earlier, sir. It shouldn't have been left to chance.'

'Nonsense. That was such an unlikely place for a doorway to be, no external evidence of a cellar anywhere outside the house. It's quite understandable.'

Ben was intrigued, 'How do you think she was moved?'

'A big black diesel vehicle in the early hours of the morning. A neighbour thought she heard it.'

'A four by four? But there are thousands ...'

'No, Ben. A taxi.'

DS York grinned at him, 'I've heard it said that the most anonymous person, the one whose face nobody notices is a motorcyclist. The second is a taxi driver.'

'Who do we know who has a driving job at night, just filling in for a friend?'

Ben caught on at once, 'Ryan Lee, and he knew a house where the people were away for a further week or more.

Chris nodded. 'He put her in the bath, covered her in water to confuse the situation even more and in that he succeeded.'

'How did he break into the house next door?'

'He didn't need to. Ryan's half-sister had a key to next door that she left on a hook in the kitchen. When she and Billy were out he carried the body next door, the work of a few minutes. He took a chance on being seen but they were lucky, it was the back door key they had, it was well hidden by shrubbery and the street light was out. He was confident that the empty property being totally unconnected to his dad, and to himself really, the connection could never be made.

'The ironic thing is that the only overlooking window is of the room Ryan was using at his sister's. It wasn't that big a risk.'

'Where had the body been to when he got it out of the Whitfields'? Not to Sharon Welland's surely?'

'In a way. She was in the shed, risky but it was only for a night or two at the most. How many people actually go to their shed at this time of year? The grass didn't look like it was mown much in the summer, never mind in late October. He must have known Billy and Sharon's routines and reckoned it was safe. He was right.

'So Billy Welland wasn't involved?'

Chris shook his head.

'But why? If Ryan Lee didn't know her, what was his motive?'

'Ryan wasn't the killer.'

'What? Then who have we been talking about?'

'No, Ryan just helped move the body afterwards. He did it for Ray Ashmore, the boy who was with Susan's brother in 1987 when he died. Ray Ashworth has a motorbike. That's his only means of transport so he couldn't use it to move the dead body. I believe he called Ryan who came with the taxi.'

DC Harris had just entered the incident room, hearing the last comments, 'But why, sir? Why did Ryan Lee do all this for a stranger?'

'This wasn't for a stranger. Ray Ashmore is his dad.'

Chapter 32

The more he thought about it, the less Ryan worried about the prospect of going to prison. Better than facing his father, and his grandmother, and his debts. Better than everyone mocking him, despising him. No more money problems, no more responsibilities. Prison would be fine, being looked after, no bills to worry about, no shopping or cooking, no need to jump every time those blasted kids next door threw things at the windows. No need to put up with Shaz's squalling kid. No need to have to work to pay rent, and nobody like Billy nagging you, suggesting every day that it was time you found somewhere else to live.

There wouldn't be much space of course, but he lived in little more than a cell now, didn't he? He wouldn't miss the exercise and he thought a spell of solitude would suit him fine, the occasional visit from his sister perhaps, but nothing to make him have to think too deeply.

No, prison would be fine. That Myra Hindley had done a degree in prison, all paid for out of taxes. He wouldn't want a degree course, but maybe in prison ... He thought himself cleverer than Myra Hindley. She got caught. They would get away with it, literally get away with murder. He gave a harsh laugh, and started coughing. And if he was caught, well then prison it would be. Perhaps he would do a degree. He would certainly be looked after, perhaps for the rest of his life; it was, somehow, a comforting thought.

As his musing continued, two men appeared at the door. He had seen neither before but instinctively knew they were police officers. He held his breath, waiting for their approach but they went straight to the John Stuart's office, the door closing behind them.

The two officers in the car that pulled up a moment later however, came straight across to his cab.

* * *

Ryan Lee slumped back in his chair in an attitude of total boredom. The heating had just been put on in the interview room, and the radiator clicked and gurgled alarmingly. The young man looked round at DC Dearing, standing behind him and eyed her up and down. Once the interview began his gaze never left the scar that disfigured Chris's head. Chris's family, friends and workmates were long used to it, and he would not indulge in vanity insofar as to grow his hair in some weird contortion to disguise it.

For some reason, today the stare was beginning to annoy him. Normally he managed to remain dispassionate during interviews but the arrogance of this youth was breathtaking.

'Susan Chell? Who? Never 'eard of her. Who the 'ell was she? I don't know her, and why would I want to do someone in what I don't even know. Why would I bash 'er over the 'ead? I wouldn't have a whatsit ... a motive.'

Chris had never held much store by motive – who knew what motivates another person, or how intense their feelings may be. He felt it was all smoke and mirrors.

'How do you know she was bashed over the head?'

'Watch the telly, don't I? There's no way you're pinnin' this on me.'

Ryan would have no way of being sure what the police had discovered, nor how far their trail had led them. Chris paused to consider his position, then continued, 'So when we take apart your taxi, there will be no evidence of this young woman having been inside it?'

'Take apart! You can't do that, mate. That don't belong to me, it belongs to John. He won't let you mess about wiv his taxi.'

'You can bluster all you like, Mr Lee, but Mr Stuart is rather anxious about his tax and VAT returns, also about the possible non-renewal of his licence to operate. He has given us full permission to search his premises, his vehicles, your locker – everything. If we find so much as a hair …'

'That would only show that she has been near the car,' his situation had not yet completely shattered the young man's aplomb, 'she could have stuck her head in the boot to take out a piece of luggage.' He exhaled deeply, relieved. 'Did she have a car? No? There you are then, she probably used taxis a fair bit.'

Chris was getting tired of this. His head was aching and he wanted to go home. 'Of course,' he said brightly, 'the car won't be searched today. The taxi's been impounded and is in our garage, and the premises? They'll have to wait until the search of your sister's place is complete.'

'My sister's place? Billy'll never allow that.'

'You're right, of course. Mr Welland strongly objects. That's why we got a Court Order. They're paying particular attention to your room and to the shed. Will they find anything Ryan?'

The confidence was gone now, and the face pale.

'Oh, and just so you know.' Chris finished up, 'we have your dad in the interview room next door.'

Ryan gave a sudden wild, whinny of laughter, portraying his despair.

* * *

Chris had suspected that, given his previous attitude, Billy Welland would refuse them the opportunity to search, so the officers had gone armed with a search warrant and were led by DS York. The sergeant's self-esteem needed a boost after the Whitfield cellar debacle. He would take the Welland place apart. Taxi-owner John Stuart had raised no such objections to the search carried out at his premises, but nothing to incriminate Ryan Lee had been found. The taxi was still with forensics, but had been valeted twice since Hallowe'en.

Chris faced Ray Ashmore across the interview table. He sat exactly where his mother sat the previous day.

'Ryan is my son. His name's Lee 'cos that was his mum's name. We were never married. I never married Sharon's mum either. I suppose I was a serial non-marrier.' He seemed pleased that he had straightened this out.

'I didn't kill Susan Chell. I admit that I was having money difficulties because of all the blackmail money I've had to pay out. The job doesn't pay well, all my savings are gone and my cards are maxed out.

Whoever killed her did me a favour, but it weren't me.'

Chris took the interview in a different direction, 'We know that you were on the boat when Susan's brother died, and after the inquest her mother shouted about you murdering him. Did you?'

'Of course not. I was ... I was very fond of Neil.'

'Then why did you agree to pay the blackmail money to Susan?'

'She threatened me that she would go to the police and tell them what she had now remembered about that day. I didn't know what she might make up about me. She was evil. I couldn't prove I hadn't done anything, so I paid.'

Ashmore shifted in his seat and licked lips that were cracked and dry. It could be just the cold, but his nerves were clearly jangling like piano wires. DC Harris watched his Adam's apple as he swallowed noisily.

'The SOCO's are searching Mrs Welland's property now. Are they going to find anything more incriminating?'

Ray pondered this question. The truth was he had no way of knowing. Ryan had come immediately in response to his father's frantic phone call and helped him undress the body and shift it upstairs from the cellar. He had a tarpaulin sheet and some towels in the back of the cab and between them they had laid the naked body in the boot.

Ray had waved Ryan off, relieved that his son had said he knew how to dispose of her, leaving Ray to check everywhere was clean and tidy.

The clothes, some of them damp, he used to

wipe the surfaces they may have touched. He emptied what water was left in the tank and used a bucket in the cellar to sluice down the walls. He was sufficiently aware to avoid using her clothes to wipe up her blood and used his own t-shirt to scrub down part of the cellar wall. He placed her clothes in a plastic bag from the kitchen and put it in his pannier, along with his t-shirt.

The t-shirt went in the bin when he got home; her clothes he left on the bike until he saw the description of them in the Sentinel, at which point he dumped them.

'Of course,' Chris continued, 'after they've finished there, they have instructions to visit your home and also to examine your motorbike.'

'You can't do that! Police turning up on the doorstep will give my dad a heart attack.'

'Your father is expecting us, Mr Ashmore. He asked what time would the officers be there. Said he'd put the kettle on.' He gave the other man a moment to digest this: 'So, what do you have to say to that Mr Ashmore?'

'I want my solicitor.'

* * *

With no more information forthcoming, Chris adjourned the interview and went to update the team.

DS York came into the incident room, 'Sir, I've just come from talking to Anthony Whitfield.'

'What took you there?' DC Dearing was curious.

'We've found a wedding ring in the Wellands' shed.' He produced an evidence bag and laid it on the desk in front of Chris. 'Neither Sharon nor Billy knew anything about it.

'Looking at photos of Susan, I thought it could be the same ring. I took it to see if Russell Chell could identify it but he's not at home, so I went to talk to Anthony Whitfield. He is prepared to swear that it's definitely hers. It's not personally engraved but it has a chased pattern. The ring, like the marriage, was barely five years old and the pattern was still quite distinct.'

Anthony Whitfield had something else to tell me. It'll be easiest to read you what he said:

'I need to get this off my chest. If Susan's death is anyway linked to her brother dying, I think it may be down to me that she was able to trace the person she blamed. It happened in the summer. I'd arranged to meet Susan as usual on a Thursday night.

'This particular evening Susan had hoped we would be going back to her flat together, but I had this job to do first. It was important, about the lease on a property, but wouldn't take long so I took Susan along to a meeting with the client. Our agency had sold shop premises to a Carly Broadbent. Loads of stuff needed doing to it, I believe it's only just opened as a café.

'It was handy to take her with me, I'd need a second witness to the documents anyway. The other witness would be the assistant who was going to be working alongside my client when the place opened, Josie Ashmore.

'They were expecting me. The two ladies were sitting together in Ms Broadbent's home. I told her I had brought a colleague as the second witness – not strictly true, I know – but I thought it would save

lengthy explanations.

'*Ms Broadbent signed the contract, then first her friend, and then Susan signed as witnesses to the signature. After the meeting Susan was white and shaking. I asked her what the matter was, and she said that she knew that woman, or at least, she knew who she was, her son was a killer.*'

The sergeant looked up from the statement. 'I asked when Susan signed the contract, whether she would have been able to see the other witness's details, her name and address, and he had nodded:

'*Yes, of course, if she was interested. Susan told me that she had gone cold when she saw the details. She said that her suspicions were confirmed, that this woman was the one who had so upset her mother at the inquest of her brother, that she didn't know what to say or do.*

'*Anthony told her to forget it, it was water under the bridge and that it was time to move on after, what was it, thirty years? He said she couldn't live in the past, they had their future to think about now.*'

'It explains a lot,' Chris was thoughtful. 'According to Ray Ashmore, Susan started blackmail six months ago when she took the flat. Two things happened. Firstly, through Josie she had found Ray, and secondly, she wrote to him, that she had information the police would be interested in, something she had found amongst her mother's possessions naming him. She needn't have said exactly what she suspected, but he was clearly sufficiently worried about something or he wouldn't pay up.'

'So what changed in October?'

'On the thirty-first, Anthony had arranged to

meet Susan at the pub. He was home for a supposed dental appointment. She went to the Pitman's Lamp to meet him, but he had driven down from the Lake District and was late. She saw Ray in there, and recognised him.'

'But she hadn't seen him for what? Thirty years? How did she recognise him?'

'By what I saw in the interview room not ten minutes ago, his tattoo; part of the tattoo is a woman's name – Josie, for his mother. Susan had seen it before when she was a little girl, and when she looked more closely at him, she knew who it was.

'She didn't want a confrontation so she left, not realising that he'd seen the necklace Neil had given her and that he in turn knows who she is.'

Chapter 33

DS Hegarty and DC Dearing had just returned from the Pitman's Lamp. The sergeant shrugged off her heavy jacket and gave her report, 'Ray Ashmore's version of that night is verified by what the landlord and some of the Pitman's Lamp customers say. He had been in the pub for a while and was heading out to the back to the shelter for a cigarette. He followed a middle aged couple who were making their way out to the car park. Susan had slipped hurrying over the car park and they had helped to pick her up. They said that a man came across and joined them, said he would see that she got home safely and took her arm.'

Chris nodded, 'Thus far he had been paying her the blackmail money remotely. Giving him the benefit of the doubt, perhaps he followed her thinking that if he could talk to her face to face, explain that there wasn't any more money, then she would understand.'

'What happened next?'

'The couple said she was laughing as they left. To be honest, they didn't want to get involved. It was cold, they had done what they could to help. They just wanted to go home.'

* * *

The interview resumed. Ray was told of the information that had come from the pub, and asked for his comments. Despite now having his solicitor sitting beside him, he seemed determined to talk, and Chris was happy to let him.

'Okay. I saw this woman at the pub and she looked familiar. What I really recognised was that thing she wore round her neck. I told her that life wasn't easy for me at the moment, and that I need the money now. My dad's shacking up with some tart and I need my own place. I'll have proper rent to find.'

'How did she react?'

'She was cool with that. She said she would have a think about it. It's weird – all the time she's talking, she's fiddling with that damned string of beads. I asked her if I could have a closer look.'

'Interesting, according to her friends and family Susan never took it off. How did you persuade her?'

'I just asked her if I could look at it, that's all.'

Chris glanced at the constable.

'Okay, Susan wasn't wearing it when her body was found. What happened to the beads?'

'When we talked in the car park, we parted company – fairly amicably I think. After she'd gone I realised I still had the thing she wore round her neck in my hand.'

'And what did you do with that *thing she wore round her neck*?'

Like father, like son, he was no quick thinker. 'I dropped it down a drain, I think.'

'You think?'

'Yes. I did. I dropped it through a grid grating on my way home.'

'I see,' said Chris 'So you dropped it down a grid?'

Ray breathed out deeply and relaxed, 'that's

right.'

'Then how come your son Ryan was able to give it to your mother for her birthday?'

* * *

The interview, Ray had thought, was going rather well. That is until that final question.

He closed his eyes, devastated. What had the boy been thinking? Of course Ryan had no idea who this woman was, nor that the necklace was possibly unique and so easily identifiable. Ray dragged his thoughts back to what the officer was asking. He looked despairingly at his solicitor, then dropped his head onto his arms. Belatedly, common sense stepped in. 'No comment,' he said quietly. Chris let the silence stretch. He well knew that most people as stressed as Ray Ashmore currently was, would need to fill that silence. He was not disappointed. The voice was a whisper, Chris had to strain forward to hear.

'She laughed at me; in the pub car park. Said her mother had suffered so much on my account, it was only right that my mother should suffer by knowing what a shit I was. She said it wouldn't anywhere near be quid pro quo, but there would be some satisfaction for her knowing that I had at last really started to pay. If I wouldn't, or couldn't continue to pay in money that wasn't her problem. She would tell my mother and the police, and I could pay with time in prison.'

'Let's cut the fantasy and get back to what happened to Susan. What happened in that cellar?'

There was a silence of some minutes. Chris began to wonder whether the other man would ever speak, then eventually:

'Okay. It was an accident. She fell against the tank, banged her head. I didn't know what to do. I could only think I had to get her out of there.'

'Banged her head in the cellar! Why on earth were you in the cellar?'

'Susan said she had something to show me, led me down there. I'd no idea why.'

The story was so thin Chris almost smiled, 'So, you maintain it was an accident. Then instead of getting help, you calmly filled the tank with water? It was not an accident that you then held her face-down in that water. She died by drowning and you killed her. Why?'

Ray Ashmore shook his head and refused to say anything more.

Chapter 34

First thing the following morning, Chris and Frances Hegarty sat in the interview room, once again facing Ray Ashmore and his solicitor. Between them on the table were two evidence bags, their contents clearly visible.

As soon as he saw them, Ashmore asked for time alone with his solicitor. Chris hoped this was the breakthrough he had been waiting for.

After Chris's introduction for the tape, Ray Ashmore sat for some minutes and stared at the contents of the evidence bags until Chris prompted him: 'Perhaps you would tell me about these two letters.'

Ashmore glanced at his solicitor and then said he wanted to tell them what had happened in his own way. His attitude had changed somewhat. He had spent some time talking to his solicitor, no doubt being guided as to the best way forward, but he was determined to have his say, and he now seemed to be telling the truth.

'She saw me kill her brother in 1987. She approached me months ago saying she knew where my mother lived. She had phoned the number she'd got from Directory Enquiries. She'd noted Mum's address from Carly's contract, that the estate agent had had her witness. She told Mum she was trying to contact Ray Ashmore, and Mum gave her my mobile number.'

In recounting it in the interview, Ray

Ashmore had laughed grimly, 'Mum asked if this was a new girlfriend. Like hell. She was poison.

'Susan told me she was leaving her husband and wanted me to provide her with somewhere to live, and for me to pay for her keep. Otherwise she would tell my mother what she knew, and go to the police and tell them what she had heard and seen all those years ago.' He rubbed his palm across his eyes, 'It was so long ago. Neil was dead, it wouldn't do him any good. Why did she have to bring it all up again?'

'Why had she not done so before?'

'She was just a little kid when Neil died, about eight years old, she wouldn't understand what we were doing with each other, would she? She said that some paperwork had come to hand that had brought it all back.'

DS Hegarty glanced at Chris, the Coroner's Report?

His solicitor interrupted with a splutter, 'Mr Ashmore, the tape. You have been advised not to say anything more.'

'I'd rather get it over with.' It was a refrain often heard in the wake of a serious crime. The relief, Chris felt, must have been enormous. Sadly, these first interviews with the investigating officers were seldom the end of the process but rather just the beginning. Perhaps it was the first interview that they found such a hurdle, the description of what they had heard, seen and done, and the necessary reliving of the moment.

'What did you do?'

'I tried to make a friend of her, I sure didn't want her as an enemy.' He paused and ran his fingers through the greasy hair, 'then she must have found out something else, I think what she had before were just suspicions. She really cranked up the ante.'

'That would be when her mother died,' Chris told him. There was no harm in him knowing, 'she had a lot more information about what happened thirty years ago. As well as the Coroner's Report and that from the Post Mortem, she also had these two letters including one from her Aunt. In it her aunt named you.'

'I read somewhere that a blackmailer could have no lasting power over his victim without the victim's co-operation, but I didn't know what to do. She was a blackmailer. She was bleeding me dry.'

'You had been paying her for months. Why did you decide to kill her now?'

Ashmore remained silent, so Chris continued.

'I said two letters. The other one was from her brother, written to you. We found it hidden in the lining of your motorbike pannier yesterday. Susan would never have seen that before, until she went through her mother's things. I believe she applied for the Coroner's Report, and it all triggered her memory.

'She contacted you by post to blackmail you. She was afraid to meet in person. She blackmailed you and had been doing for six months. The money you sent in a parcel each month to a PO Box in Hanley centre. I think she threatened you with making the letters public.'

Ashmore nodded, 'First she said that in her mother's things was a letter from Vivien Jennings, her aunt, from thirty years ago. Vivien and her husband had been at the inquest. The letter begged her not to become bitter or feel hatred for me and it gave my name.

'Susan said that letter and another one had

passed to her when her mother died. And then she remembered. Remembered going down the garden that morning and seeing through the boat window something she had not understood. She remembered him begging his friend to stop and calling the friend Ray. Remembered two naked bodies, positions and movements she was too young to understand.

'She remembered the tears streaming down her brother's cheeks and clearest of all, she remembered an arm around her brother and a hand clasped over his mouth to silence his cries an arm with a tattoo that said *Josie*.

'I wasn't absolutely sure it was her at first, even when I saw the necklace, but when I followed her into the carpark and she told me her maiden name – then I knew.'

He ran his hand around the five o'clock shadow now prominent on his jaw.

'I had a motorbike back in the eighties – still have, it's my only means of transport – nobody would have heard it because I used to ride quietly down the towpath and leave it under the bridge under the A53. Walking the few yards along the towpath I would wait for Neil to row across in the little inflatable dinghy that they kept tied to the boat's stern. No one would know if I was there.

'I loved her brother. I loved him and wanted him and would have looked after him, but that day he laughed at me and pushed me away. I thought it was the start of a great romance – for me it was. But he quoted something about trying everything once, although it had been a fair few times more than just once. The idea of love with another man had intrigued him – what kid of that age isn't intrigued by sex of any sort. But then he told me it had sickened him. He couldn't bear to touch me again and didn't want to speak to me.

'I tried to explain that it wasn't dirty or smutty, it was love. I loved him, but he just laughed. Laughed and said he didn't know what love was but when he was older and he did, it would be because of a woman. I tried to take hold of him, put my arms around him, but he pushed me off – really hard. I fell and banged my head on the bulkhead. I felt sick then. I didn't know if it was the bump, or that he didn't want me, but I was so angry.' He paused, 'Really, really angry. I said something I had heard on the telly, and said it in the same tone of voice, *If I can't have you no one will.* He laughed at me.'

He raised red-rimmed eyes to the detective.

'I was right there, wasn't I? He was still laughing as he went through to the bedroom. He put on the rest of his clothes: *Lunchtime,* he said, as if nothing of any importance had happened, and for him it hadn't, but my world had just ended.

'I saw red, I picked up the fire extinguisher fastened to the saloon wall and I hit him across the back of the head. He fell into the water, between the boat and the quay. Then I used the boat hook to hold him under. I don't know how long for, until he wasn't blowing bubbles any more. Then I figured he would be dead, that was the only way I could make sure he never spoke about it to anyone. I was frightened. We were both so young.' He looked at his solicitor.

'I knew it was against the law even if we'd been eighteen and neither of us were. This was 1987. I looked it up later. The Sexual Offences Act had come into place in 1967 but only for consenting adults. But she was there, watching, sucking on that string of bloody beads she always wore. I tried to grab her, but she took off up the garden. I knew I was going to go to prison if Neil'd said anything, but if he'd fallen off the boat and I'd try to help him, then no-one would ever know.

'It seemed the kid was struck dumb afterwards. I didn't know how long she'd been there, how much she'd seen. I had to give evidence to the Coroner. I was dreading her being called but I reckoned she was just a little kid – kids don't understand do they? I reckoned if they did call her I'd just have to try and outface her.

'In the end, she didn't have to give evidence. She wasn't even there. I gave them my version of what had happened and what I had seen. A while later my mum told me that the family had moved away. That was such a relief. I have tried going out with women, but it's not right for me. I've had partners over the years and have fathered a child, but my mind kept going back to Neil and how much I loved him.

'When she phoned me after that night at the pub I told Susan we should meet and lay the ghosts to rest. I told her lies about Neil, that he had attacked me and that the Coroner's Report referred to that attack. I could explain it all to her properly but not on the phone. After all, I reasoned with her, I was there and defending myself. Her mother wasn't there and nor were the people who wrote the stuff in that report or the aunt's letter.

'She gave me the address. As soon as I arrived she made it clear that she didn't live there, that she was looking after the house for a friend. She wasn't going to give me her real address. She thought she was so clever.

'I said I was the only one who really knew the truth. Didn't she want to really know the truth? She just gave me a sly look. Then she told me what I dreaded, that she too had been there and seen it all. The attack, me holding him under the water, my tattoo, everything. She hadn't understood at the time, but piecing it together with the Coroner's Report, she did now. She knew exactly what had happened and who was responsible.

'She told me how I'd driven her mother to lose her mind; and had ruined her own life. She was sent to live with relatives she hardly knew and who didn't want her.

'Then she played her ace. She had another letter, found among her mother's stuff. God knows why the old woman had just kept it and done nothing about it, she really must have been away with the fairies.'

The detectives glanced at each other, as Ray continued: 'I thought that on the phone she had been talking about the letter from her aunt, explaining to her mum that it wasn't my fault and she shouldn't bear a grudge, but there was this other letter as well.' He glanced down at the table, 'The one Neil had written to me. Susan took it to the Whitfields' house with her and hid it so I couldn't find and destroy it. I eventually calmed her down. Said it wasn't fair not to let me see the charges she was laying up against me. How could I explain if I didn't know what had been said against me?

'She agreed to go and get it. I followed her. It was ridiculous, she climbed through this little hole in the wall, down to a cellar. God knows why she put it down there. I kept it after I killed her – perhaps through fear or maybe for sentimental reasons, I don't really know which – it was all I had of Neil. In it he asked me not to do it anymore. It said that all boys wonder about sex, experiment even, but Neil didn't like it. It wasn't who he was and he had found a girlfriend, at school, a nice girl.' He snorted derisively, 'I would like her. On and on in the same vein.

'He said that he had first been uncomfortable, then disgusted by what I did to him and wanted him to do to me. It sickened me I can tell you.'

'If this was a letter to you, how come it was never sent?'

He shook his head, 'No idea. Perhaps he changed his mind. It's certainly some of the stuff he was saying on that last visit. Maybe he wanted to show some strength in saying it face to face.' He looked away, 'He'd have been better posting the blasted letter.'

While he could never condone blackmail, Chris thought all this went some way to explaining Susan's need to control her own life, and certainly her aunt had been right in suggesting that Susan was not a nice person. But Ray Ashmore hadn't finished speaking:

'After I'd read it, I couldn't allow her to live.'

Chapter 35

'After you'd smashed her head against the fish tank and then drowned her, you emptied the tank and the water flooded into the drain in the corner of the cellar. You were stuck with a dead body in the cellar of the Whitfields' home. What did you do?'

'I knew I couldn't even get her up the stairs from the cellar on my own and I'd never get her out of there, I only had the motorbike. I phoned my son. He was working but he came as soon as he could. It must have been the early hours of the morning by then.

'Ryan said he had access to an empty house next door to his sister's. He said he would take the body somewhere and I should go home. He told me much later that he'd dumped the body at the Frasers' as being totally unconnected to me; he thought that the connection could never be made. He dumped the towels on somebody's bonfire. We thought that if the clothes were found elsewhere it would make it harder for the police,' he seemed to realise who he was talking to, 'for you – to find out what happened.

'We stripped her and put her in the taxi and then he drove away. The Wellands' garden has access for cars round the corner in the road at the back, so he was able to get her into the shed with no-one any the wiser. He told me to go home and contrive a row with his Grandad as a sort of alibi. That wasn't hard – we've done nothing but row just lately – then and go to bed. I didn't know what happened then, but he phoned me next day to say he'd got rid of her, she wouldn't be found for days. She was only a skinny little thing and he'd not had too much trouble carrying her upstairs. I was going to take her clothes and stuff over to the other side of Stoke to confuse things. The bloody phone kept going with texts. Where was she? Why hadn't she turned up? Why?

'I told Ryan I'd hang onto the clothes for a while, we didn't want them found too soon. It'd be better if they were found after the body, unless they were put somewhere they'd never be found. He said that we should put them somewhere they definitely would be found, but he'd tell me when to dump them.'

'Was it you who used Susan's phone to text her boyfriend?'

He nodded, 'These messages kept coming in and Ryan said he had an idea for muddying the waters more as long as she wasn't found too soon. And then he laughed. He was bloody enjoying himself.

'I dumped the clothes and the phone as soon as he told me the description had appeared in the paper. I didn't know the silly sod kept those bloody beads.'

* * *

'But what exactly did Josie at the café do?' DS York wanted to know at the subsequent team meeting, when Ray Ashmore had been taken to a cell.

'It all came out in the end. He seemed relieved to be able to talk about it at last.

'He went to the Bookends Café twice on opening day, but not to support his mMum. He first went to the café to try to get a roof over his head, to either see if Josie would put him up, or if she would try and talk some sense into his dad.

'He told his mum he'd call up to the café because he hadn't seen it yet, but then when he saw the tickets it gave him an idea. He asked her if he could look at the kitchen and she was surprised that he was interested. He never had been before.

'He commented on how small it is and then asked her about the pile of tickets. She told him about the suggestions ideas and he read few of them aloud. The café was really busy of course that first day, so she had to leave him for a while – long enough for him to pocket a blank. Then the doorbell pinged and Carly puffed through into the kitchen.'

Chris perched on the edge of the desk, in front of the photographs of the dead woman.

'He took the blank with him. He hadn't completed it in the café. It wouldn't do to have either his mum or Carly see him filling one in, as presumably they would go through them later and there wouldn't be one with his name on. So he had to return later. At about four o'clock he brought the card back, along with some champagne – well – sparkling wine really. Said it was for the two of them to celebrate their success. He took it into the kitchen, ostensibly to open the bottle, and slipped the card in amongst the others.'

* * *

DC Dearing asked Chris would they ever be able to prove that Neil Jennings' death was murder.

'I'm pretty sure, he's all but admitted it, hitting him with the fire extinguisher and holding him under the water. He said he was in a panic and didn't intend to kill him. With Susan dead he can pretty much say what he likes but he's made a fairly robust confession.

'Only the two of them were there, but we have proof of the sodomy and we know now about Susan's murder and that can be firmly laid at Ray's door, with his son Ryan as accessory. We have means, opportunity and now a strong motive for the murder at the canal side in 1987. There is no statute of limitations on a murder charge.'

'Perhaps he's hoping that a jury will see some mitigation for the murder of Susan, she was blackmailing him after all.'

'Yes. And the crimes against her brother are so long ago. Thank Goodness that isn't our decision to make.'

* * *

That evening in front of the fire with his two little girls playing on the rug Chris told Pete Talbot the outcomes of the day. Ray had revealed the recurring nightmare he had suffered over the years and which had resurfaced since Susan's death: what actually happened to Neil. She realised what she had seen, what it meant, and the identity of the other man she had seen with her brother, except he wasn't a man, he was a teenager and irrespective of age, homosexuality was a crime in 1987.

'Neil was of an age where he was beginning to discover girls. He didn't like what Ray did to him and told him that was it. He threatened to tell his parents who would tell the police. Ray was more afraid that the police would tell his parents. Ray was scared of Bob then, but he loved Josie and would not want her hurt.

'This was half term week, hence the thirtieth

anniversary.' Pete paused to top up his beer, 'There was some hero-worship of Neil, she often looked through the boat windows to see what he was doing, hoping he would come and play with her.

'There had been various youngsters on the boat through the week. How did Susan know the sodomist was Ray?'

Chris smiled. 'He has a distinguishing mark, a tattoo. Susan had never seen one close up, she was fascinated. They were a lot less common in 1987, and much more of an indicator about social class. In October in the Pitman's Lamp car park Susan saw that tattoo again, which helped her to put the picture together.'

'I don't understand.'

'The tattoo says *Josie*, in a heart.'

Chris paused to bring them both fresh beers from the fridge, while Pippa took the little girls up to bed. He wondered whether these sessions would continue in a few weeks' time, after Pete's marriage.

'The flat Susan moved to in Hanley was her mother's old place. When her mother died she found both letters, applied for a copy of the Coroner's Report, and started digging.

'She also found the original PM report giving details of the sodomy. Ray was never charged on grounds of lack of evidence. He was there but no one else saw what happened. Susan was in shock at the time, and said nothing – she either couldn't speak or hadn't understood that it was deliberate. Did she think they were playing and go asking to join in? I can imagine a movement as she climbed onto the boat alerting Neil, and that maybe Susan never forgot his face, his eyes tortured, but Ray oblivious for some time. She would be watching, her focus fascinated by the tattoo on his arm.

DS Hegarty took up the story: 'She began to remember what she actually saw and recognised the tattoo as belonging to the person she saw; remembers looking through the window of the boat seeing Neil and the other man semi-clothed and Neil being struck on the head with something red and metal. Definitely deliberately.

'Now she had recalled clearly what actually happened she goes after him. Outside in the pub car park, she referred to the tattoo.

'Like boys do you, young boys like Neil was? Then who's Josie?'

'Leave Josie out of it,' he had shouted at her, unaware of the cliché. Josie is my mum.'

'I know her,' Susan had sneered, 'the old bird who's opening a caff. Well, well. Wouldn't she like to know about her boy and what he's been up to?

'I fancy going to a big café opening. Perhaps they'd like it livening up? What if someone was to get up and announce that her son was a pervert and a murderer? What if the police were to arrive? What fun we would have.'

An eye for an eye was only fair in her view. She was determined his mum should suffer like hers had. This meeting happened when she went to pub to meet Anthony. He was late getting there because of the length of his journey from the Lake District, once he eventually got away from Diane, who had been suspicious.

Ray was in the bar when she arrived. He took the opportunity to follow her and when the old couple had gone, he told her he was not paying any more.'

'How did he know who it was?'

'He saw her necklace. He had been with Neil when he bought it for her.'

Chris thought back over the conversation and nodded:

'Ray Ashmore told us he hadn't thought about Neil for over a decade. He felt no guilt about that. He'd moved on. Susan asked him if he knew what date it was and he told her.

'She could tell it meant absolutely nothing to him. Then she told him it was the anniversary of Neil's death; thirty years she'd lived without her brother because of him. It had not taken Ashmore a moment to remember it all and what had really happened to his beloved Neil. He was terrified.'

Hegarty settled herself by the fire whilst Chris replenished beers for Pete and himself.

'How did she contact him again?' Pete wanted to know.

'She phoned Ray later that day. Said she had been thinking since she saw him in The Pitman's Lamp earlier. That was when she agreed that they meet later that evening and she gave him the Whitfields' address.

* * *

After charging Ashmore, Chris went to find DS York. Josie Ashmore had been arrested on suspicion of assisting an offender.

'All I did was help my boy when he needed it. Any mother who wouldn't do that, shouldn't be a mother at all.'

'You lied to the police – never a wise move. You didn't see Susan at the café opening did you?'

'No. If I'd seen her I'd have chucked the golden ticket there and then, hardly hung on to it. Her address would have gone into my memory and then the ticket into the bin.

'I suspected later that Ray was there for some particular purpose, nothing to do with supporting me. I suppose Carly told you he was there?'

'She saw no reason not to. It would never occur to her that you or he were involved in a murder.'

* * *

Chris and Pete Talbot sat in the kitchen and had gone through the case in minute detail. Now all that was needed was to prepare the paperwork for the Crown Prosecution Service, a job that would take most of the following day.

Pippa's sister-in-law, Florence, was picking up Laura and Rachel's bricks off the floor and launching them at the toy box in the corner. She seemed pensive.

'Before I go back home Chris, I was wondering ... could I do some work experience with you during the summer?' They prefer us to set up something we're interested in, otherwise we have something dire inflicted on us, like a boring accountancy office.'

Chris thought a moment, but shook his head. 'You can't, I'm sorry, Florence. This is the Major Crimes Unit remember, you'll give the powers-that-be apoplexy. There would be all sorts of confidentiality breaches and goodness knows what other objections from on high.

'Also, take this current case. It crosses into another area of police jurisdiction. It just happen to involve Pete this time, which makes it relatively straightforward, but not all forces are as accommodating.'

'Why did you have to involve another force?' Florence wanted to know, 'Surely where the body is found decides who investigates?'

'Not necessarily. In this investigation, the body was found in Newcastle, but the clothes of the deceased were found in Stoke, near to where she was supposed to have been staying. We never know whether we could be blundering into an enquiry another force has ongoing. For instance if they've spent months setting up the right situation for a drugs bust, or for arresting leaders of a vice ring, we could wreck all that if we go blundering in, even if we're asking questions about something completely different. So we work together.'

'I thought it would have to be a No. Boring accountants' here I come.'

'Hang on,' Pete was pouring more wine for the adults. He was used to thinking before he spoke; an unguarded comment at the wrong time could compromise an investigation, but extra personnel were always useful and he had known Florence a long time. He felt sure he could find something.

'What you could do is perhaps come into the general office at Bethesda Street. We're altogether a bigger set-up than Chris's, we could hide you.'

'What!' Florence was stunned.

Pete broke into a laugh, 'Just kidding about the hiding bit, but there are more of the routine jobs around the place. You wouldn't be able to go out of the office with the detectives or anything, and sadly it would probably be making the tea more than anything, but a vital role – every police force runs on tea. If you're prepared to go to the cake stall every now and then as well I'm sure you'd be valued as a member of the team for a few weeks. Can't promise it'll be more interesting than accountancy though.'

Florence beamed. She had been focused on joining the police for a couple of years and had not wavered.

'Oh, I know I can't start in CID, I'll have to work my way up.'

The three officers smiled between themselves.

Frances Hegarty suggested, 'You may prefer uniform in the long run, you never know. Not all the beat coppers are there because they couldn't progress any further, many stayed in uniform through choice.'

'Oh, no! Chris snapped' Florence was adamant. 'I reckon that, handled properly, by the time Chris is ready to retire, I'll just about be ready for promotion to DCI.' She sounded so definite that no-one cared to argue with her.

With difficulty Chris dragged his mind away from Susan Chell and her brother, whose only memorial was a rotting boat in a neighbour's garden.

'Well, now the future of policing is in good hands after my retirement,' Chris smiled, 'we need to talk about what is required of me, if I'm to give the bride away at the undisputed wedding of the year.'

If you have enjoyed reading this and other books by Alison Lingwood, please leave feedback on amazon.co.uk

Printed in Great Britain
by Amazon